ONE
LITTLE
SIGH

BOOKS BY SHANNON HOLLINGER

CHIEF MAGGIE RILEY SERIES

The Girl Who Lied

Their Angel's Cry

The Shadow Girl

Best Friends Forever

The Slumber Party

SHANNON HOLLINGER

ONE LITTLE SIGH

Bookouture

Published by Bookouture in 2024

An imprint of Storyfire Ltd.
Carmelite House
50 Victoria Embankment
London EC4Y 0DZ

www.bookouture.com

ISBN: 978-1-83525-485-1
eBook ISBN: 978-1-83525-484-4

To Sully, for always bringing smiles and levity to my day, no matter how dark the writing gets.

PROLOGUE

He looks so peaceful on the back seat. Curled on his side, eyes closed, long lashes dark against his pale skin. Everything about him so tiny and perfect. He doesn't belong here.

But that doesn't stop him from being lifted from the car, his body limp and surprisingly heavy as he's carried through the night, the way lit only by the ethereal glow of moonlight filtered through thick clouds above as he's taken to a place where the sun never shines, a spot perpetually stuck in the shadow of a slumbering giant. But the mountain feels awake now, a menacing shadow at their back, a silent witness to what's about to happen.

The body beneath him trudges forward, sweating though the air has a bite to it, savagely cold in this corner of the valley where winter never seems to cease. It sinks its fangs in deep, working its way to the bone as they make their way to the edge of the lake.

Hesitating on the shore, the person casts a glance over their shoulder. They're alone. No one knows. It's not too late to turn back. Only, it is.

This has to be done.

Steps thud hollowly against the wooden planks, the sound spreading out into the night, slow, reluctant, like the beating of a dying heart. The wind wails as it sweeps over the frozen surface of the lake, snatching greedily at the child in their arms, his bare feet frigid cold through the fabric against their thigh. Goosebumps tighten their skin. Adjusting their grip on the boy, they continue on, just them and the mountain, watching at their back.

And then they reach it. The end of the dock.

They squint out over the ice that spreads along the top of the water like a toxic oil slick. April, and the only place the lake is still frozen is here, in this evil little corner eclipsed by the stony peak.

Spotting what they were hoping for, a thin patch on the surface, they squat and hold the child out, over the weak spot. Then slowly lower him, his feet breaking through the crust. His ankles disappear, then his calves, his knees, each and every part of him, until finally only his head and shoulders remain. The lake accepts him, drawing him under, until with one little sigh, it claims him, and he vanishes.

And then it's done. This night never happened.

1

MAGGIE

Sometimes there's a moment, a fleeting instant in your day, where you forget all your troubles—who you are, what you've done, what's been done to you. Then in a flash reality comes crashing down, reminding you of all the things you'd rather forget. But as I wake up to a fresh day, opening my eyes to the morning light, and find my fiancé, Steve, watching me, reality seems blissfully far away.

"Morning," he says.

"Were you watching me sleep?" I ask.

He's propped up on an elbow, the side of his head resting on his hand. The skin at the corner of his warm brown eyes crinkles as he grins, lifting his free shoulder in a shrug. "Maybe."

"That's not creepy at all," I joke.

"Or is it romantic?"

"No, I'm pretty sure it's creepy."

"What if I told you I was lying here, watching you, thinking of what a lucky man I am?"

"Then I'd probably tell you it's a little early in the day to be drinking," I say, returning his grin, hoping my morning breath isn't too bad as I wiggle forward on the bed, closing the distance between us. We kiss, and for a brief moment, my carefree instant seems to last an eternity.

Then there's a scratch at the door. A dog whines, needing to go outside. Steve groans as I pull back. We give each other a meaningful look, a promise of things to come.

"I've got to go into the department, anyway," I say, and just like that, the real world I've been avoiding falls down on my shoulders.

"But we're still on for dinner tonight, right?" he asks as we tug clothes on. "With my family?"

"Of course. Wouldn't miss it."

I give him a smile that I hope doesn't betray my nerves, because the truth is, there's a part of me that would miss it. I'm afraid to meet his family. What if they don't like me? What if they see the darkness I work so hard to hide? What if they tell Steve to cancel the—

"If you have any ideas about the wedding..." he says, trailing down the hall behind me. "You know my mother will probably try to seize control as soon as she gets here."

Diane's the only member of Steve's family that I've met, and though it was a bit of a disaster at first, we've ended up developing a comfortable relationship. And she's supposed to be the difficult one to get along with. I tell myself I'm worrying for nothing. I tell Steve, "But maybe that's a good thing."

He gives me side-eye from under raised brows. "You say that now," he deadpans.

We step outside after the dogs, and I suck in a sharp breath. Bite my tongue to keep from cursing about the cold because, even though it's mid-April, it's freezing out. Literally. It seems like Coyote Cove has yet to get the memo about springtime. I squint at the thermometer attached to the beam framing the door, searching for the little red line that should be much higher by now.

Though as I turn to watch the dogs scamper across a yard

where bright green shoots are emerging from a landscape that's still mostly mud from snowmelt and catch a glimpse of the lake shimmering in the early morning light, mountains painted in muted pastels in the hazy distance beyond, I realize the trade-off.

"But you might regret that decision," Steve says, wrapping his arms around me to keep me warm. His breath forms little clouds of vapor as he adds, "When you're walking down the aisle in a big fluffy dress with puffed sleeves..."

"Will there?" I ask, leaning back against him. "Be an aisle, I mean?"

"Well, where were you thinking of for a venue?"

"I don't know." The wedding is only two months away. I'm fairly certain that most couples have decided this by now. And sent out invitations. Or at least ordered them. We've done none of those things. Gesturing toward the view, I say, "We could do it here."

He lets me go to open the door for the dogs. Says, "There's not much room."

Stepping back into the warmth of the house, I ask, "How much do we need?"

And though I don't speak the thought out loud, it echoes through my head: *It's not like I have many people to invite.* Is that why I've been so lackadaisical about the wedding planning? Because even though I'm looking forward to being Steve's wife, part of me is dreading the ceremony.

What will everyone think? That I'm an orphan? But that doesn't explain my slim handful of friends.

I have no tribe.

I know Steve doesn't care. He understands how difficult it is for me to let my guard down, to trust. That when you see the worst that humans inflict on each other, it's hard to let anyone in —especially when you're inspecting everyone you meet, searching for the secrets they're hiding.

He's silent as he beats eggs in a bowl, and I'm grateful that he's let the conversation drop. I fill the coffee urn with water. Reach into the fridge, grab the cheese, and hand it to him as he passes me a filter from the cupboard. Isn't this what's important? The intricate dance of working together.

"We'll meet you at the department before dinner and head over to the inn together."

I straighten up from filling the dog bowls, feeling like I've missed something. Steve's voice has a hint of strain to it. His posture as he shifts the eggs around in the pan is tense.

"That's not necessary," I say, kissing him on the cheek. "I'll just meet you there."

"No."

I startle at his abruptness. Turn to stare at him.

"My family will want to see where you work, anyway."

It sounds like an excuse to me. Is Steve worried that I'm not going to show? Is he having second thoughts? Am I? But most importantly, how did I manage to mess this day up already?

2
MAGGIE

Pulling into the parking lot at the Coyote Cove Police Department, I breathe a sigh of relief. This is my sanctuary. The one place where I feel like I'm in control. Where I'm confident in my actions and decisions.

Only, now that I'm here, I wonder if I shouldn't be. Maybe I should have arranged to take the day off so I'd have been there to greet my future in-laws when they arrived. But maybe they'll appreciate some time alone together, just family, to catch up before they have to make nice with a virtual stranger. I don't know. I'm not good at things like that.

It's not that I'm antisocial, exactly, just easily overwhelmed by the minutiae of life that seems to come so naturally to everyone else. Small talk, pleasantries, event planning—I grimace, thinking of the details left to plan for our upcoming wedding, which is all of them.

I'm looking forward to us starting our life together. It's just that I wish there was a way to get from this point in time to that one without having to suffer through all the decision-making it's going to take to get there.

And I'm worried, because Steve's mother, Diane? This is

her kind of thing. Am I going to be a huge disappointment as a future daughter-in-law because I don't care what color the flowers are? Or even if there are flowers? If I let her make all the choices, will I be setting myself up for a lifetime of being steamrolled about things I possibly do care about?

I make a note to ask my receptionist, Sue, for her opinion when she gets in this morning. Then I remember that it's Saturday. It'll just be me alone with my thoughts for nine hours, which is never a good thing.

Reluctantly, I push open the door to my Jeep and step out into a morning as gray as my mood. The icy bite to the air takes my breath away, a shiver wracking through my body, as I hurry to get inside.

When I first moved here, I was told I'd get used to the cold by the time my first winter was over, but I've given up hope. I don't think I'll ever grow accustomed to northern Maine temperatures, my blood too thin from decades spent under the Florida sun, years where I yearned for a release from the heat, not quite understanding what the alternative might be. I never realized how good I'd had it. What I wouldn't give now for a balmy day, the warmth of the sun on my face.

But that was another life, though not necessarily a better one. One where I was a metropolitan detective instead of a small-town police chief, a member of a close-knit family rather than estranged from my parents, and the older sister of a beautiful, precious baby brother who was stolen from us.

And the man who destroyed all those things—my family, my life, my career—still walks free. Suddenly, I don't feel the cold anymore, the red-hot coal of my rage flaring beneath my skin, my fist curling painfully tight around the keys I'm using to unlock the door.

This is why I shouldn't be left alone. This is what happens. I start thinking about everything I've lost instead of everything I now have. The tortured past that I've worked so hard to leave behind instead of the promising future Steve and I are building together. The vendetta I've yet to settle, the one that could cost me everything, and probably will. The one I should forget about but just can't seem to abandon.

Because the man who stole my baby brother has yet to pay for his actions. One day, I'm going to fix that. And that single act will change everything I've known and become. I'll no longer be one of the good guys.

I used to be okay with that thought. Used to know in my heart that it would be worth it. But somehow, everything's gotten complicated. Now my heart is confused, and I'm not quite sure what I want anymore.

I think about Steve's face when I left this morning, the crease of tension between his brows, and wonder if he somehow suspects the turmoil going on inside my head. Or if maybe he's just worried about me meeting the rest of his family. I'd be if I were him.

The thought is interrupted as tires squeal behind me, raising the hair on the back of my neck. I turn in time to see a car speed into the lot. Instantly, I suspect that I should have been happy with the frigid, uneventful day I was worried about only moments ago, but a dark part of me, the part I'm not very proud of, can't help but be relieved by the distraction.

The engine remains running as a car door creaks open. Shoes slap frantically against the pavement, closing the distance between us. All it takes is one look at the woman running across the parking lot, at the anguish on her face, to know this is going to be bad.

3

STEVE

This is a mistake. I shouldn't have brought them here. It isn't safe. But at the same time, how could I not? Because nowhere is safe for them now, not their homes or mine, and it's my fault. I wish I could tell them of the danger they're in, but they wouldn't understand.

Not my baby sister, Izzy, who was fearless as a child and now, as a grown woman, one who gave up a lucrative career as a psychologist to work with at-risk youth at a halfway house in Boston, is even more so. She gives me a brief hug before commenting on the silver that's grown in at my temples since the last time I saw her, lips curving into the same impish grin she's worn since she was a toddler.

She ruffles my dark hair like I'm the younger sibling before dropping to the floor to meet her "niece and nephew," Tempest and Sullivan. The two terriers take to her immediately, stumpy little tails wagging so fast they're a blur as the dogs cover her with kisses.

Grandpa Joe wouldn't understand, either. A decorated war veteran who served multiple tours in Vietnam, the octogenarian pulls me in close, the muscles under his chunky tweed sweater still firm from regular workouts. He makes a joke about hardly recognizing me as he releases me, then he, too, ruffles my hair.

And my mother, Diane, most certainly wouldn't get it. She frowns in disapproval as she tries to smooth my hair down before offering me her cheek for a kiss, then her dog, Laurel, for another kiss. She sets Laurel down, watching her frolic off with the terriers before putting her hands on her hips and surveying the room.

"Where's Maggie?"

"At work."

She gives a noise not unlike a growl. No, my family definitely wouldn't understand the danger they're in.

"I'm worried about her."

I have to bite my tongue not to agree, though I'm sure the causes of our concern are quite different. It took everything I had not to beg Maggie to stay home this morning. The only reason I hadn't was because she would have known immediately that something was wrong, would have demanded that I tell her what.

She's already under enough stress. I have to try to work this out on my own first. So I've kept the fact that I'm being blackmailed by my childhood best friend from her.

But no matter how hard I try lying to myself that I'm concealing what's happening for her benefit, the truth is that it's because I can't bear the thought of the look that would be in her eyes if she found out the secret that Wesley, recently released from a fifteen-year prison sentence for manslaughter, is holding over me. If any of my loved ones discovered that dark truth about my past.

"She works too much," my mother says.

"I know, I agree. But we'll be meeting up with her later, before dinner."

I know Maggie thought it was weird that I insisted on meeting her at the police department, but she'll be there alone today. There'd be no one to say what time she left if she didn't show. The inn is on a long stretch of dark road where too many bad things could happen. But there's only one bad thing in particular that has me concerned.

My mother sniffs and glances around. "Where's the mood board I suggested the two of you create for the wedding? I can't wait to see the aesthetic you're going for."

I silently curse to myself. Maggie and I had discussed my mother's suggestion. And we did, in fact, have a stack of ideas we'd been giving each other for our "board."

The front from one of the boxes of frozen enchiladas Maggie frequently eats for dinner when she gets home late that I cut out, proposing that we make it the cornerstone around which we plan the rest of the wedding. A picture of orange tiger lilies ripped from a magazine that Maggie had given me in return, suggesting that we use them as centerpieces, arranged in glass bowls with enchilada sauce instead of water. A photograph I'd printed off the internet of a woman from the '70s in an ornate rust-colored gown with matching makeup that I'd left taped to her bathroom mirror with THIS!!! written on it in Sharpie.

The truth is, neither of us is the mood board type, and the whole thing had turned into a running joke. Instead of admitting it, though, I say, "Maggie and I thought it would be nice for us to make one together. As a family."

Instantly, the steely look in my mother's eyes softens and I feel a wash of guilt. It should be true. I wish it were. But now it's just another task to add to my already insurmountable list.

One, keep everyone safe. Two, prevent my family from ever discovering that Wesley Banks has resurfaced. Three, find a way to remove Wesley and the threat he presents from my life. Permanently.

4

MAGGIE

The young woman's hands twist into knots on her lap. A steady stream of tears flows down her puffy, reddened cheeks. She struggles to catch her breath between sobs, wipes her swollen nose on the shoulder of her jacket, leaving a shiny trail behind.

"Jenny, please." I crouch beside the chair behind Sue's desk, where I've sat her in an attempt to get her to calm down enough to tell me what's wrong. Taking her hands in mine, I gently squeeze them until she lifts her eyes to meet my own. I hold her gaze and smile encouragingly. "Tell me what's wrong."

"He's gone."

"Who's gone?"

"My baby. PJ."

"PJ?"

I feel my body go rigid, blood hardening in my veins like lava in magma tubes. When I first moved to Coyote Cove, Jenny was the receptionist at the local veterinarian's office. She'd been bright, bubbly, young.

I'd thought nothing of it when another girl answered the phone the next time I'd called to make an appointment, when I saw Jenny walking around town first with a baby bump, then with a baby, though that was years ago now. Since then, I've seen her on dozens of occasions, each with the child in her arms.

Though I try, I can't for the life of me recall ever seeing the boy's face—it's always been nestled against Jenny as he clings to her with fierce devotion. I swallow down a lump of guilt as she nods, her voice raspy as she says, "Patrick James."

Rubbing my dry lips together, I clear my throat, find my voice. "When was the last time you saw him?"

"Last night. I peeked in on him when I got home from—" Her voice breaks, tone going high enough to break glass.

"From where?"

"The bar. I was at the Loose Moose with a couple of friends from school." Her expression begs me to understand, to not judge her, or tell her she deserves this, as she explains. "It's the first time I've hung out with them since I found out I was pregnant."

"There's nothing wrong with going out," I assure her. "Who was watching him while you were gone?"

"My husband, Greg. And his mother was there. And two of his kids from his previous marriage, the oldest and the youngest."

"And you've talked to all of them this morning? None of them knows where he is?"

She shakes her head, fist held to her trembling mouth.

"How old is PJ?"

Her voice is barely a whisper. "He just turned four."

"Has he ever disappeared before? Maybe gone out on his own, exploring?"

"No, never. He's never out of my sight when he's awake."

"Did you notice any signs that the house might have been broken into? That someone else may have been inside?"

Jenny gulps before answering. "They wouldn't have had to break in. We never bother locking the doors. Don't really have anything to steal. Only..."

I duck down to find her eyes, which have dropped to her lap. "Only what?"

"Only, last night, when I got home, the door was locked. I figured my mother-in-law had done it on purpose, you know? To show her disapproval of me going out. Or just to be a, well... you know. I had to use the key from under the mat to unlock it. But I... I was drunk. Too drunk. I don't even remember if I took the key out of the lock after letting myself inside."

Her body jerks in a series of spasms as she curls herself into a ball, drawing her legs up on the chair, dropping her face to her knees. "This is my fault. It's all my fault."

"Let's not get ahead of ourselves," I say. "I'm going to call Lieutenant Kishore, have him contact our reserve officers and start organizing a search party. Then we'll go to your house and take a look around. With any luck, he just decided to take a walk and he'll already be back home by the time we get there."

But if she's heard me, she doesn't acknowledge it. "It's so cold out. He'll need his hat. He always gets an ear infection if he doesn't wear his hat."

"Maybe he thought to take his hat with him?"

She unfurls one of her arms from the tight knot she's drawn herself into, reaches into her pocket in slow motion, a look of horror spreading across her already stricken features as she withdraws her hand, a red knit cap held in her grasp.

The beanie is obviously well loved or, at least, well worn, with frays and pulls in the maroon yarn. Yarn the exact same color as blood. My stomach feels like it's turning inside out as I stare at it, overcome with the sensation that I'm looking at a premonition.

5

MAGGIE

The house before me has seen better days. A sagging roof looks like it might buckle under the weight of the clouds hovering above it. The exterior walls are covered in Cape Cod shingles the color of decay, gone in places like missing teeth. Plywood covers a broken window like an eyepatch, and the entire structure appears to list to the left, though that could be an optical illusion caused by the half-collapsed front porch.

"Greg's first wife got the house in their divorce. After that, he decided to never have anything worth taking again," Jenny explains, rotting boards groaning beneath her feet as she races recklessly across them.

She tosses the unlocked front door open wide, charging into a living room that remains dreary despite obvious attempts to cozy it up. A middle-aged man, one at least twice Jenny's age, sits beside a boy on a threadbare couch. Both have their eyes glued to the TV in front of them. Their thumbs move frantically as they work the game controllers clutched in their grasps.

"Is he back?" Jenny asks, the hope in her voice tugging at my heart.

The man frowns but his gaze doesn't leave the screen. "You haven't found him yet?"

"No, I haven't found him yet! I told you he's missing! Have you even bothered to look?" The level of her voice triples, the tone tinged with panic.

"Don't go getting all worked up now. He's probably just hiding somewhere. Give me a minute and I'll help you look."

"He's not hiding! He's gone, Greg!" Jenny snatches the remote from the coffee table in front of them and turns the TV off.

The boy, who must be around ten, gapes at the blank screen before bursting into tears. Jumping to his feet, he runs down the hall, his disappearance accentuated by the slamming of a door.

"What's gotten into you?" Greg turns toward her and notices me standing by the front door. The color drains from his face. His voice is full of disbelief as he says, "You called the cops?"

Jenny steps closer to me, seeming to shrink under her husband's gaze. She nods reluctantly, like she wishes she could deny being the one to bring me into their home.

"What's all the fuss about?"

An older woman shuffles into the room on dirty slippers, a lit cigarette dangling from the corner of her mouth. Her lips draw back in a sneer when she sees me. She exhales a cloud of smoke in my direction as she asks, "What's she doing here?"

Jenny ignores the question. "Have you found PJ?"

I watch as Franny Warner drops heavily into an armchair. It's not even 9 a.m. yet and her eyes are already bloodshot and out of focus. And yet she manages to glare at me, obviously still pissed that she lost her license when she couldn't pay the fine for the OUI I issued her earlier in the year for drunk driving. Ashing her cigarette on the floor, she takes a long drag before replying, "It's not our job to keep track of your kid."

"He's Greg's kid, too!" Jenny covers her face with her

hands, sobbing into them, the composure that I'd worked so hard to help her achieve now completely gone. "He's just a little boy."

"Calm down, Jenny." Greg stands up, pauses for a moment, eyeing me before he approaches his wife and settles a hand awkwardly on her back. "I told you he's probably just playing a game and hiding in the house."

She shakes his hands off, teeth bared as she hisses. "Don't you think I checked? He's gone, Greg. I... I'm worried someone might have taken him."

They stare at each other for a long moment, an intense, silent exchange taking place between them. As I watch, he seems to shrink before my eyes. Finally, swallowing hard, he turns to me and says, "What do we do now?"

When a child goes missing, a clock starts. The longer it takes you to find them, the worse the odds become that you will —at least alive. I already have a search party organizing. I need to determine if we're actually going to need to use it, if little PJ Warner is indeed missing, or simply hiding somewhere in the house like Greg seemed so convinced of only moments ago. And if he is gone, I need to talk to the members of this family and determine who knows what, fast.

Because the clock is ticking.

If the child wandered off, Coyote Cove is mostly wooded, which further complicates matters. And if PJ didn't just wander off, if something else happened to him... I think about Jenny not remembering if she had left the key in the lock last night, then do my best to shake off the sense of doom that's wedged its way under my skin like a splinter. We'll cross that bridge when we come to it. *If* we come to it.

But first. "I'm going to need to speak with everyone who was in this house last night and this morning. If you could please gather them all for me, I'd appreciate it."

I hold Greg Warner's gaze until he turns and trudges down

the hallway to collect his children. As soon as he's gone, I take a quick look around the room, cataloguing the sparse furnishings, none of which could provide a hiding place for a four-year-old boy.

"I'd like to help you check the house again real quick," I tell Jenny, "make sure that there isn't a spot you overlooked where PJ is hiding before we proceed."

She nods, then silently leads the way out of the living room. I dig my hands deep into my jacket pockets as I follow, fingers crossed. I don't believe in luck, but in this case, I'll take all of the help I can get. Because I have to find this little boy.

I know firsthand what can happen to a family when they lose a member. I've failed before. I can't fail again.

6

MAGGIE

Five years ago

It's Maggie's first day off after nine in a row on the job. She loves what she does. Loves putting the pieces together until they fit, loves tracking down criminals and holding them accountable for their crimes, loves truth and justice and the American way.

But sometimes, it's a lot. Bearing witness to the horrors that people inflict on each other. Immersing herself in the inhumanity of humanity. It makes her wish she had a dog to come home to, a loving, loyal creature that she could trust.

Not that she has time to take care of anything, including herself, but one day, maybe. Until then, she's going to eke out whatever joy she can find in life, and today that includes catching up on some much-needed rest, which is exactly what she does.

She wakes late, lingering in bed, relishing the luxury of having nothing to do. Dozing until her bladder insists she gets up, which she does reluctantly. Throwing on an old college t-shirt and a pair of gym shorts, she starts what she anticipates will be a lazy day.

Carrying her breakfast outside, she settles onto the back porch. Opens her laptop and brings up a local news feed. The verdict is due today on the Gordon Barkley case, a man she arrested for murdering his elderly father. The tweaker had needed money to feed his addiction and thought smothering his own flesh and blood would be a good way to get it.

It had been an easy collar to make, Gordon's skin cells found under his father's fingernails, fibers from the ratty sweatshirt he always wore recovered from deep within the murdered man's nasal cavity, multiple neighbors seeing the son run from the house with a TV tucked under his arm the day of the crime, confirmed by a pawn slip from a local shop.

But Maggie's one of those detectives who feels a case isn't truly closed until the jury renders its verdict. She follows all of her arrests until sentencing. So she makes herself comfortable, pulling her feet up onto the chair and balancing her plate on her knees.

A warm, gentle breeze carries the promise of a scorching day and the aroma of her new cinnamon bun–flavored coffee. She breathes deep, relishing the fresh air. Takes a bite of English muffin, savoring the taste of the butter lathered into the nooks and crannies. But she stops chewing when she thinks she hears the newscaster say her brother's name in his slightly clipped tone.

Maggie's gaze jerks sharply from the butterfly she was watching and lands on her mother's tear-streaked face, the image grainy on the computer screen. The plate with her breakfast flies off her knees, shattering as she scrambles toward the laptop, grabbing it in an attempt to wrest the truth from it as the camera feed shifts to her dad. Not believing what the broadcast is telling her, she springs from her seat and dashes inside.

Her baby brother, missing.

Last night his bed had lain empty and she hadn't known. No one had bothered to tell her.

It didn't make sense. He'd been playing in a park in broad

daylight, yet no one saw a thing. Not her mother, nor the other parents, nor their kids. And Brandon knew better than to wander off.

Her mind races as she thinks of the park, the same one she'd played in as a child, in the same neighborhood she'd grown up in. The area is developed. No empty lots, no drainage ponds, no woods. And the news said the search crews had gone door to door, checked every yard and outbuilding, anywhere a small child might hide, and had turned up empty.

So where had he gone?

She thinks of Brandon, with his chubby cheeks, the spray of freckles across his nose, his shining eyes and infectious smile. The curious joy she'd felt when his first word had been "Magga." The way he'd climb into her lap whenever she visited, which she didn't do nearly enough. It just isn't possible.

He can't be gone. But chances are, he would have been found by now if he had just strayed off, which meant...

A stranger had him. Her baby brother had been taken.

It's the worst-case scenario.

Nausea crawls up her throat, the taste of butter sickening on her tongue. The clock has started. The first twenty-four hours after a child goes missing are the most vital, and those are already over. The first forty-eight hours... She swallows hard, not wanting to think it.

This morning, while she'd been in bed, thinking there was nothing to do... She'll never forgive herself.

Why hadn't anyone thought to call her? Her parents? Her supervisor? One of her colleagues?

She needs to organize another search. Pull video footage. Conduct interviews. Someone must know something. Little boys don't just vanish into thin air.

Except when they do.

It strikes her like lightning, leaving her breathless and reeling. All the atrocities she's seen. The horrors she knows are true.

She dials her parents. The house phone rings as she grabs her car keys. Her mom's cell as she shoves her feet into an old pair of sneakers she'd left discarded by the entryway. Her dad's line as she runs to her car, not bothering to lock her front door. The calls ring and ring and ring.

But no one answers.

7
STEVE

I'm in a cold sweat, heart jackhammering as I peer around the corner. My gaze bounces off my mom, reading with the dogs on the couch, to my sister and grandfather, hunched over the coffee table playing a game of chess. Feeling like a criminal, I slink down the hall and into my bedroom, closing the door silently behind me.

"I told you not to call," I whisper angrily, barely able to hear myself over the pulse thundering in my ears.

"That's not the way this works, and you know it. *You* aren't the one who gives the orders in this little relationship of ours. Not if you want me to keep playing nice."

I sit on the edge of the bed, cradling my head in my hands. Wondering how it is that I came to find myself in this mess.

Taking my silence as agreement, Wesley continues. "I've been patient enough, old friend. It's time for that favor you owe me."

I bite my tongue to keep from spitting out that I don't owe him any favors. That I don't, in fact, intend to give him anything. Even if it were something small, something easy, he'd just ask for more later down the line.

8
MAGGIE

It had taken only minutes to check the small house for PJ and confirm that Jenny was right—he wasn't anywhere. Not under any of the cabinets or beds, not in the closets, and certainly not in the little storage room that was his nursery, a space too small to park a car, but that Jenny had decorated into a place he must have loved. Now that room is off limits, waiting to be processed as a potential crime scene.

As I looked, I inspected every window that I came to, checking that the locks were on, scanning the sills for signs that they'd been opened recently—a leaf blown inside, a live bug struggling to get out, a dent in the layer of dust that covered each ledge—but there were none. There were also no footprints in the mud outside them, and the carpet beneath each was relatively clean and completely dry to the touch.

Which means that whatever happened, whether PJ left on his own or was taken, he went through the front door. The question is, would he have left quietly with a stranger, without making a fuss?

"I have a search crew on the way," I tell the family, slowly letting my gaze run over the members one by one.

there are no misunderstandings, if you don't meet with me, the deal is off."

"We don't have a deal," I remind him.

"Oh, I think that we do. Because I really don't think you want me bothering anyone else with this. They all look so peaceful right now. Gramps and Izzy playing chess. Your mother reading. And all those adorable doggies. Three now! Hmm. But your fiancée's not here. I wonder where she could be right this moment?"

My blood chills in my veins, hardening into ice. He's here, watching us right now. I want to run into the living room, start pulling all the curtains and blinds shut, and I will. But first.

"When?" My voice comes out as a whisper.

"Tomorrow. Three o'clock."

"Where?"

"I'll let you know that when it's time."

"But—"

"It's a small town, Steve-o. Doesn't take much time to get around. You just be ready, and you'll make it on time. At least, you will if you're lucky."

The line goes dead. It takes a part of me with it. I knew this was bad. I knew Wesley was dangerous. But for some reason, I'd really expected him to keep this between us and play fair. Maybe that makes me almost as crazy as he is.

considered allowing me into her home a good deed, like I was some kind of charity work. I'm sure she disinfected anything she thought I had touched as soon as I left."

"That's not true."

"We'll have to agree to disagree on that one, buddy. She was always funny about me, especially when your little sister was around."

I can't say anything about that because it's correct. In hindsight, it's like my mother had some kind of sixth sense about Wesley. About what he'd turn into one day.

Almost as if he can read my thoughts, he says, "Not that I can't see why now. Izzy sure is looking good these days. Baby girl got fine."

"That's enough." I can't stomach anymore. Can't listen to any more of the filth coming out of his mouth, wondering if it's a veiled threat. Or a not so veiled one. "You leave her, leave them all, out of this. This is between you and me and no one else."

"Sure, of course. Your choice. It's all your choice. Give me what I want and this all goes away."

"You still haven't told me what that is yet."

My eyes grow damp. I feel like I'm eight years old again and the only boy in the neighborhood who can't pop a wheelie on his bike. Like I'm fourteen and can't talk to the girl I like without choking up and making a fool of myself. Like I'm seventeen and can't wrap my head around calculus no matter how hard I try, my failing grade threatening to squash my hopes of getting into a good college.

Only, the consequences of this failure could be deadly.

"I will. But not like this," he says.

"Like what?"

"Over the phone. We need to meet. In person."

"What? No way. That's not happening."

"Whatever. Like I said, this is all your choice. But just so

"You haven't even told me what you want yet," I say, speaking slowly to keep my voice tempered.

"You know, I've got to hand it to you, Steve-o. You sure are a lucky man."

Something in his tone makes my skin bristle. My teeth grit together. An imaginary fist clenches around my throat until it's too tight to swallow.

"A hot cop fiancé. A couple of dogs. You got yourself a nice little setup to play house with there, don't you?"

I wipe at the sweat that's sprouted on my brow with the back of my wrist.

"Of course, let's not forget about your family."

My legs start trembling. I feel helpless, trapped between the urge to tell him to shut his mouth and the fear of the repercussions if I antagonize him.

"Grandpa Joe got old. I mean, I suppose it has been almost twenty years since I last saw him, but still. He used to be such a badass. I'm not ashamed to admit that I was more than a bit intimidated by him back in the day. But not anymore."

I should have known. I thought I was protecting my family by bringing them here, where I could keep an eye on them. Instead, I've put them at even greater risk. There's got to be a way to fix this.

"Your mom looks almost the same, though. Funny how money can do that to a woman. Stop her from aging. Of course, she still has that look on her face. You know the one. Like she's better than everyone else. Like the mere mortals of the earth offend her. Especially me. Even when I was a little kid, she didn't like me."

"You know you were always welcome at my house when we were growing up," I rush to say, not wanting this lunatic to feel like he has some sort of vendetta to settle with anyone but me.

"Not by choice. She only tolerated me because we were such good friends." He gives a bitter laugh. "She probably

Jenny, chestnut-colored hair pushed back from her face in greasy clumps, chewing on her nails as she paces the room with a wild look in her eyes. Franny, head hanging low over her chest in the recliner, mouth slack and slightly open, possibly sleeping —or, more likely, passed out. Greg, slumped limply on the couch like he's boneless.

The young boy who'd been playing a video game when I arrived sits beside him scowling, arms crossed over his bony chest. A teenage girl, phone clenched in a white-knuckled grip, is wedged into the far corner of the couch.

"Is this everyone who was here last night?" I ask. When no one answers, I prod, "Mr. Warner?"

"Don't know what time Jenny finally decided to drag herself home last night, but yeah, the rest of us were here."

"And no one else?"

"Who else would there be?"

"Dylan," Jenny says, coming to a stop behind her husband and staring down at the back of his head.

"Dylan was at a friend's house last night," he says.

"Who's Dylan?" I ask.

"His oldest son. From his first marriage," Jenny explains.

I look at Greg. "Where's he now?"

"Dunno. Probably still at the friend's house."

The girl mutters something about *"great parenting"* under her breath.

"And you are?"

"Does it really matter?" Greg asks.

The girl raises wary eyes to mine. "The daughter from the first marriage."

"Amanda," Jenny supplies, tone exasperated. "Her name is Amanda."

"And this guy?" As I nod toward the little boy, his scowl deepens, causing his ears to jut out even farther from the sides of his head.

"Doofus." A teenage boy struts into the room, drops onto the couch between his sister and his brother, pinning a bit of them both under his lanky legs. Amanda rolls her eyes and shifts free while the younger boy protests.

"Hey."

"Don't blame me, squirt, I didn't name you."

He puts his brother in a headlock, gives him a noogie hard enough to turn the boy's face bright red.

"Dylan," Jenny pleads. "Can you please leave him alone right now? This is serious."

The teenager squinches his face up. Confusion clouds his features as he notices who I am.

"Hey. What's going on?"

"Your brother's missing," I say. "If you could all just settle down a moment—"

"No, he isn't. He's right here."

"Your other brother."

"PJ?" he asks. He leans forward so he can see Jenny. "The little guy's missing?"

Jenny nods, a high-pitched whimper escaping from her throat.

"But that's... I mean..." He looks around the room, wide-eyed. "There's no way. I've never seen such a momma's boy before. The kid's practically still attached by the umbilical cord. He wouldn't have just taken off."

"She was out last night." Franny speaks up for the first time from the recliner. "Boozing it up."

Jenny makes a noise of protest.

"Maybe he left to try and find her," Dylan suggests.

Amanda whispers, "But it was so cold last night."

"I checked on him when I came home," Jenny says. "He was still here, in his bed. He was sound asleep."

The atmosphere in the room shifts as the small amount of hope PJ's family has been clinging to shrinks a little more. I feel it myself—it's getting harder to stay positive. Harder to believe that PJ went exploring and is just waiting for us to find him. Harder to deny the grim reality that someone took their little boy.

"This is important," I say, knowing that the search party will be arriving any minute now. "Did any of you see or hear anything out of the ordinary last night?"

"Like what?" the youngest boy asks.

"Jamie." His father says the name as a warning.

"No, it's all right." I squat in front of the kid. "Like, did you see anyone who wasn't supposed to be here? Or hear someone coming or going?"

He shoots a worried look at his brother. Dylan holds the boy's gaze as he ruffles his hair. "The little dwarf here could sleep through a bomb explosion and not wake up."

"How about the rest of you?"

The family looks at each other, seeing if there's anyone who isn't shaking their head no. There's not.

Standing, I search their faces as I ask, "Do you have any idea what direction PJ might have gone if he did go out on his own?"

No one does.

"Where do you go most often when he's with you?" I ask Jenny.

She shifts uncomfortably, staring at her hands as she says, "Nowhere. Just town."

"Do you usually walk or drive?"

"Drive."

"Okay, then. We'll start the search along the roads and spread out from there."

I don't mention that PJ would have been spotted already if he had stuck to the roads between here and town. By the looks on the faces of the family around me, I don't have to.

9

MAGGIE

My muscles vibrate, nerves strumming my tendons like guitar strings, my body longing to burst into action. But searching for a missing person is a slow process. You have to be careful, thorough, methodical. You have to take your time, no matter how much you'd like to run full speed ahead.

The reserve officers await my signal. The civilians who heard about a lost child and chose to come join us today exchange nervous glances, wondering at the hold-up as I squint at the landscape in front of me. I imagine what this next step will look like, trying to predict the problems we might encounter, but it's impossible.

This search becomes more difficult—and dangerous—the moment I give the go-ahead to proceed. It's my duty to keep these volunteers safe. But there's a little boy missing. And he could be out there. Raising my hand high, I gesture forward.

No one speaks as we leave the road and enter the woods. Trees tower high overhead, a mix of pine and maple and birch. Though the fresh green of new buds is just beginning to sprout on winter-bared limbs, there are enough evergreens to effectively block out the sun overhead. It's like dusk has fallen, and with it, the thermometer.

I shiver and pull down the sleeves of my jacket over my hands, chilled by the shadows and the thoughts that lurk in the darkened corners of my mind. Leaves crunch loudly underfoot. A stick cracks. Someone sneezes. But I don't hear the sound I long to hear most right now—that of a child.

The silence crawls under my skin, making it tight and itchy, until I can't take it anymore. Cupping my hands to my mouth, I yell, "PJ?"

I crane my head, listening for an answer, but none comes. There's only the sounds of the searchers and the infinite distance before us. We could walk for days without coming upon signs of civilization.

Between that and the unseasonable temperatures, hovering just below freezing, if that little boy is out here in these conditions on his own, he doesn't stand much of a chance of lasting long. Perhaps that's why the searchers with me remain mute, the mood somber as we thread our way through the woods, looking for any sign of the child.

I try not to think about how far north we are. How remote. How different this search would be if neither of those things were true. To do so seems defeatist. And yet, I can't deny what the sick feeling lodged like a stone high in my throat is trying to tell me.

Because Coyote Cove is like no place that I've ever been before. Once you've left the scant streets of the town, there's a vastness to the valley, a sense that it's never-ending, that you could walk a lifetime without hitting a barrier.

But more than that, there's something about the place that suggests someone could easily be swallowed up, never to be seen again. Maybe it has something to do with the feral feel of the northern Maine landscape, the fanged bite of the air. Or maybe it's because in the five years that I've been here, I've learned that these shadows hide a darkness the likes of which I've never encountered anywhere else.

Whatever the reason, a sense of déjà vu wraps tight around me, refusing to be ignored. Because I've been here before, haven't I? Maybe not here, in this forlorn section of the north woods, but in my life.

A child missing. An overwhelming anxiety that I won't be able to bring him home.

Though I'm doing my best to keep it together, to maintain my calm exterior, I can't manage to fool myself. It's all a lie. On the inside, I'm screaming.

Because it's happening all over again.

10

MAGGIE

Maggie bursts into the squad room, struggling not to break out into a run as she crosses the bullpen. She looks around at her colleagues, seeking answers, her actions frantic, manic, but no one will meet her eye. It's eerie, like she isn't even there. Like she's ceased to exist.

She wonders for a moment if maybe she has. If Don from cybercrime's coffee is so interesting because she isn't really passing by his desk right now. If Joni from narcotics isn't purposely ignoring her, staring up at the flickering fluorescent lights overhead as she brushes by in the hall. If maybe she's still at home, collapsed on the floor in a puddle of loss and grief.

But her rap on Sheriff Brewster's closed door is loud and undeniable. She's here. She's just on her own.

An excruciatingly long moment passes before the sheriff answers, "Come in."

Wiping her damp palms on her shorts, she takes a deep breath, doing her best to compose herself, then enters the room.

The man before her continues reading the paperwork on his

desk as she enters the room that smells of boiled cabbage and dust. Her gaze runs over the stacks of boxes, shelves overflowing with files and books, before settling on her boss. She stares at the thinning hair on the top of his head, at the shiny scalp visible through the wisps, surprised to see that the little that remains hasn't started to smoke under the intensity of her gaze.

Finally, Sheriff Brewster looks up. "Detective Riley," he says, tone holding a mild element of surprise. "Aren't you off today?"

"What's being done in the Brandon Riley case? Who has it?"

He straightens in his chair, runs a hand over his balding pate as if finally feeling the heat as he asks, "Relative of yours?"

"He's my brother."

The crease between his eyebrows deepens as he frowns, regarding her. "Quite an age difference, isn't there?"

Maggie bites the inside of her cheek to keep from shouting. She could explain that her mom was in her late forties when she gave birth to Brandon. That what she'd thought was menopause was a change-of-life baby instead. That obviously there's a huge age gap between her and her sibling since she's old enough to be his mother herself. But time is ticking, and she doesn't want to waste any more of it than necessary. So she just nods instead.

"Take a seat," he says, gesturing to one of the worn chairs in front of his desk, cheap vinyl meant to look like leather. She stares at it like it's a disease-ridden needle. Forces herself to perch on the edge as Sheriff Brewster leans forward over his desk, his expression blank, unreadable.

The sheriff is old-school South. Slow. Methodical. Refusing to be rushed beyond his own pace and demanding the respect he thinks he deserves. The worst move Maggie can make right now is to lose control. She needs to keep her cool. But for the first time in her career, she resents the man sitting across from her.

She tucks her fists under her legs so she won't be so compelled to use them. Digs her nails deep into the palms of her hands, using the pain to steady herself. Focuses on her breathing, not entirely understanding how her body is functioning right now.

"We've conducted a thorough search of the area," Sheriff Brewster explains. "We sent patrols door to door. Checked every yard. Had the copter up running infrared. But..." He holds his hands out toward her, palms up. "Nothing."

"So what's next? Do we widen the search area or—"

"There is no we on this, Maggie. I understand your desire to help, but you need to keep your distance from this investigation. You can't be involved."

The air leaves her body like she's been punched in the gut. "But—"

"No buts. Not if you want to keep your job."

A hard coal of anger ignites inside her. The two bites of breakfast she ate this morning rise up the back of her throat. She feels like she's going to erupt.

Who better to work this case than her? She has a box of awards and commendations, or has he forgotten? That seems unlikely, since he never hesitates to trot her out and parade her in front of the media when the department needs some good PR. A tremor starts deep within her body, a rage she must somehow contain unless she wants to be cut off completely.

Her voice sounds reedy as she asks, "Then what is your next step? Sir. Are there any suspects?"

His gaze breaks away from hers, eyes shifting to the side. His already ruddy skin turns a little redder.

"What is it you aren't telling me?" It's a whisper. A plea.

Sheriff Brewster sighs wearily. "The truth is that we have nothing to go on. There's been no sign of your brother. No evidence." He clears his throat and shifts in his chair. "We haven't even been able to find any witnesses to confirm that your brother was there at the park before your mother says he went missing."

Maggie reels back in her seat. Her eyes grow wider, then

wider still, until they feel like they're going to bulge right out of their sockets. Her trembling growls stronger, her body visibly shaking now. She feels like a rocket getting ready to launch.

"We both know the stats on missing children cases, Maggie," he says softly, not unkindly. "A majority of them have familial connections."

Her head shifts from side to side. Is that why her parents haven't called her? Because they're under investigation? Because they somehow blame her for what they're going through right now?

"We don't have anything else to go on right now."

"Then you aren't looking hard enough."

"Maggie—"

"Who's pulled the case?" *she demands. Someone isn't doing their job. Isn't looking hard enough. Someone is missing something. She wants to know who.*

"Detective Hawkins."

"No."

"Excuse me?"

"Hawkins is an idiot. The man couldn't even find his own foot in a sock."

"Detective Hawkins is a valued member of this department."

Maggie huffs. "If Detective Hawkins were a woman—or a minority," *she says as she stands, unable to sit on her disgust any longer,* "or anyone besides your godson, he wouldn't even be a member of this department, and we both know that's true."

She looks hard into his eyes, challenging him.

The sheriff's voice is low and steely as he says, "I understand that you are under a great deal of strain at the moment, Detective, so I'm going to overlook the lapse in judgment that compelled you to challenge my integrity, this one time and one time only."

It's unbelievable. Her whole career, everything she's spent her entire adult life working for, is a joke. She has to get out of here. She spins on her heel, turning her back on her boss, and stalks toward the door.

"I'm serious, Riley," Sheriff Brewster calls after her. "You stay away from this investigation. Don't let me find out that you've been meddling."

But the warning falls on deaf ears. Someone has to do something to find her brother. Someone has to bring him home. And it's become clear that someone is her—no matter what the cost.

11

MAGGIE

I squeeze my arms tighter to my sides, fighting off a shiver. Blink against the gray haze that's making it harder to see, blurring the trunks of the trees. Try being casual as I check the time. It's almost four. Still early in terms of the day, but this far north, the sun will be setting soon. Once that happens, darkness—and the temperature—will fall fast.

Already my cheeks feel hard and frozen, my eyes stinging from the cold. I know I should call it for the day. I need to get my search party out of these woods safely. But no matter how cold and uncomfortable we are right now, a child would be faring much worse.

Especially one who's without shoes or a jacket. Jenny's tearful confession that all of PJ's outerwear was accounted for had torn at my heart, a tear that was enlarged as she begged to be allowed to join the search party. But I couldn't agree to that, couldn't allow any of the family to join our efforts to find their youngest member, no matter how much they wanted to.

As much as I hate to even consider it, until we find the boy, they're not just parents or siblings or grandparents—they're suspects. And even if they weren't, I still wouldn't want them with us. Because if PJ *is* out here on his own, unprepared for the brutal elements we're facing, the outlook is grim. They don't need to see what we might find.

The radio strapped to my shoulder crackles. A second later, my lieutenant's voice carries through the speaker. "Chief, you there?"

"Yeah, Kal. You guys find something?" I ask hopefully. His team had been tasked with searching the area immediately surrounding the Warner house. When that failed, he led them into the wilderness beyond, to the east, while those who went with me searched along the road and entered the woods to the west.

"Unfortunately, no. I just wanted to let you know that we're down another two members."

Squeezing my eyes shut, I curse. We've got less than an hour of light left to search by. If PJ is out here on his own, we need to find him while there's still a chance that this is a rescue mission and not a recovery. And if he is out here, I can only imagine how scared he is. How miserable. How cold. All things that will only get worse after dark.

With each hour that has passed, more members of the search team have fallen off. Not that I can blame them. Many of these men and women need to work to survive. They can't afford to incapacitate themselves to find a child who may no longer be alive. And no one wants to be the one to make the discovery if that's the case.

I check the time again. As much as it pains me to do so, I say, "It's getting late. Let's give it another half hour and then call it for the day. Get everyone back to their vehicles before it's too dark to see."

"You sure? I don't mind staying out later, got a few guys on my team who feel the same way."

I draw a deep breath. "I'm sure."

Only I'm not. What if we're giving up too soon? What if

tomorrow, when the search reconvenes, we discover that if we'd only looked a little longer, gone a little farther, we would have found him? What if it's not too late now, but it will be then?

"Roger that. Over and out."

Immediately, I want to radio Kal back and tell him to keep his team at it as long as they're willing, but I can't. It's my responsibility to make the calls that will keep these people safe, no matter how hard they are to make. If I choose the wrong one, the weight will be on my shoulders, my cross to carry.

But if I'm being honest with myself, my gut's telling me that it's already too late to bring PJ Warner home alive and well. And if I'm being *really* honest, I've thought that from the start.

12

STEVE

I've checked every window. Every door. The bulkhead to the basement. I've done everything I can to make sure that this house is secure, that the people inside it, my people, will be safe, but it doesn't feel like enough. How could it?

There was a time when there was no one I was closer to than Wesley Banks. We'd grown up in the same apartment building. Been friends since kids are capable of that kind of thing, earlier than that, even, if you count the time we spent in diapers, drooling in a playpen together while our mothers kept company.

By the time we started school, we were inseparable. It was us against the world. The two amigos because we didn't need a third. We were even roommates in college, first in the dorm, and later off campus. For almost two decades of my life, I would have sworn that our friendship would last forever. That there was nothing that could have ever come between us.

But one fateful night proved me wrong.

In an instant, our unbreakable friendship shattered into a million irreparable pieces. Even then, though, I wasn't scared of Wesley. There hadn't seemed a reason to be. Because what happened was horrible. It was unforgivable. But it was an accident.

Only, all these years later, I've come to realize that maybe it wasn't.

I denied the little pieces of the puzzle that didn't add up. I never tried to put them together to find out what I'd see. It didn't seem necessary. Wesley was out of my life forever, and that was enough.

Until he tracked me down.

It seems impossible that the first call was only months ago. Probably because every second since has seemed an eternity. Looking around every corner. Waiting for the hammer to drop.

Wesley wants something from me, and he's not going to stop until he gets it. But how can I give in to a known murderer? And then there's a thought I've been avoiding, one that chills me to the bone and makes me more afraid than I've ever been of anything before in my life. One that makes me sick to think how far out of my league I'd be if it was true. But as much as I've been avoiding the prospect, I can't deny that it's possible.

What if my old friend is a serial killer?

The reason I hadn't heard from Wesley all these years wasn't because he was respecting my wish for him to leave me alone. It was because he was in jail, serving a fifteen-year sentence for manslaughter as a plea bargain down from murder. A murder other than the one I knew about.

Now the guilt is nearly overwhelming. If it were just me Wesley was threatening, I'd let him do what he wants. I know that I deserve it. Because if I had only said something, if I had spoken up twenty years ago, he wouldn't have been free to kill again.

But I'd been too concerned about protecting myself. He'd told me that I was just as much to blame for what happened, and I believed him. Now I realize that wasn't exactly true.

Because all those little fragments of details I chose to

ignore? They paint a much different picture than what I spent the intervening years believing.

Why had I passed out after only two beers, one of which Wesley gave me? What were we doing out on that vacant country road, so far from where we were going, from where we had been? What was the girl doing out there by herself, with no vehicle, well beyond walking distance from the party, where I had witnessed her laugh at Wesley's advances? Wesley had always hated being laughed at.

Now, in hindsight, it seems so obvious that I wonder if I wasn't purposely blind to the truth. Because as much as I want to believe otherwise, there's a chance that I still would have helped Wesley bury that poor girl's broken body under an oak tree that night. It had been my car that hit her, after all. And though I'd been passed out in the back seat until the force of the impact woke me, no one saw who drove away from that party, as Wesley was quick to remind me.

I had my whole life ahead of me. Would I have chosen to risk my future for a girl who was already dead? Regardless, it's now clear that I should have spent the last two decades living in fear. The reprieve was undeserved.

"What are you looking at?"

I jump, a yelp strangling in my throat as I spin to face my sister.

"Is someone out there?" Izzy asks, frowning as she pulls the curtain to the side to peer out.

"No." I yank the curtain back over the window, ushering her away before she can ask any more questions. "Is everyone ready?"

"Yep, just waiting on you."

I trail behind her into the living room. Look guiltily at the three dogs resting on the pillow by the hearth. I *really* don't want to leave them. I don't want to leave the house. It makes me feel vulnerable, exposed, like I'm tempting something bad to happen. But to change our dinner plans now would seem too suspicious. Squatting beside them, I give the pups a pat and a kiss, whisper that I love them.

"Honestly, darling, don't you think you're spoiling them a bit?"

I arch an eyebrow at my mother, who packed more luggage for her dog, Laurel, than my sister brought with her. She pretends not to notice, keys jangling in her hand as she heads for the door.

"What are you doing?" I ask, jumping to my feet and hurrying to head her off.

"What do you mean?"

"I'm driving," I say. I'd counted on leaving a car behind, so Wesley would think that someone was home. Assuming, that is, that he isn't out there right now watching us leave.

"Steven, don't be absurd."

"You don't know your way around."

"I managed well enough the last time I was here. Honestly, dear, the town's not that big."

"I insist," I say, snatching the keys from her hand and giving her my best smile. "I thought it would be nice for us all to drive together. Kind of like old times."

She gives me a look like she doesn't believe me, but she doesn't argue, and for that, I'm grateful. I tug my jacket on even though I feel like I'm overheating, not even noticing the cold as I herd everyone into the vehicle. My chest feels tight as I get behind the wheel. I take several deep breaths to erase the spots from my vision. I have no idea what I'm going to do about Wesley, but whatever it is, I've got to figure it out, fast, before Maggie finds out and cancels the wedding.

13

MAGGIE

I tell myself that we've done everything that we can for the day. That tomorrow, PJ Warner will turn up just fine—in a neighbor's shed, a barn, a garage, a place where he'll have spent the night safe and warm and sound. And even though I don't believe it, I tell myself that I must, because otherwise, trying to assure his family, trying to go about the business of living my life, eating and sleeping and breathing, without becoming overwhelmed by guilt and grief would be impossible.

I try not to think about what his poor mother must be feeling right now as I stare at the map of Coyote Cove pinned to the wall under a sheet of plexiglass, feeling hopeless. There's just so much wilderness to get lost in. It would be impossible to search it all, and quite honestly, I'm not sure it would be the best use of our time to try.

Using a black dry-erase marker, I shade in the area my team searched today. "It's a rough guess, but it'll have to do," I say. I pass the marker to Kal as he hands me a cup of coffee.

He nods, running his fingers through his hair, leaving it standing on end. He considers the map for a moment before coloring in his own search quadrant, a section that includes the

Warners' yard and radiates out in a half-moon. Then he steps back beside me and we stand, shoulder to shoulder, regarding the map.

"How many miles do you think your team covered today?" I ask quietly.

I hear a hard swallow before he says, "At least three."

I know it's a low estimate. I know because it's the same number I'd have thrown out had he been the one to ask the question. I'd have said three and thought six. Not a far distance for an adult, but what about a small child?

Grabbing a red marker, I step forward and draw a big circle with the Warner house at the middle. Use the legend in the corner to guesstimate that it's ten miles. There's no way around it. Tomorrow, we need to search ten miles out in every direction.

It won't be an easy task, but we'll find a way to get it done. I've been promised that the help I requested from the state police earlier, once I confirmed PJ was missing, will be here first thing in the morning. They've agreed to send two dozen officers, a couple of crime scene techs, and a search dog. If PJ's out there, we'll find him.

But what if he's not?

I push the thought away, trying not to think of my own brother, of the fate that befell him when he was far too young. I try, but I fail. Because the quiet is haunted by the whisper of every breath my baby brother never got the chance to take.

Grief clutches me tight, squeezing my throat, my chest, my heart. I stare at the map before me until it blurs. The sound of laughter carries from outside, and I feel a pang of jealousy that some people get to travel through life unscathed while the rest of us are forced to carry the tattoo of our loss on our soul for eternity.

Kal clears his throat. His voice is gentle as he asks, "What do you think the odds are that he didn't wander off?"

I lift my eyes to his. His head bobs, signaling that he's read the truth in my eyes.

"Any ideas who?"

As much as it pains me, I don't have a choice. I've been wracking my brain for alternatives, but at this moment, they just don't exist. "No suspects yet besides the family."

"You want me to start pulling backgrounds?"

I hesitate. What I really want is a larger suspect pool. It feels foolish to hold out hope, but maybe tomorrow, when the crime scene technicians arrive, they'll find some evidence that points in a different direction. Some fingerprints, maybe, or a hair that doesn't belong.

Before I can decide on an answer, the door swings open, a gust of cold preceding the visitors into the room. I jump at the unexpected intrusion, blink rapidly to collect the tears from my eyes before clearing my throat and turning to face the interruption with a plastic smile forced across my face.

"Maggie." The frown Steve wears deepens as he takes in my expression.

I do my best to swallow my shock, try to relax in her embrace as his mother brushes by him and wraps me in her arms. "Darling. How have you been? You look tired. Are you eating well?"

Before I can answer, she withdraws, grabs me by the arm and holds me on display to the others. "Sweetheart, this is Grandpa Joe. And this"—she gives me a half turn until I'm facing a pretty dark-haired woman only several years younger than myself—"is Steven's sister, Isabelle."

"Izzy," she corrects, smiling warmly as she disentangles her mother's arm from mine. "Mother, let her go, you're hogging her."

Her eyes, calm and understanding, hold mine for a moment before she folds me softly into a hug. Everything about her is soothing, from the scent of vanilla that surrounds her to the tickle of her voice as she whispers in my ear, "Just give me a sign and I'll create a diversion for you to run." She gives me a quick squeeze before releasing me and I laugh nervously, trying to conceal the shock of it all.

"It's so great to finally meet you both," I say, giving Izzy a look of gratitude before turning my attention to Grandpa Joe. "I've heard so much about you."

Grandpa Joe's eyes twinkle as he gives me one of Steve's lopsided grins, and for a moment, I'm struck by how similar the two appear. It's like pushing fast-forward and seeing what my fiancé will look like in forty years. But there's one obvious difference that strikes me right away.

While Steve is reserved and shy, his grandfather obviously is not. The old man gives me a wink as he takes my hands in his. "Hopefully it was the PG version."

As he sidesteps the swat Diane aims at him, I catch Steve's concerned gaze from over his shoulder. *You all right?* he mouths.

I give a small nod, not wanting to let him know that, once again, I forgot. Not just about dinner tonight at the Foxtrot Grill with his family, but even that they were coming to town at all.

I've got this horrible habit of letting my personal life become overshadowed by my professional, and it's got to stop. If this marriage is going to work, I'm going to have to prioritize family, and since I don't have any of my own anymore, that means his. But I need a moment to catch my breath and prepare myself for the night ahead.

"This is my lieutenant, Kal Kishore," I say, grabbing him by the arm as he tries to fade into the background and giving him a gentle push forward to divert the attention from me.

Kal greets my future in-laws with an ease that I lack, buying me the temporary reprieve that I desperately need to collect myself. Taking a step away, I press my spine against the wall, using the chill of the surface to cool my feverish skin. The knots that had drawn my muscles tight relax their stranglehold.

"What's this I hear about the little Warner boy gone missing?"

And just like that, I find myself floundering once again. I gape at Margot Graves as she storms through the door, tossing it shut behind her. A tsunami of guilt crashes over me as the tiny owner of the local motel stalks across the room, stopping in front of me with her hands fisted on her hips, demanding answers. Every head in the room jerks in my direction.

Are they judging me, the woman who only seconds ago was pretending like nothing was wrong when a little boy has vanished? Was there something I should have done differently? How do you find a balance?

The truth is, I've never known. Even before my brother was taken, I'd never been what one might consider normal. My social skills have always been lacking. My priorities have always been skewed. And yet, when I look at Steve, hoping to find forgiveness, I find concern and acceptance instead.

"Oh. Sorry." Margot sounds subdued as she looks around the room. "I didn't realize you had visitors."

"Maggie, darling, is this true?" Diane asks. "How tragic."

Steve wraps an arm over my shoulder, tucking me close, as if trying to protect me from everyone's stares. I glance at Kal and quickly look away. I'm supposed to be the leader here. It feels like just one more way that I'm failing.

"We haven't found him." I say the words like I'm admitting a dirty secret, head hanging low in shame.

"You look at the father yet?" Margot asks. I give her a desperate look, trying to convey that now isn't the time to discuss this, but she doesn't take the hint. "You should talk to his ex. Ask her about the time he forgot about that boy of theirs in the back seat of his truck. Poor kid sat there roasting all day while his daddy tossed back cold ones at the Loose Moose. Been ten, twelve years, and that boy still ain't right."

I think about the teenager I'd met earlier, Dylan, and wonder if she's correct. Had there been something off about him? But he'd been at a friend's house when PJ went missing.

His father, Greg, however, had been home. Remembering how disinterested he'd been in his youngest son's disappearance, I can't help questioning if he'd learned his lesson all those years ago, or if he was still walking the line of a neglectful parent.

This time, when I meet Kal's eyes, it's with authority. His lips press into a tight line and he gives a slight dip of his head, a signal that he understands the unspoken directive.

"Thanks, Margot. I'll be sure to look into it."

She gives me a curt nod, all business, and turns to leave. Stops dead in her tracks as her eyes land on Grandpa Joe. "Who are you?"

His eyes alight with mischief as he gives a little half bow. "Your date for this evening, madam."

She points a thumb over her shoulder as she spins to look at me. "Is this guy for real?"

"Come to dinner with me and find out."

Diane rolls her eyes, muttering something under her breath. Izzy giggles and Steve blushes. But there's something in Margot's expression that I've never seen before. Hope.

I give Steve a look. He raises his eyebrows, wondering if he's read it right. My smile is small and eager.

"Margot, this is my grandpa, Joe, my mother, Diane, and my sister, Izzy," he says, stepping forward. "We were just leaving for dinner at the Foxtrot Grill, if you'd like to join us."

She squints at him with her shrewd, raisin eyes, wrinkled face puckered in suspicion. "I wouldn't want to intrude."

Steve gestures toward his grandfather. "You'd be doing me a favor."

"Well, as long as we both agree that you'll owe me one."

Pointing a finger at Joe, she says, "Don't you go getting any ideas, now."

"I wouldn't dream of it."

"I never said you couldn't dream about it." Margot gives him a wink before leading the way out the door, leaving us all slack-jawed behind her.

This could be a very big mistake. Or it could be my saving grace. As long as it takes the pressure and focus off me long enough to get me through the night, which one doesn't really make a difference.

I turn to Kal, wondering if I should invite him. I feel like I should. I'd like for him to join us. But before I can extend the invitation, he says, "I'm going to get started on that research we talked about. Then I'll outline the perimeter for the search tomorrow. Print out some maps for the teams to use as reference."

I know I should be grateful, but I can't help feeling ashamed instead. Because I should be the one staying behind.

I have more riding on this case than anyone can know. I can't afford to mess up. Only, as I've learned in the past, it doesn't matter what you can afford. One way or another, life will find a way to make you pay its price.

14

MAGGIE

Five years ago

Maggie drives the streets of her parents' neighborhood, eyes peeled, on the lookout for signs of her brother, something that strikes her as suspicious or out of place, anything really, because she has to do something. She can't just stand by and watch. Not when the stakes are so high.

She coasts past the Moores' house, where the neighborhood kids used to gather to play kickball in the front yard. Pauses at the stop sign at the corner of the Kellers', who used to give out full-sized candy bars on Halloween. Stares through the dining room window of what used to be the Vangartens' house, where a new family is gathered around the table.

This is a safe neighborhood. The kind of place where parents don't think twice about letting their children walk to a friend's. Where the kids get set loose, roaming the streets in packs as they play.

Or maybe it's all an illusion. Maybe the safety is in the numbers. Because if what she believes is really true, her brother would be at home right now, where he should be.

Parking along the curb in front of her parents' house, she envisions Brandon inside. Maybe he'd be watching his favorite cartoon right now, or scribbling in one of his coloring books, or playing in his sandbox out back. Maybe he'd be wearing the special Scooby-Doo shirt she'd had made for him with a little cartoon Brandon standing with the rest of the gang.

Despite what she'd hoped, neither of Maggie's parents come outside to meet her. She looks at their cars in the driveway as she pulls out her cell and dials again. Pretends not to notice the shadow moving behind the bay window, peering outside. Imagines that she can hear the unanswered rings all the way out here on the street as the vehicles grow blurry behind a film of tears.

She has to make this right. She has to bring her family back together. And she knows there's only one way that's going to happen.

Ending the call, she drops the phone on the passenger seat and pulls back onto the road feeling lost and confused. She's been given a direct order not to interfere in the investigation. But how can she not? Isn't it worth risking anything if it means recovering the one who means everything?

She pulls into one of the handful of spaces at the park. Gazes, shocked, at what she sees. There's not a single squad car or patrol officer in sight. There's no police presence at all.

Instead, there are over a dozen citizens contaminating the scene as they go about their business. A young mother pushing her daughter on the swings. A father teaching his son how to shoot a basketball. A flock of older women power-walking their way around the perimeter. All of them carrying on like a little boy wasn't snatched from this very spot the day before, right beneath his mother's eyes.

Her brother is still missing! Shouldn't they be looking for him? What about combing every square inch for evidence?

Maggie exits her Jeep, falling in step behind a couple pushing a stroller. She keeps her pace slow, casual, not wanting to draw attention as she walks the northern border of the park. She stops often, studying every scrap of trash she comes across, checking every bench, scanning every vehicle that drives by and every yard she passes, knowing that the answer is here somewhere. She just has to be smart enough to find it.

Rounding the corner, she strolls along the eastern edge. Her chest is growing tighter. Each step seems a little harder, her feet growing heavier. But she refuses to lose faith.

The sun stabs at her eyes, impaling them on sharp beams of light as she shuffles along the southern stretch of the park. She squints against the glare as her fair skin sizzles in the heat.

And then Maggie sees what she's looking for. She darts into the street. Tires squeal as a car stops short to avoid hitting her. She holds up a hand in apology to the driver, but her gaze never leaves her target. Reaching the door, she starts pounding like a relentless woodpecker.

After what seems like an eternity, an older man answers. "No solicitors," he barks, pointing to a sign affixed to the wall above the doorbell.

"Does that work?" Maggie asks, pointing.

Scowling at her suspiciously, he follows her outstretched finger to the camera mounted onto the eave at the corner of the house.

"Who are you?"

She fumbles her wallet from her pocket, flipping it open to her sheriff's department ID as she repeats herself. "Does that work? Does it record?"

"Wouldn't be much use in having it if it didn't."

"How far does it reach?"

"Far enough."

Maggie draws a deep breath, resisting the urge to grab the man by the shirt and shake him until he cooperates. "Does it reach the road? The park?"

The man rolls his eyes. He takes a step back, preparing to shut the door.

"Please." Her voice breaks over the word. "A little boy went missing from the park yesterday."

The man pauses, his face softening. He rubs an age-spotted hand over the thin hair on the back of his head. "I heard about that," he says. "Unfortunate business. You're one of the investigators?"

His expression hardens again as he takes in her disheveled appearance, her unprofessional clothing. She wants to tell him yes. She wants to pull rank, summon whatever clout her badge affords her, but to do so would be crossing a line.

So, instead, she begs him. She begs him with her gaze. With her tone. With her words as she whispers hoarsely, "He's my brother."

His eyes narrow, dropping back down to her ID, still open between them. His lips move as he silently mouths her surname. Riley. The same as the one that's been plastered all over the news.

"It's not your case?" he asks.

She shakes her head.

"So shouldn't I be sending whatever I've got to the person in charge?"

Her fingers blanch as they tighten on her wallet. Her hand drops to her side. Though she doesn't say it, technically, yes. But she's not leaving without the footage. As if sensing her thoughts, he shifts his weight nervously, stepping back from the door.

"Can't you do both?" she asks. "Please."

She wants to explain that she's never done this before—asked a citizen to do anything other than exactly what they should. She isn't a rule breaker. Or even a rule bender. She's not one of those rogue cops who make up their own laws as they go along.

Detective Maggie Riley has a box of awards and commendations to attest to that. But in this moment, that's not who she is. Right now, she's Brandon Riley's big sister, and she'll do anything to find him. Anything.

15

STEVE

The Foxtrot Grill is unusually packed. Bodies crowd the space, elbowing for room around the bar. The noise level surges as a nearby group bursts into laughter. The smells of perfume and cologne and sweat and food combine into a nauseous mixture. It's too much, too hot with all these people in here. It's sensory overload.

I drain my water glass, hoping to cool off a bit as I scan the restaurant for the dozenth time, searching for a potential threat. There's a door to my left, a hallway that connects the grill to the inn on my right. Diners fill the seats in between.

Is anyone paying too much attention to my table? Is Wesley lurking somewhere in the shadows? How easy would it be for someone to sneak up on us without me noticing? The thought has me spinning in my seat, checking behind me.

I can't believe that it's come to this. That this is my reality, a tightrope of paranoia and fear. Not even being able to enjoy my family's visit because I'm so concerned about what threats could be lurking around every corner.

My survey of the room ends with Maggie, seated across from me at the far end of the table, my mom on one side, my sister on the other. She laughs at something Izzy says, and though it appears genuine, I can tell by the small things—the crease between her eyebrows, the set of her jaw, the small lines bracketing her mouth—that she's as tense as I am. Knowing Maggie, the guilt from trying to enjoy herself while a child in her jurisdiction is missing is eating her alive.

She glances up, catching me watching her. Her face softens for an instant, the strain easing, but then as quickly as it relaxed, it pinches into a frown. Her head tilts slightly to the side, a question.

I force a smile, doing my best to convince her that I'm fine. That there's nothing to worry about. And as if the unspoken lie wasn't bad enough, I try shifting the blame for my behavior, darting a quick glance between my grandfather and Margot and rolling my eyes. Maggie settles back in her seat, reassured, at least for now. Returns her attention back to my family.

If I'm not careful, I'm going to blow everything. I need to do a better job of acting normal, but I'm wound so tight that just the idea of sitting still and making idle conversation seems impossible.

Grabbing my beer, I drink until I've emptied the glass. It clunks loudly as I set it back on the table, my hand heavy, my movements weighted. But it has the desired effect. I feel my body relax, sinking into the chair beneath me. It slows the barrage of thoughts whirling like a tornado through my mind, and suddenly, everything becomes clear.

I need to tell Maggie the truth. I'm in over my head, and even if I wasn't, the health of our relationship and the happiness of our future depends on it. As hard as it's going to be, I have to do it.

Grandpa Joe's chair scrapes across the floor as he shifts beside me, drawing my attention. He leans forward in his seat. I watch as his hand inches across the table, closer to Margot's. As his gnarled, age-spotted fingers brush against hers. I notice the sparkle in their eyes, the color in their cheeks.

This is what I want for me and Maggie. This is what I need the future to hold. I need to believe that forty years from now, I'll be lucky enough to still be able to hold her hand in mine.

But will we ever get that chance if I tell her the truth?

My chest tightens at the thought. I don't think it's a gamble I can take.

So even though I know I should confess and come clean about everything, I vow to myself that I won't. I can't. From this moment forward, I'll do whatever it takes to keep her from ever finding out. As long as I get to keep her in my life, I'll find a way to live with the consequences, whatever they may be.

16

MAGGIE

I discreetly check my phone under the table. It's getting late. The cold snap seems to have brought everyone out tonight, making the Foxtrot Grill unusually busy. We still haven't received the appetizers Diane insisted on ordering for the table, much less our entrees. I do the math, calculating how long the meal will take, travel time, the tasks I have to do when we get home...

Even if everyone decided to call it a night as soon as we got back to the house—which I seriously doubt will happen—by the time I finish working out the logistics for the search tomorrow, there will be precious few hours left to sleep. Not that I'd be able to, anyway. Not knowing that little PJ Warner is still unaccounted for. So maybe it's a good thing I'll be kept so busy.

Still, I shake my head when Gail asks if I want another glass of wine before she heads to the bar to get the rest of the table their refills. But I can't help noticing that Steve's ordered another beer, his third, or is it his fourth already? He usually doesn't drink so much, especially not so fast.

His glassy gaze meets mine, and I give him a sympathetic smile across the table. He looks stressed. Steve never looks stressed. At least, not until recently. I search my memory, trying to pinpoint when it started.

Is it his family? Or maybe it's just the situation. Joe and Margot sit on either side of him, their heads bowed close as they lean across the table toward each other.

Gail returns with the drinks and several plates of appetizers. My mouth waters as I eye the dish closest to me, and I realize I haven't eaten all day. I have to force myself to take modest portions as they make their way around the table.

"You must have an early morning tomorrow," Izzy says, noticing that Gail takes my empty wineglass after topping off my water. "Should we be keeping you out so late?"

I cover my mouth as I finish chewing, forcing myself to swallow too soon, the stuffed mushroom traveling down my throat like a rock.

"No, it's fine. It's easier to stay distracted."

"Can you talk about it? I mean, are you allowed?"

I take a long sip of water, buying time. Until I discover what happened to PJ, this is an active investigation. I'm reluctant to say anything until I know more, not wanting to tip off a guilty party or injure an innocent one.

"There aren't really a lot of details yet. This morning, a four-year-old boy was discovered missing from his bedroom."

"His poor mother," Diane says. "Do you have any idea who took him?"

"There's no evidence that he was taken. He may have just wandered off."

"Well, surely with a four-year-old she had some child-proofing in place. Safety locks, deadbolts or chains higher than he could reach, doorknob covers..."

"Um. What?"

"Doorknob covers. You pop them on over the doorknob to make it harder for tiny hands to use them."

I chew my lip, staring at a spot on the tablecloth while I try to remember if I saw anything odd about the door handles at the Warner house.

"Knob covers probably wouldn't still work for a four-year-old, Mother."

"True, although who knows what advances they've made since my time. I'm still trying to get sticky residue off my door-frames from the top locks I had to use when Isabelle here was little. It was impossible to control her as a child. She got into everything."

"I guess some things never change." Izzy gives me a wicked grin as she tips her wineglass in her mother's direction before taking a large gulp. "Do you need any help with the search tomorrow?"

"Oh, I wouldn't want to impose. This is your vacation," I say. "Besides, conditions are pretty miserable right now."

Diane sniffs. "Hmph. There's not a miserable situation available that my daughter's managed to pass up so far. She seems to thrive on pushing me to the edge of worry."

"Yes, Mother. My enjoyment of the outdoors and challenging myself is all about you."

I shift uncomfortably in my seat, wishing I wasn't trapped between them.

"Well, maybe if you spent less time focusing on yourself, you'd have found a husband by now."

Izzy scowls. "That's such old-fashioned thinking! Life isn't about finding some man to take care of you, Mother. I'm perfectly capable of taking care of myself. Besides, Maggie's made it this far without being married, and look at her, how successful she is."

An awkward smile freezes on my face as I realize she's being serious. It seems like a lifetime ago since I considered myself anything near successful. My past life, where I was a detective in Florida. Before Brandon got snatched, before my career derailed, before my personal life burned to the ground around me, leaving me covered in wounds and ashes.

But maybe I *have* managed to climb my way back up the ladder. Which means I have it all to lose again. I can't think like this.

I shoot a desperate look across the table to Steve, trying to catch his attention as his mother and sister continue to bicker with me in the middle. Praying that he'll notice and come intervene, like he usually would. But he doesn't. He never even glances in my direction as he flags Gail down and orders another beer. As soon as she's moved off, his gaze drops back down to the phone cupped in his hand.

Something strange is going on with him, and though I'll be the first to admit that a visit from family is enough to cause erratic behavior, I have a funny feeling that in his case that's not it. The feeling grows as I watch his face, his expression growing sadder as the seconds pass. Something's wrong. Really wrong. And I'm worried that whatever it is, it has to do with me.

I stare down at my plate, focusing on eating while I struggle to get my emotions in check. I've got to hold it together. I just have to make it through the night. Then tomorrow. Then the next day. Baby steps. Sometimes, that's the best you can do.

But as I chew a mouthful of now tasteless food, I realize it's what I've already been doing. I'm not sure my steps can get any smaller. And each one forward has been more reluctant than the last. Especially now, with this case.

Because this—a little boy missing, my personal life in the balance? I know how it ends.

Pretending I don't is agony. Every comment I make, every smile I fake, feels like another strip of skin that's been peeled back and flayed from the rest of me, each piece a chink in my armor, leaving me vulnerable and exposed. But if there's one thing that I've perfected over the years, it's the mask I wear.

No one seems to notice my performance as I feign my way

through the meal, being the Maggie they all want me to be. The one that I wish I were. Even Steve doesn't notice as he ushers us all out into the parking lot once the meal is over. Then again, I'm fairly certain he's drunk.

I watch with relief as Diane grabs the keys from his hand and gets into the driver's seat of his car. When Izzy calls shotgun, all he does is blink, like he doesn't understand what's going on.

"Nonsense," Diane says, pointing at her grown children as if there's an argument she has to break up. "Grandpa Joe will sit up front."

"That won't be necessary," he says with a grin. "Ms. Margot has invited me back to her place for a nightcap."

"Wait. What?" Steve shakes his head like he's trying to clear it.

"You kids have fun. Don't wait up."

"No." Steve's face tightens, the muscles in his neck straining beneath his skin.

Grandpa Joe's head cocks to the side. "I don't remember asking for permission."

"You need to come home with us. Now."

The older man's chest puffs out. There's a rasping sound as he rubs his knuckles across his chin. He smirks as he gives a mock salute, then gets into Margot's car anyway.

Steve lurches as if he plans to go after him, but Izzy stops him, taking him gently by the arm. "Steve. What's the big deal? Let him go."

He turns toward her, mouth open, but whatever words he was going to say escape. His shoulders slump, and he nods defeatedly.

I'm not sure what just happened, but it wasn't normal. I study him closely, but he appears fine. That's when I realize—maybe I'm not the only one wearing a mask.

17

MAGGIE

It's still dark when Kal and I knock on the Warners' front door the next morning. Jenny answers, the young mother looking as if she hasn't slept in a week. Her eyes are puffy and bloodshot, the bags beneath them tender and bruised looking. Her skin is sallow and blotchy, her hair oily and lank. She moves back and allows us into the house with an air of defeat, like we're executioners.

We step inside, into a dim space lit only by a single lamp, two crime scene techs following close at our heels. She gestures halfheartedly toward the hall and our destination, then returns to her spot on the couch, settling into the middle of a nest made of photographs of her son. I linger near the door, studying her as Kal helps the analysts carry their gear to PJ's room, wishing I could do something to alleviate her grief, knowing that I have to find a way to bring her child back.

But the house already has the feel of a place of bereavement, grief and loss permeating every corner. Hope has already been abandoned. I give Jenny one last look before joining the others, and it's clear—this is not a woman who thinks her son is coming home.

I know that everyone handles the worst life throws at them differently. Some are eternally optimistic. Others immediately assume the worst. Despite this, I can't help wondering if there isn't something more to Jenny's reaction, like something she knows that she isn't telling us.

I watch as one of the techs removes a boxcutter from the outside pocket on one of her bags and uses it to break the seal on the tape I'd placed on PJ's door yesterday. The room is tiny, too small for all of us to fit comfortably, so I give my instructions from the hall, keeping my voice low so we don't disturb the slumbering members of the family.

"I want every inch searched. Every print lifted, every fiber collected. Get a ten card from each of the family members for exclusionary purposes before you leave. I'd like one of you to process the bathroom across the hall as well. It's a shared space, so I don't have high hopes you'll find anything useful, but still..."

Even though Kal and I will be leading a search effort to find PJ as soon as the sun rises, his bedroom will be processed for any hint of a crime. I bite my lip, glancing down the hall toward Jenny. Lean forward, my voice barely above a whisper as I say, "I know you know the drill, but be thorough with the ALS. I want samples of anything you find."

The alternative light source will detect things that can't be seen with the naked eye, like bodily fluids. And blood that's been cleaned. It's a chilling thought, one that makes my stomach ache and my throat grow tight, but it has to be done.

The older of the two techs gives me a curt nod and starts unpacking one of their equipment bags, a sign that they're all set and ready to begin. So we leave them to it, Kal and I retreating back through the house, and though it's much more comfortable inside, despite the tense atmosphere, we head out into the cold. We need to talk before the search begins.

Kal checks behind us as we shelter from the wind at the corner of the house. Voice low, he says, "I pulled Greg Warner's background last night after Margot's accusation. He's had multiple OUIs."

It shouldn't be a surprise. It's the same charge—operating a motor vehicle under the influence of intoxicants—that I'd filed against his mother, Franny, earlier this year.

"Including on the day of the incident that Margot referenced last night. According to the report, he'd forgotten about his son in the back seat of his car while he spent the day at the Loose Moose, drinking. If a passerby hadn't noticed the child and gotten him help, Warner might have faced manslaughter charges. The boy was taken to Memorial Hospital over in Lincoln and treated for heatstroke."

I rub the back of my neck as my muscles tighten. None of this information bodes well for Greg's parenting skills, though Dylan seems to be healthy enough now.

"Has he ever been charged with anything intentionally violent?" I ask. "Any history of child abuse?"

"No," Kal answers. "Although he did get in an accident while following the ambulance to Lincoln that day. Blew over twice the legal limit."

I curse under my breath. Greg Warner's past is a strong case for poor judgment. And proof that the man is, or at least was at one time, a neglectful parent.

"What about the rest of the family?"

"The grandmother's record reads the same."

I nod. I'd already been well aware of Franny's run-ins with the law.

"The rest are clean. Not even a parking ticket."

We fall silent, watching as a string of automobiles arrives, lining the road in both directions as they park. A frigid wind nips at my flesh as people exit their vehicles and wander over, a small crowd gathering at the foot of the Warners' driveway. A faint glow on the horizon hints at a sun that has not yet risen.

It's not even dawn, and already the search party is much

larger than yesterday, many of whom I recognize. It's one of the benefits of living in a small town, I suppose. As word of mouth has spread, everyone who's able has decided to help, friends and neighbors all wanting to do their part to help bring the little boy home. I wish I could share their optimism.

"Guess we might as well get started, huh?" I ask.

Kal nods, giving me a tense smile, and we approach the gathering. Two dozen staties stomp their feet, trying to keep warm. A thickly furred German shepherd has its nose buried in PJ's red woolen hat. Lifting its muzzle, it spins in a circle before lying down. The handler frowns and offers the cap to the dog again for another sniff.

I squint as the first ray of light crests over the mountains. I can't in good faith send anyone out until it's light enough to see, but by the time I'm done talking, it'll be close enough.

"I'd like to thank everyone for coming out this morning." My voice sounds shaky. No sleep, a gallon of coffee, and a little boy in peril will do that to you. So will an ominous feeling lodged deep in your gut that the efforts you're about to lead will prove futile. I shake my head to clear the thought before continuing.

"In a few minutes, I'll split you all into teams and assign each a quadrant to search, but first, I'm sure I don't have to tell any of you how to stay safe out here, but please do keep the other members of your group in sight at all times. Also, I don't think anyone is going to disagree that conditions are less than desirable right now."

An annoyed mutter comes from the crowd.

"If you start feeling weak or disoriented, if the cold gets overwhelming or you stop feeling cold, please let your group leader know immediately so that they can get you to the nearest shelter."

Another murmur makes me pause. I scan the people clustered before me for the source, find several faces creased in annoyance. Several more join them as an older man shoves his way through the crowd. Kal catches my eyes, gives me a nod that he's seen him and moves in his direction.

Half of my attention stays on the situation as I continue. "I'd like to begin by briefly searching the area we covered yesterday on the off chance that PJ backtracked during the night. And—"

The man shakes his head as Kal approaches. He points at me. I hold a finger up to the searchers and smile tensely as he closes the distance between us. Cupping a hand around my elbow, he guides me a dozen feet farther from the group. Kal watches, shifting from foot to foot, waiting close by while the old man's hot breath, strong with the scent of coffee and halitosis, slaps against my cheek as he whispers in my ear.

My stomach plunges and acid rises in my chest at his words. Pulling away, I check his expression, searching it for any sign of deception. There's none, just rheumy, sad eyes sunk deep within the folds of a weathered face that's nodding sadly. I look at the crowd that's gathered, locals and law enforcement all watching curiously, waiting for directions.

I know I should say something, but I can't. I don't have the words. Though I suspect, as I push my way through the mob and hop into my Jeep, take off down the road with my lights and siren running, that they can guess what it is that I can't bring myself to say.

18

MAGGIE

I pull into the dirt lot and park, my chest tightening as I stare out the windshield at the scene before me. Rattlesnake Mountain towers over the area, casting this corner of Beaverhead Lake, an inlet that would roughly constitute the beaver's nose, in an eternal dusk. Whereas the rest of the water is silver and glinting, this portion is leaden and dull, as if something rotten lurks beneath.

Steeling myself with a deep breath, I push the door open and climb outside. Here in the mountain's shadow, where the sun rarely shines, winter is still in effect. The ground is slick beneath my feet, a sheen of wind-slicked snow frozen over its surface. Pulling my jacket zipper up high under my chin, I make my way cautiously toward the dock before me, my gaze pinned to a lone figure at the far end of its length.

A shudder runs along my spine, rippling under my skin. I've never been one for superstitions, but I'm ruled by my gut, and right now it's telling me that this is not a place I want to be. The vibe is bad, off, like curdled dairy sitting out on a hot summer day.

I'm acutely aware of the stone giant looming over my shoulder, lurking like a predator. Which would make me the prey. I shake off the feeling and force myself forward.

My boot slips as I step up onto the pier, legs threatening to go out from under me. I get a brief image of myself going down, landing hard, the impact unforgiving and jarring. By some miracle I manage to keep my balance, but there's no denying that there's a tremor to my gait, a distrust in my footing as I walk.

The wooden planks thud hollowly beneath my feet, the boards dark and weathered, ends crumbling with rot like decaying teeth. Ice spreads from either side like an infectious rash, a flesh-eating virus devouring the healthy skin in its path. A low, eerie moan fills my ears, the wind singing its lament.

As I get closer, the details of the form before me take shape. The man is on his knees, sitting on his heels, his body slumped. His head hangs forward, low, chin almost resting on his chest. It's the posture of defeat... or something worse.

He turns his face away from me as I approach. Wipes at his eyes as he scrambles to his feet. I scan the area, but I don't see— and then I do.

I gasp, stumbling back a step. But it's not the still form of the little boy before me that has me feeling so stunned. It's not the way the upper half of his body rises through the icy surface of the lake like the masthead on a ship. It's not the parted lips that look like they've been stained by a blue popsicle, or the cloudy haze of his half-open eyes, or the lavender tinge to his skin. It's not the way his pajamas, covered with a dog wearing a police uniform, have frozen on his thin frame.

It's not even the knowledge that Jenny Warner is going to be absolutely destroyed when I have to break the news to her that her son has been found. No, it's not the dead child before me that has me reeling. It's that the little boy looks so similar to one that I used to know and love, one that, like this one, was lost far too soon. If I didn't know better, I'd think the body was my brother's.

I step closer, slowly sinking to my knees on the dock beside him, assuming the position my silent companion has just abandoned as he steps to the side to make room. Staring down at the child, so tiny and frail looking, so cold, I resist the urge to take PJ Warner's hand in my own, because even though it's possible this was just a very unfortunate accident, I have to treat it like a crime scene. I can't risk contaminating any evidence that might be present on the body.

Tugging my glove off, I fumble my phone from my pocket and type out a text to Kal letting him know where I am, and that PJ Warner has been found. Requesting that he escort one of the forensic technicians currently processing the Warner house here instead, to a rotting pier hidden in the shadow of a mountain where the corpse of a child that looks too familiar emerges from the last bit of ice on the lake.

Now that I'm looking closer, though, I see the differences. Brandon had chubbier cheeks. A smattering of freckles across the bridge of his nose. Wider-set eyes. I hadn't noticed the resemblance in the photographs of the animated little boy Jenny had shown me yesterday, but then again, he doesn't look quite like the same little boy anymore.

He's too still. The light that sparkled behind his eyes extinguished. Maybe it's not the resemblance that's left me feeling so blindsided as much as the fact that I find myself faced with such a close replica of the image I've been haunted by for the last five years, that of my baby brother's body, lifeless.

My breath is wheezy and shallow, the shards of my broken heart taking up the room inside my chest that my lungs need to inflate. I should have expected this. Prepared myself better.

At four years old, PJ was the same age that Brandon had been when he'd been stolen. This case was bound to dredge up some memories. And somehow I'd known, hadn't I? Had felt the ache deep inside from the start warning me that just like my family, there'd be no happy ending for the Warners.

"Can you tell me what happened? How you found him?" I ask.

"My uncle and I got here before first light this morning."

I glance at the two fishing rods and tackle box beside me. It seems obvious, but I ask anyway. "For?"

"To fish. It's been so cold, they're still hanging out in the deeper parts of the lake, but they like the dock. Only spot they're biting right now that you can get to without a boat."

"When was the last time you were here?"

"Day before yesterday."

I turn to face him. He's still looking away, staring out over the lake.

"Two days ago? So, Friday?"

"Uh-huh."

"Same spot?"

"Yes."

"How often do you come out here?"

"This time of year? Most days. Best way to make the budget stretch right now."

"But you didn't come yesterday." I get to my feet, move until I'm in his space and he has no choice but to look at me. "Why not?"

He snakes a hand under his beanie to scratch his head. Pulls it down over his ears when he's done. "I wasn't feeling well. My uncle was going to come without me, but he decided to stay home, too."

"How long were you out here on Friday?"

The man shrugs. "'Til noon, at least."

"And when you got here this morning, this is the way you found him?"

"No." He shakes his head. "He was under the ice. The hole we've been using froze over, so I stuck the gaff down through, started poking around, trying to break it up, and that's when I snagged him. As soon as I saw what I'd... Well, I wasn't quite sure what to do, so I left him as is."

I turn back to the broken patch of rime and take a closer look. There's an area about two feet square that looks thinner than the rest. PJ's body is at its center. The little boy went missing somewhere between 2 and 8 a.m. Saturday morning, but there's no telling when he went into the lake.

"Does it freeze back up every night?"

"Usually not by this time of year, but it has been lately."

Which means it was likely frozen when PJ got to the lake. But *how* had he gotten to the lake?

I think back over the route I took to get here. The Warners live about twenty miles away, on the other side of the Cove, which means that PJ would have had to walk all that distance and pass through town to get here, all without being noticed. Could a four-year-old have done that on his own?

It's not likely. Which means odds are strong that this wasn't an accident. Someone knew exactly where PJ Warner's been all this time. They knew because they'd put him there.

19

MAGGIE

Five years ago

Maggie stares at the computer screen, the words before her barely legible. Her eyes ache, feel dry and gritty. She rests her ear against her palm, her head too heavy for her neck. She knows she should get some rest, or some food. At the very least, a cup of water to quell the dehydration that's made her mouth so dry that the insides of her cheeks have drawn painfully tight against her teeth.

But she can't. Because the second she looks away might be the one before a breakthrough. The two minutes it would take to quench her thirst means an extra two minutes that her brother's missing.

She groans as she hits another dead end, checks the list beside her, and types in the next license plate number. It had taken her hours to go through the video footage she received from the man who lived alongside the park. Hours spent screenshotting every vehicle that drove by the camera the morning her brother went missing, enlarging the shots and running them through filters until the tags became legible.

As the name and address for the next plate come up, she scrolls to highlight and then copies the information. She's not exactly sure what she hopes to find, only that she has to keep looking. Someone knows something. If she has to, she'll interview the owner of every single car that drove by in hopes of finding that person.

Clicking the next tab, Maggie accesses the registrant's driver's license. Prints a copy, then opens the next tab and enters the information into the National Crime Information Center, or NCIC, search engine. So far, most of the drivers' records have contained only minor offenses. A handful had been charged with more serious crimes, a few had even served time. Those are the ones she'll start with.

The results load, and she hits print. Almost starts the process over again with the next license plate number, when a word on the screen snags her attention. She throws her hands in the air, away from the keyboard as she reads, afraid she'll do something to make the words vanish. Draws a shaky breath, not believing she almost missed this.

It's like someone has cracked an egg over her head. She feels the warm goo of the yolk as it oozes down her face, over her skin, burning through the numbness and restoring her senses. And what it leaves behind is pure rage.

Standing, Maggie grabs the report from the printer, holds the pages clenched in a shaky fist as she looks for her cell phone. Curses the entire time it takes her to find it wedged in the crease of her office chair. And while she scrolls through her contacts. And while the call rings.

A groggy, "What?" ends her tirade.

"Will Todd."

"What? Who is this?"

"It's Detective Riley. I found him."

"Found who? Your brother?"

"No." Her head shakes emphatically though he can't see it. "The man who took him."

"Listen, Riley, what time is it?"

"What does that matter?"

One of the same words she muttered only moments ago gets repeated back to her. "It's 3 a.m. Call me in the morning and we'll talk."

"No! I'm telling you, this Todd guy has my brother. We need to pay him a visit right now. Keep him occupied while we're waiting on a warrant."

"Based on what?"

"He was driving by the park just minutes before my mom made the call that my brother was missing. He's got a record a mile long, a whole slew of charges, sexual abuse against a minor, sexual assault of a minor, false imprisonment, kidnapping... All the offenses were against boys under the age of six. I'm telling you, Hawkins, this is our guy. He did it. This pedophile took Brandon."

"We can't go banging on people's doors in the middle of the night just because you have a hunch."

"Just being at a park is a violation of his parole."

"Does your footage show him actually stopping and getting out of his car?"

"But—"

"He's got a record. I heard all that. But he's still got rights. What proof do you have that he took your brother? Anyone see him do it? Just cause this Todd guy got busted in the past, that doesn't mean he's guilty this time."

"He was right there when my brother was snatched!"

"If your brother was snatched."

"What?"

Detective Hawkins heaves a heavy sigh. "Maggie. I hate to have to do this, but no one saw your brother with your mom at the park. Not one person remembers her having a little boy with her."

Maggie's skin is too tight. There's a lump in her throat so large she can feel it pressing against the backs of her eardrums. "You can't possibly believe that my mom had something to do with Brandon's disappearance?"

The question is met with silence. After a long moment passes, she checks her phone, makes sure the call hasn't dropped. She clears her throat.

"And is this just your theory or—"

"The sheriff's with me on this. There just isn't any evidence to prove otherwise."

"Is there any evidence to support it?"

Again, there's no answer.

"I see. So we're just making up our minds without even investigating now, are we?"

The sound of him clearing his throat is loud over the line. "We've confirmed that you were at the department when your brother went missing, but I have to ask—"

"You're not actually doing this, are you?"

"I'm just doing my job. It's nothing personal."

"Are you serious?"

"I'm sorry—"

"You are sorry. You're a sorry piece of—"

This time, the silence is because the call has ended. But the investigation is just beginning. Because Maggie knows she's onto something. It doesn't matter if she's the only one. She'll just have to be enough.

20

MAGGIE

I sit in my Jeep with the engine running, guarding the entrance to the dock, doing my best not to feel guilty about being safe and warm while a child's body is stuck in the ice behind me. I scan my surroundings, trying to distract myself from the thought. The parking area is empty, a desolate wasteland of dirt and trash. A faded Doritos bag sticks halfway out of a crest of frozen mud, rumpling in the wind as I watch.

Rattlesnake Mountain looms before me, casting us all in its shadow. I stare at its craggy peaks, remembering the last time I came into contact with the stone giant. The memory squeezes me in an ominous grip.

I glance around, searching, even though I know I'm alone, and tighten my hold on my cell phone like it's my link to reality. Put it on speaker so that Kal's voice fills the car. I hear his turn signal clicking in the background, the low hum of his tires as he leads the state police from the Warners' house to our crime scene.

The Warners' house, which will never be the same again. Whose youngest member will never return. And whose patriarch has a past record of being a neglectful parent. I assure myself that doesn't mean he's responsible. While a majority of child abductions can be attributed to a family member, less than fifteen percent of those cases end in murder.

Yet those cases do exist.

My own parents had been suspects when my brother disappeared. I'd always wondered if that's why they had pulled away —because they were ashamed. But who am I kidding? My parents didn't just pull away. They abandoned me, even after I had done everything within my power to reveal what had really happened to Brandon.

But I failed to bring him back. Just like I failed PJ Warner.

"So what now?" Kal asks over the radio.

The state police have jurisdiction over major crimes in the state of Maine. But this is my town. This case might not be a priority to them, but it is to me. "Once you get here, I want you to oversee the staties. Keep your eyes and your ears peeled. Anything they find, I want to know about it."

"You got it."

"I've asked the gentlemen who discovered the body to come in later this afternoon around three to give a statement. Hopefully, you'll be done with the state police by then and you'll be able to sit in. But as soon as you guys get here, I'm going to go break the news officially to the Warners."

"What are you going to tell them?"

I know what he's asking. "There are no injuries from what I can see."

"So it could be an accident?"

"It could."

"It's an awfully long way," Kal says.

"Awfully," I agree. I swallow hard, trying to work up some spit before adding, "And he would have had to walk through town. You'd think someone would have seen him."

But maybe someone did. Maybe that's how PJ got all the way out here. Or maybe this was someone's intention all along—

to steal a child from his bed and leave him here, in the middle of nowhere.

But there are plenty of better places in the valley to leave a body. Did they think the lake would keep their secret? Or did they want the boy to be found? I can think of only one reason that would be true.

I stare out the windshield, as if searching for an answer, and feel my body sag. The barren landscape around me is hard and unforgiving. It won't give up its mysteries easily. I let a long moment pass before I say, "We need to do a deep dive on this family, see if they're hiding anything. Can you fill out a subpoena for their financials and send it off to get approved?"

"Consider it done."

"But also... keep your mind open. It's too early in the investigation to rule anything out. All we know for sure is that a little boy is dead, and we need to find out why. Nothing else matters besides that. Agreed?"

"Of course," Kal says. I know I haven't told him anything he actually needed to hear. But I'm working up to what really needs to be said.

"And—" I draw a deep breath. I keep my voice low because it's the only way I can keep it steady. "This case is hitting a little close to home for me. If I stop making sense..."

"You won't," he says.

I let the words wash over me. I know that Sue's filled him in on my history, about Brandon, and though my lieutenant and I have known each other for less than half a year, in that time, I've grown to respect him in a way I do few others. His confidence in me restores my faith in myself.

"We're pulling off the highway now. I'll be seeing you soon."

We end the call, and once again, I find myself alone in the deafening silence. Staring at the mountain before me. And feeling the entire weight of it on my shoulders.

21

MAGGIE

"I don't understand." Belinda James, Jenny's mother, looks at me through tear-ravaged eyes, her arms wrapped tight around her grieving daughter. "What are you saying?"

I lower myself gingerly to the edge of the couch, rub at a worn spot on my pants as I perch there. The search party has been dispersed, the volunteers sent home. It's just me and the family and the terrible news that I bear.

"Mrs. James." I duck my head, trying to draw her daughter's attention as I say, "Jenny. We need to consider the possibility that PJ didn't find his way into the water by accident."

Jenny looks at me, her eyes flashing behind their curtain of tears, hard and angry. "Tell me something I don't know."

I study her face. Grief affects people in a variety of ways. But while her anger isn't a surprise, the confidence behind her statement is.

"Is there something you'd like to tell me?" I ask.

"She's just blowing off steam," Greg says, looking up from where he's been sitting on the armchair, head cradled in his hands, since I broke the news that PJ had been found. "She's just, that's what she does. She's young. Too young," he mutters under his breath.

"I'm old enough to have taught my son to know better than to go outside on his own, much less go near the water," she shoots back.

"He was my son, too."

"Too bad you didn't seem to realize that when he was still here."

Greg's face darkens. There's something unsettling about how quickly his grief is abandoned, how easily he turns on his wife as he seethes, "Who do you think you're fooling, Jenny? We both know that motherhood hasn't been anything like you'd hoped it would be when you traded your dollies in for the real thing."

It's not uncommon for marriages—or entire families—to dissolve over the untimely loss of a loved one, especially a child. It seems the easiest place to channel your heartache is into blame. I stand, positioning myself between them before the argument has a chance to escalate. "Please. I understand how difficult this is."

"Do you?" Jenny glares at me with narrowed eyes.

I allow myself a moment of vulnerability, letting the shutter I keep my emotions hidden behind to open briefly as I return to my seat beside her on the couch. "I do."

She looks away from the part of me I've allowed her to see, dropping her gaze to her hands, wringing each other like dish-towels on her lap.

"But right now, I need you, I need both of you, to work with me to figure out who could have done this."

I try not to be too obvious about the close eye I'm keeping on Greg, watching as he nods and leans back in his seat.

"Can either of you think of anyone who might have wanted to hurt PJ?"

There's a long moment of silence. But there's plenty being said, even if I can't hear it. My gaze darts between the couple as they exchange a long look between them.

Finally, Jenny says, "No, no one."

"Have you noticed anyone strange hanging around lately, maybe showing him a bit more attention than they should when you take him out in public?"

They both shake their heads.

"What about his half siblings?" I ask.

"Now, wait just a minute." Greg jumps to his feet, towering over me. "My kids don't have anything to do with this."

"I was asking if you thought any of them might have noticed anyone," I say, though that's not what I'd meant at all. I'd purposely baited him to see his reaction. And he failed. If he truly thought his children were beyond suspicion, I doubt he would have reacted quite so vehemently.

"Oh." Once again, the man deflates. "They're at their mother's now. Are you going to go talk to them?"

"I am, Mr. Warner, but first, before I do, I have to ask, do either of you have anyone in your life who you think would want to hurt you in this way?"

I was half expecting another outburst. Instead, the man seems to wither and shrink in on himself. And if that isn't strange, the look he's exchanging with his wife—again—sure is.

"No. There's no one. We don't have a clue about who could be behind this. We haven't done anything wrong."

Something about his words snag my attention like a stray thread against a splinter. *We haven't done anything wrong.* It seems an odd thing to say when you're being questioned about the circumstances surrounding your son's death.

I sharpen my attention on him, cataloguing his body language, the sweat that has sprouted on his upper lip, the hardness that's entered his eyes. I shift my focus to Jenny. There's no denying the grief that holds this woman in its clutches, and yet, I can't shake the feeling that the Warners are keeping something important from me.

There's a long, uncomfortable moment of silence, then Jenny bursts into tears.

"Chief Riley, please," Belinda says, folding Jenny in her arms and trying to soothe her. "My daughter's suffered a great loss. Do you really have to do this right now?"

I stare at Jenny, wondering at the outburst. Are those crocodile tears? Is she just trying to get me to stop asking her questions she doesn't want to answer?

As I've done many times over the years, I try imagining what my own mother's reaction must have been like when she was interrogated about Brandon's disappearance. When she realized he wasn't coming home. Had she sobbed? Raged? Withdrawn?

But just like usual, it's a picture I can't form. I should have been there. Should have witnessed it firsthand. Shouldn't have been cut off and excluded from a loss that was mine, too. Am I being too insensitive right now? And is that why?

I nod and mutter, "I'm sorry. Sorry for your loss and... We can speak again when you're feeling better."

"Come on, honey. You should go lie down."

I watch as Belinda helps her daughter to her feet, supporting her as they disappear down the hall. The sound of Jenny's weeping ceases with the soft click of a door shutting.

I turn back around, facing Greg. The man shifts uncomfortably, looking like he wishes he could shrink into a speck and disappear.

"Mr. Warner," I say, realizing that he never responded to my question, "Is there anything you think I should know? Something that might have any bearing on what happened to PJ?"

His eyes dart nervously. He scratches at a spot on his arm.

"Sir?" I prod.

He draws a deep breath and exhales loudly. "I don't know what happened," he says, sounding defeated. "None of this makes sense. Are you sure that it wasn't an accident? Isn't it possible that he walked out to the lake and fell in?"

"It's possible, but it doesn't seem likely. That's a very long distance for a child his age to travel on foot."

Greg's gaze is distant and unfocused. He absently fingers a small hole near the hem of his shirt, making the flaw larger. I lean forward as his mouth moves, waiting for a sound to come out.

"What are you doing here?" Franny Warner taps a cigarette out of a pack as she shuffles into the living room wearing a dingy bathrobe. "Aren't you supposed to be out looking for the kid?"

Greg jumps up, looking relieved as he crosses the room to his mother. His voice is low as he says, "They found him, Mom."

"What?" She squints at him for a moment as if confused, then looks to me for an answer. "That true?"

"Why don't you take a seat?" I ask.

"If I wanted to sit, I'd be sitting," she says, shoving a cigarette between her withered lips.

Greg gives me an exasperated look. His reluctance to be the one to break the news is etched across his face.

"Mrs. Warner. I'm sorry to inform you that PJ was found by a couple of fishermen in Beaverhead Lake this morning."

Her eyes harden as she stares at me. Patting her pockets down, she withdraws a lighter and fires up, exhaling a cloud of smoke in my face. Her voice is steady as she asks, "Who do you think put him there?"

"Why would you assume it wasn't an accident?"

She takes another long draw off her cigarette. Takes her time before answering. "Because that boy was attached to his mama's hip. Wouldn't go anywhere without Jenny. Greg here couldn't even get him to bed that night because he insisted on trying to wait up for her."

I look at him with a raised eyebrow. He shrugs. "Didn't seem like it was worth getting in a battle over. Eventually, he passed out on the couch. When he did, I carried him to bed, then followed suit myself."

"What time was this?"

"Late. Almost midnight."

"Was anyone else still up?"

"Just Mom."

Franny takes a deep drag of her cigarette. "I went out, had my final smoke, then called it a night."

Remembering Jenny confessing that she had to unlock the door, that she couldn't recall if she had left the key in the lock, I ask, "And you locked up for the night?"

"I turned off all the lights when I came inside, if that's what you're asking."

"What about locking the front door?"

"Never bother. Someone wants in, that flimsy little lock ain't gonna stop them."

"Jenny says the door was locked when she came home."

Franny eyes me sharply. "Well, I didn't do it."

I look at Greg. He shakes his head, a furrow appearing between his brows as he frowns. "Uh-uh."

"How'd she get in if the door was locked?" Franny asks.

"She said she used the key under the mat."

Greg's frown deepens. "If there was a key under the mat, I never knew about it. You sure she wasn't just so drunk she imagined it? Or dreamed it? I mean, where's the key now?"

"I don't know, Mr. Warner."

"Well, there you go. What more proof do you need?"

I chew the inside of my cheek to keep from responding, because the truth is, he has a point. But there's also the possibility that Jenny had left the key in the door, and it was used by whoever took PJ. Or even that someone in the house had taken it after Jenny came home to conceal their attempt to lock her out, not knowing that PJ was gone. I can't rule anything out yet.

So far, this family has done nothing but raise my suspicions. Somebody here is lying. Or everybody is.

22

MAGGIE

The door to the Warners' house shuts firmly behind me. I descend the stairs carefully, my bones heavy, my heart weary. A little boy is dead, and I'm not entirely sure that his family cares to help me find out the truth. Something about the thought seems unimaginable to me.

When it was Brandon... but it isn't him, I remind myself. It doesn't matter how grateful I would have been if someone had actually shown some initiative about getting to the truth about what happened to my brother. It doesn't matter what I would have done, what I did do, in search of that truth.

I'm lost in thought, climbing behind the wheel of my Jeep when I hear someone calling me in a loud whisper. Looking around, I spot Jenny peeking her head around the corner of the house, gesturing wildly. Slipping back out of the vehicle, I close the door quietly and hurry over to her.

"Jenny? Is everything okay?" I feel ridiculous the moment the words leave my mouth. Of course everything isn't okay. Nothing is. Her son is dead. But there must be a reason she followed me out here. "Do you want to talk?"

She cranes her head as she checks around, making sure

we're alone. When she's satisfied, her teary eyes meet mine. There's something desperate in them. More than that, there's something else I recognize all too well... guilt.

"What is it?" I ask, even though part of me is afraid to find out what it is this woman has to tell me.

"We deal drugs," she says softly. Her head drops, hanging in shame.

"What?" I'm sure I must have heard wrong.

"Greg and I. Not a lot. Just enough to cover the bills."

"What kind?"

"It used to be just weed, but..."

But marijuana is legal now in the state of Maine. Which means that the criminals who once sold it have been forced to make a choice. Stop dealing or deal something else.

"But now?"

"Heroin," she whispers.

I bite my tongue to keep from cursing. Now the defensive comment Greg had made about not doing anything wrong makes sense. Because they had been doing something wrong, hadn't they? Is that what this is all about? Had PJ Warner been killed because of a drug deal gone bad? Was his death retaliation?

"Do you think that could have anything to do with what happened to PJ?" I ask.

A high-pitched whimper escapes from Jenny's throat. "I don't know, but... I'm worried it might."

"Did anyone make any threats?"

"No."

"Did you upset anyone?"

She shrugs. "I don't think so."

"Then what would make you think that's the reason that someone might have hurt your son?"

Jenny stares at her feet. Digs the toe of her shoe into the

mud. "I was so worried about getting caught. And I... I would bring PJ with me. To help."

I pinch my eyes shut against an approaching headache. A memory of Jenny carrying PJ plays on the back of my lids, the little boy grabbing at her, the bulge of his diaper bulky beneath his pants as he squirmed.

Why was he squirming? Surely it made it harder for her to carry him. And had he been grabbing, or pushing at her, like he was struggling to get down. But if that was the case, why didn't she let him walk on his own?

It hits me with the force of a brick, my breath whooshing painfully out with the blow as it clicks into place. "You put the drugs in his diaper," I say, stunned.

She's actively sobbing again now as she nods.

"You must think I'm the worst mother ever."

It would be unkind to answer, so I don't.

"Please, you have to believe me. PJ was my everything. I'd give my life if it would bring him back. I... I need to know what happened to him."

She needs to know, so she'll stop blaming herself. But I'm not entirely sure she should. I give the woman before me a long hard look before pulling a card out of my pocket and handing it to her. "You have email?"

She nods.

"I want the names of everyone you've ever bought or sold from. Send them to that address. Immediately. I've wasted enough time already." Then I turn on my heel and return to my car.

I need to get out of here. I need to think. I need to find out the truth behind little PJ Warner's fate. Not for his mother, but for the child whose life was cut heartbreakingly short. And for Brandon. And maybe even a bit for myself.

23

MAGGIE

I pull into my spot at the Coyote Cove Police Department quicker than I should, tossing the door open before I've even come to a complete stop. I jog across the lot and up the wooden ramp, not even feeling the cold. March inside and, like a balloon that's sprung a leak, I deflate. I'd been running on adrenaline, but suddenly it's gone.

"Everything all right?" Sue asks, looking at me over the top of her glasses.

I drop into the seat beside hers, nodding, even though I'm not sure it's true. But just being here, with her? It's a relief. As much as I consider myself a loner, there are times when I need a distraction to keep me out of my own head, and this is one of those times.

I just feel so... angry. Outraged, really. Right now, there's nothing I'd like more than to inflict a little violence on Greg and Jenny Warner. I just don't understand how people rationalize making such poor decisions. How they can be so selfish as to endanger what should be most precious.

Staring at the cartoon character on Sue's pajama pants, I

feel my rage lessen a little. "What's that?" I ask, gesturing toward the yellow rectangle wearing pants.

She stands, giving me a better view, and looks down at her legs, frowning. "You don't know who SpongeBob is?"

"Should I?"

"Kids love him."

"He's terrifying."

"No, he's not."

"He really is. I don't know why they put such creepy eyes on kid's characters. Probably to give them nightmares."

"You should see his pet snail, Gary," she grins, handing me a cup of coffee before reclaiming her seat.

Shaking my head, I take a long sip, letting the heat burn away some of the fog clouding my brain. Sue realizes that I don't really care who the scary yellow thing on her pants is. She knows that something is up. Yet she gives me the space I need, waiting patiently for me to find the words to tell her. Somehow, she understands me.

Finally, I say, "The Warners are drug dealers."

"They're what?" Sue's mouth drops open. "You're kidding me?"

"I'm not. Jenny told me in secret as I was leaving their house. She's worried it might have something to do with what happened to PJ."

"Do you think it does?"

"It's too early to know. She's going to email me a list of everyone she's dealt with, both buyers and sellers. When Kal gets back from processing the scene with the staties, I need him to start running backgrounds on everyone."

"That poor woman," Sue says, slowly shaking her head. "I can't even imagine. To not only have lost a child, but to think that she may have something to do with what happened. And you know it was probably her husband's idea."

I stare at her for a long minute. She meets and holds my

gaze until I'm the one who gives and looks away. But I can't let the statement drop. Because as I think of my own parents, wrongly accused of having something to do with their son's disappearance, of the detective who chose to focus on them while the real perpetrator was given ample time to cover his tracks, I'm not sure that Jenny does deserve any sympathy.

I mutter, "I wouldn't feel too bad for her. She trafficked the drugs in his diaper so she wouldn't get caught."

Sue's eyes narrow and her hands curl into fists. Her jaw juts forward as it tenses. And what she suggests should happen to parents like the Warners? It's less than kind and extremely illegal.

This is why I'm here. Because I knew she'd understand.

As much as I love Steve, this isn't a trait we share. And that's okay. He's calm. Even-keeled. He balances me out, is the water to my fire. But sometimes, the flames don't need to be extinguished. Sometimes, they need to be fanned. And this is one of those times.

24

STEVE

I flip the edge of a curtain aside to peer out the back window, then pace across the kitchen. Check the time on the oven, then pull my phone out to confirm and make sure I haven't missed the call. It's two fifty. I'm supposed to meet Wesley in ten minutes. The only problem, or at least, the first problem, is that he still hasn't told me where.

Setting the cell on the counter, I force myself to take a seat. Stare at it, willing it to ring. Scratch at the red welt that's formed on my right arm, then the one on my chest. Try to ignore the creeping sensation as the hives spread like poison through my body. Awaken the screen again, but still nothing.

I should have known that he'd pull something like this. Keep me waiting on tenterhooks until the last minute so that I'm left scrambling to meet him on time.

I can't just keep sitting here doing nothing. Snatching the phone up into my sweaty palm, I march to my bedroom. Close and lock the door before pulling the comforter down, revealing the item I hid there after Maggie left this morning.

The black metal of the gun is dull like a cottonmouth's scales and has the potential to be just as deadly. I briefly debate zipping the weapon into one of my jacket pockets before deciding to tuck it into the back of my waistband instead. I pull out my shirt, check my silhouette in the mirror, then grab my coat and keys and head for the front door.

"Heading out?" Izzy asks from her seat on the couch under a pile of dogs.

"Just have a quick errand to run. I shouldn't be long." My voice sounds tense and strained.

"Want some company? I feel like we haven't gotten to spend any one-on-one time together."

Looking at my sister's hopeful expression, I feel another little part of me break.

"Next time, I promise."

I hate myself, hate that I'm the one who just made her face crumple like that, hate that I don't even pause on my way out the door to make sure she's all right. Most of all, I hate Wesley for putting me in this position in the first place.

Sliding behind the wheel, I start the engine. The car clock says two fifty-five. Even if Wesley called this very second, there's no way I'd be able to make the meeting on time. The business district of Coyote Cove is minuscule, but it takes more than five minutes just to reach the edge of town from here.

I draw deep, controlled breaths, trying to keep my sense of helplessness from becoming crippling. The gun digs into my back as I pull my seatbelt on. I welcome the pressure, the firearm the only small semblance of control I feel I have. I'm imagining the look on Wesley's face as I pull it out and confront him with it when the phone rings.

Two fifty-seven.

"Hello?" I try not to sound as panicked as I feel.

"You ready?"

I stem the flow of curse words ready to slip off the tip of my tongue. "You know there's no way I'm going to be able to make it anywhere by three now, right?"

"You better." His voice sounds different, the undertone of amusement replaced by something dark and threatening. But maybe I just imagined it, because a second later, the glee is back as he says, "I mean, you just have to cross the street, dude. You haven't gotten that old and out of shape on me that you can't handle that, have you?"

"What?"

"Meet me at your lady's place. And hurry it up, the clock is ticking."

The line goes dead. A droning buzz fills my ears. I realize it's my pulse as I stare at the phone in my hand in horror. He wants to meet at Maggie's house.

This is a total power play on Wesley's part. He wants me to know who's boss. And, I'm sorry to say, it's working. He's backed me into a corner. There's nothing like desperation to make you ignore common sense.

25

MAGGIE

Five years ago

Maggie checks her GPS, then edges her Jeep up onto the shoulder of the road, pulling right up against the tree line. Hits her interior lights, making sure they won't come on as she cracks her door open and slips out into a night lit by only a sliver of waning moon. There are no streetlamps out here. No neighboring houses to be seen.

There's just her and the darkness, the hum of insects and the chorus of frogs. She creeps along the woods, palmettos snagging at the sleeve of her black shirt, the fabric of her black pants. She can barely see her hand in front of her face, but she moves confidently, quietly, slinking through the shadows as if she's one of them.

Maggie isn't entirely sure what she's doing, only that she had to come. It's been almost forty-eight hours since her brother went missing. Hawkins obviously isn't going to help. She can't let another second be wasted. Especially not if Brandon's with someone like Todd.

She's been doing her best not to think about what might be

*happening. What might have already happened. But the only
way to keep those thoughts from her mind is to keep busy.
Curling her hand around the weapon holstered at her hip, she
quickens her steps.*

She's parked at a distance to keep the element of surprise on
her side. Todd's house should only be another several hundred
yards ahead. But that's dozens of miles from the nearest town,
from help, should she need it. She refuses to let herself consider
that, instead focusing on her anger, using her rage to fuel her
forward momentum.

Maggie comes to a sudden halt, one foot still raised, as a
sudden movement rustles the grass where she intended to step.
Takes a deep breath, listening as the low-lying creature retreats
into the woods, before continuing. It figures that a man like him
would live out here, far from civilization, keeping company with
the other snakes and rats.

Then she sees it, a break in the trees, the glint of moonlight off
a pane of glass as the grass cedes to bare dirt. Lowering herself
into a crouch, she jogs across the open expanse, watching the
windows for signs of movement.

The sulfurous stench of swamp grows stronger. Something
plonks, making a small splash. She imagines deadly reptiles
cutting silently through the water. The kind that would welcome
a free meal and make short work of a body. But whose body?
What is it that she intends to do?

Pressing herself against the side of the house, she looks inside.
A small kitchen hides somewhere under a layer of filth. She
squints at the dirty dishes and food containers, searching for signs
of her brother. Seeing none, she skulks to the next window. Then
the next. Then the next.

A living room gives way to an office. Both empty. And then
she reaches the bedroom.

Maggie's hands curl on the window ledge as her eyes land on
Will Todd's sleeping form. The man has gained weight since his

last mugshot was taken, but there's no mistaking the bulbous nose, the giant forehead, the greasy look of his oversized lips, now open and slack. She curls her fingers around the frame and tries to silently pull it up, but it doesn't open.

She needs to get inside the house and find her brother.

Looking around for something to help her break in, she notices how much lighter it's gotten. The first rays of dawn have crested the horizon and painted the sky with faint streaks of gold. She can see a line of cattails moving in the breeze at the edge of the swamp. She'll have to hurry.

There's a heap of junk near where Todd's parked his car, only a dozen feet away. A crowbar on top catches her eye. Perfect.

But as she moves toward it, she fails to notice the tin can laying on its side in the weeds in front of her. She kicks it, sends it flying into the vehicle. Winces as a voice yells from inside the house, "Who's there?"

Without thinking, Maggie scuttles down the driveway, back to her car, and climbs inside. Starts the engine, then stops, hand halfway to shifting the gear. She can't leave without finding her brother. But she's lost the element of surprise.

Hot tears run down her cheeks as she pounds the steering wheel with her fists. She'll have to return tonight. This time, she'll be prepared to do whatever it takes. And she won't be leaving without her brother.

26

MAGGIE

Unlike her ex-husband's house, Loraine Garner's appears neat and well cared for. The porch I find myself on looks like it's been recently swept and a pretty wreath in spring colors adorns the door, seeming to challenge the lingering cold. I knock and step back, fixing a neutral expression on my face, friendly, but not happy.

The door opens and I find myself having to drop my gaze so far my neck aches to meet the eyes of the woman who stands before me. I recognize her as the receptionist from the local dentist's office, but I'd never realized how tiny she was—I've only ever seen her sitting. But while Greg Warner is easily six feet, his ex-wife is under five. And though we've never made more than small talk before, she greets me warmly, as if we're friends.

"Chief Riley! It's lovely to see you. How have you been doing?"

It's an awkward question to respond to, one for which the truth never seems appropriate.

"It's nice to see you, Loraine. Do you mind if I come in for a moment and speak with you and your children?"

The muscles of her face tense beneath her skin, yet she keeps the same broad smile plastered on. "May I ask why?"

"I'm afraid I have some bad news about their half sibling, PJ."

She blinks hard. Swallows loudly. But doesn't invite me in. I decide to change tack.

"Do you mind if I ask you a few questions about your marriage to Greg Warner?"

"Um."

"How long were the two of you married?"

"Thirteen years."

"And you had three kids together during that time?"

"Yes."

"What kind of a husband was he?"

"Good enough, I suppose, all things considered."

"What's that mean?"

She shrugs. "I mean, we were awfully young when we got married. The same things that seem fun then turn into major warning signs when you're older and wiser."

"Like?" I prod.

Her cheeks color. She doesn't answer.

I'd like to discover if she was aware her ex-husband dealt drugs without revealing that I know. Remembering his arrest record, the jeopardy he put one of their kids in, I ask, "Has Greg ever had a drug problem? I heard something about him forgetting your son in the car once?"

"Drugs? No. But alcohol?" She studies her nails as she says, "I mean, when you're a teenager you don't stop to ask yourself, 'Hey, it's cool that he's a party guy right now, but is this going to be an issue in the future?' Then one day you're getting a call that your child's being treated for heatstroke because your husband left him in the car while he spent the day drinking with his buddies."

That jibes with what Kal had told me he'd read in the case file.

"Then was stupid enough to take off drunk after the ambulance and get in a wreck."

I want to ask more details, but keep my mouth firmly shut so I don't interrupt as she continues to talk.

"Luckily, no one got hurt, but the legal fees almost sank us. And I was so naïve. I saw what an alcoholic his mom was, but it never even occurred to me until that day that it was possible Greg could ever become like her."

She winces as she confesses, "In a way, it felt like my fault. For a long time I told myself that he wasn't like that when we first got married, but now? If I'm being honest? It was probably only because there were times when we couldn't afford it. But eventually he stopped caring about that. And showing up for work. And paying bills."

"So he wasn't bringing in any money when you were married? Didn't have anything he did on the side to bring home a little cash?"

"I wish." She catches me studying her and laughs. "I know what you're thinking. All that, and yet he was the one to leave me. Trust me, I kick myself every day over that. But the truth is, besides that one time he forgot about Dylan in the car, he was much better at being a father than a husband."

Her answer is a surprise. I remember how unconcerned he'd been when PJ first went missing. "Was he a hands-on parent?"

"Oh, yeah. He was always playing with them, tending to them. Honestly, he was a little better at it than I was, in the beginning. Of course, I was pretty young when I had our first."

"How young?" I ask.

"Nineteen." She makes a face. Her tone is sharp and bitter as she says, "The same age *she* was."

"You mean Jenny."

"Yeah." It's practically a growl.

"Is that what happened?" I ask. "Between you and Greg."

She smiles, but there's nothing nice about it. "I didn't even have a clue. Came home from work one day to find him waiting with divorce papers he'd printed up online. Said we couldn't afford an attorney 'cause he was expecting another baby." Loraine laughs. "Like I would want to help make things easier on him."

"Did you ever meet Jenny?"

"A few times. Had to before I'd let my kids go over there and stay with them."

"What'd you think?"

"I knew she'd be trouble."

"And why's that?" I ask, leaning toward her like I'm just a woman gossiping and not a police officer conducting an interrogation.

"For one, that baby didn't look a thing like Greg. I wouldn't be surprised if it wasn't his, and he just got duped into marrying her."

"And two?"

"Greg didn't love her. Didn't even like her, as far as I could tell. That baby wasn't even six months old before he was over at my house, trying to rekindle the old spark."

"And?" I ask when she doesn't continue.

"And I told him to get bent. He made his choice. Not my fault that it was the wrong one. Not that I would have wanted him anyway after he cheated on me. But I knew that situation was a ticking bomb. It was only a matter of time. If I were you, I'd be looking into what happened to that poor child as more than an accident."

I study her face, wondering what she knows. And how. She still seems awfully bitter about the collapse of her marriage. Bitter enough that I'd expect her to tell me about Greg dealing if she knew about it. But bitter enough to hurt a small child to get her revenge?

I decide to play stupid. "You think that one of them hurt PJ? Do you think Greg would be capable of that?"

She shrugs. "I really couldn't say. But either way, if you ask me, that kid got lucky."

I stumble back a step, her words knocking into me like a shove to the chest. She has the decency to try and look contrite, but there's something ugly hiding underneath. Satisfaction.

The temperature has dropped, and it isn't just because it's unseasonably cold. I stare at the woman before me, taking her measure. Yes, Loraine Garner is a woman scorned, but she's also a mother. That she would be so callous about the death of another woman's child has me concerned.

"Ms. Garner," I say, reverting to formality. "Would you mind if I spoke with your children now?"

She looks like she wants to say no. Instead, she tells me, "Stay here." Turning sideways, as if she doesn't dare show me her back, she calls her kids to the door. It seems obvious that, despite her initial friendliness toward me, she's decided that I'm not a friend.

Amanda is the first to respond, jogging down the stairs. She stops short when she sees me, exhales a soft, "Oh, no." She catches Jamie by the arm as he runs past her, pulls him to her side, and keeps him pinned to her as they approach the open door.

She stands there for a moment before straightening her spine and lifting her chin. Her voice wavers as she asks, "How's PJ?"

I press my lips together. There's no easy way to say this, so I'd rather not do it more than I have to. As if sensing the cause of my reluctance, she yells, "Dylan!"

"What?" he says, appearing at the top of the stairs. Amanda steps to the side, pulling Jamie with her, so Dylan can see me.

He runs a hand over his hair, ruffling it as he slowly descends to join us.

Reaching the landing, he joins his siblings, the three of them standing shoulder to shoulder in the doorway before me. Loraine hovers behind them.

"I'm afraid PJ was found this morning. In Beaverhead Lake."

Amanda's eyes fill with tears. Jamie's face and neck turn red. Only Dylan seems unfazed.

"How'd he get there?" Dylan asks.

"That's something that we're still working to determine."

"Do you have any suspects?"

Eyeballing the teenager in front of me, I ignore the cold creeping through the fabric of my uniform slacks as I ask, "Do you have any suggestions?"

He doesn't answer. After the silence has lingered uncomfortably long, I ask, "How did you feel about PJ?"

Dylan shrugs. "He seemed cool enough, for a little kid. We didn't really get to spend much time around him."

"Because you spend most of your time here?"

"No. Because Jenny didn't want us to."

Amanda steps in to explain. "Jenny was one of those, what do you call them? Helicopter moms? She was nervous. Afraid she'd screw it up. I'm not sure it was so much that she didn't want us spending time together as much as she was afraid to take her eyes off PJ for a second."

"The homewrecker had no problem taking her eyes off him long enough to go get drunk and slut it up with her skank friends at the Loose Moose, though, did she?" Loraine spits. The friendliness she'd greeted me with is gone, her smile now a sneer. For such a small woman, she harbors a huge amount of anger.

How did she know Jenny was out the night PJ went missing? Did she see her at the bar, or is it something she learned through town gossip? I file the question away for later.

"How did you guys get along with her?"

Amanda shoots a nervous glance at her mother. "Fine, I guess."

"No problems?"

No one answers.

"How about her relationship with your dad?"

Again, my question is met with silence.

"Did anything happen between them that night that—"

"Nothing happened," Dylan interrupts.

"You were at a friend's house that night, weren't you?" Recalling the name from the statement I took, I add, "Larry Ross?"

"Yeah."

"And you stayed there the whole time?"

His face twists up, eyes blinking hard as he says, "Well, yeah. Of course."

But his reaction suggests he might be lying.

"Then how do you know?" I ask.

He shifts nervously under my gaze, declining to answer.

"If I ask Larry, is he going to tell me the same?"

His eyes meet mine. He gives me a hard look as he says, "Yes."

"You're sixteen, correct?"

"Uh, yeah. So?"

"And how about you?" I ask the youngest boy. "Your name's Jamie, right?"

He looks from side to side at his siblings. Amanda gives a small, barely perceptible nod. "Uh-huh."

"How old are you?"

"Ten."

"And how did you feel about Jenny?"

"We hate her. If it wasn't for her, my dad would still be living at home with me and my mom."

I glance at Loraine. She's smirking. "I think we're done here," she says, stepping forward, ushering her children back from the door.

As she closes it in my face, I can't help feeling like there's something I'm missing. Something besides a scorned woman's contempt for her replacement. And I have a nagging sensation I just can't shake that those kids are hiding something.

27
STEVE

How is it possible that Wesley knows Maggie owns the house across the street? I can't remember the last time either of us went over there—it's been months. There's been no reason to. It's locked up tight and uninhabitable, a hole in the roof from where a tree fell during a snowstorm. We're still waiting for the repairs to be made.

It means Wesley's been doing more than watching us. He's been researching us. For the first time, I suspect this wasn't just a last-minute lark of his, to blackmail me.

While growing up, he was the rash and impulsive one, always rushing to action without thinking. But it seems my old friend has learned some new tricks. My chest tightens as I realize how much effort he's likely put into what he's doing. He's probably been planning this for a very long time. Like the fifteen years he was in prison.

Shifting into drive, I steer the car one-handed, using the other to wrestle the gun out from under my waistband. I tuck it under the seat as I cross the street and pull up in front of Maggie's house. If Wesley's prepared for this meeting, he'll expect me to come armed. I need to do the unexpected, lower his defenses so I can catch him off guard next time. I force a swallow past the lump in my throat at the fact that I'm already expecting there to be another meeting.

I take a quick look around, noting that there are no vehicles here except mine. How did he get out here? Where's he coming from? And what kind of game is Wesley playing? I really wish I didn't have to find out.

Opening the door, I exit the car before I can change my mind and hurry up the front steps. My breath fogs in clouds as my numb fingers barely manage to fumble the key to Maggie's front door into the lock. It opens with a creak, the hinges stiff from cold and disuse. I step inside, flicking the light switch as I wonder where I should wait when a voice behind me makes me jump.

"Three o'clock on the dot. See? I knew you could do it. You always were punctual, weren't you?"

My heart skips erratically inside my chest as I turn, and there he is. Wesley Banks. My old best friend.

He's bigger than I remember, his lean form more muscular. But the years haven't been kind to him. Or maybe it was prison that eroded the contours of his youth into a face formed of craggy ridges and stone.

Though he wears his slightly too long dark hair in the same unruly style I remember girls loving when we were younger, and there's no mistaking those nearly black eyes of his, I almost don't recognize him, wonder if it isn't possible that I passed him any number of times on the street without realizing how close I was to evil.

"Go on." He gestures toward the house with his head.

I walk sideways, unwilling to turn my back on him as I enter, unable to take my eyes off his jacket, the right pocket bulging with something much larger than just his hand. He pulls the door shut behind him, then gives a mock shiver.

"Brrr. They really don't pay cops enough, do they? Yours

can't even afford to heat her house. But I suppose there's really no need since she's shacking up with you, is there? I gotta say though, I never saw you as the type who could handle a redhead, much less one with a pair of handcuffs. Well done."

"Why are we here?" I ask.

"Geesh. Here I was thinking maybe we could catch up a bit first, but I guess you always were all business. All right, have it your way. First things first. Empty your pockets."

I pull my jackets pockets inside out, proving there's nothing in them.

"Now take off the coat and drop it."

I do as he says.

"Pull up your shirt."

I roll my eyes.

He finally shows his hand—and the gun held in it. "Do it."

I say a silent prayer of relief that I left my own firearm in the car as I obey.

"Turn around."

I circle.

"Pull your pants legs up."

Once we've finally finished playing his game of Wesley says, he leans his back against the door, crossing his arms as he smirks. "Man, the surprises just keep coming. I remember you as being more predictable. I really expected you to be armed or bugged or something. I'm kind of disappointed. I guess people really do change."

"You always loved to hear yourself talk, so that's the same," I say.

He tilts the gun a little more in my direction, eyebrows raised. "Well, someone put on his sassy pants this morning."

"Can we cut the bull, already?"

"You always did think you were something special, didn't you?" Wesley's lips curl into a smile. His obsidian eyes glitter with malice. "I've waited a long time for this. To see what you're really made of." His expression darkens, gaze turning almost black. "And I'm gonna give you a chance, I really am. But I don't think you've got what it takes. So just know, when you fail? I'm going to rip your happy little life to shreds. And then I'll do the same to everyone in it."

I brace myself as my legs threaten to buckle. A sharp pain lances through my chest. I'm worried it's my heart. Because it's clear that this man right here hates me. Whatever he's going to demand, I suspect he doesn't want it as much as he wants to destroy me.

28
MAGGIE

I hurry back to the police department, late for my meeting with the Greenleys, the men who discovered PJ's body in the lake this morning. Spotting their truck already in the lot, I pull in and park beside it, relieved to see Kal's vehicle is here, too. I jog up the ramp and duck inside in time to see Kal shaking their hands.

"Gentlemen, thank you for coming," I say, leading the men into my office and gesturing toward the guest chairs in front of my desk.

I wait for them to get settled before taking my own seat. Leaning back, I study them for a moment. The older one strips off his hat, gloves, scarf, and jacket, folding them neatly onto his lap. His scalp glistens through his sparse gray hair, and a bead of sweat rolls down his weathered temple.

My own shirt sticks to the small of my back, and I have to fight the urge to fan myself. I glance over at Kal, leaning against the wall to my left, and notice dark spots at the armpits of his uniform. There's no denying that it's uncomfortably hot in here.

I shift my focus to the younger man, watching as he squirms. Though his companion has the rough tanned skin of an outdoorsman, his own complexion is relatively pale. His flesh looks soft, doughy almost, and though it's covered with a sheen of sweat, he has yet to so much as undo the zipper on his thick winter coat. It makes me wonder what he's hiding.

Pressing the speaker button on my desk so that Sue can hear clearly and transcribe their statements, I give them both a friendly smile and say, "I'd like to begin by thanking you both for your time and cooperation. I know that it can't have been easy for you, and I appreciate your help with this. Can I get either of you something to drink?"

Both men shake their heads, though the younger one swallows so hard I can hear it. I know he's thirsty. It's more than a little suspicious.

Pulling the notebook I'd used earlier to take their preliminary statements from my shirt pocket, I flip it open and skim the page. "Just to confirm, you're Walter and Ned Greenley?"

I pretend not to notice the way the older man cuts his eyes toward the younger one, the unspoken conversation that occurs between them as I confirm the spelling of their surname, their address, and the fact that they are uncle and nephew, a fact that will make it easier to verify their identities.

"This shouldn't be too hard. We just need to confirm the details you provided me with earlier for your official statement. Ned," I say, addressing the younger one. "Can you please walk me through the events of this morning again?"

He shrugs and wipes the sweat from his eyes. "There's not much to tell. We got out to the dock before dawn. Carried our gear out to the end."

"And this is something you do frequently? Almost daily, you said, this time of year?"

"Yep," Walter supplies.

"And you were there for the same reason on Friday?"

"Correct."

"But not Saturday, because Ned was feeling ill?"

"That's right."

I turn my attention back to Ned. "Then what?"

"Our hole had iced over, so I stuck the gaff down and gave it a stir to break it up, only it snagged on something and didn't want to come free." He back-arms his forehead dry. The motion pushes his hat up, which he hastily tugs back down. "I kept pulling, and that's when I saw what it had gotten hooked on."

Walter crosses himself as he says, "I reached down and checked the poor boy, but it was too late."

"And then?"

"Then I drove out to the Warners' place and told you. You know it from there."

"Did you touch the body at all?" I ask Ned.

"No."

But he doesn't look too sure.

"Why'd you stay with the body instead of getting help?"

"My uncle knows his way around better."

"How long have you been in the area?"

The younger man looks at Walter to save him. When his uncle remains silent, he says, "Three years."

"Three years," I repeat. "That seems like plenty of time to get familiar with the area."

His face flushes as he says, "I don't go out much."

The guy's clearly hiding something. The question is, what is it? And more importantly, does it have anything to do with my case?

"Well," I say, pushing my chair back from my desk and standing. Ned springs to his feet, eyes flashing as he looks around the room as if seeking an escape. "Thank you both for your time."

"That's all, then?" Walter asks.

"For now, yes. I'll just need you to read over your statements and sign for me."

The printer whirs as Sue makes two copies of the form she's

just typed. I hand each man a pen. To my disappointment, the younger one fails to remove his glove to sign. And while Walter's signature is neat, Ned's is messy and illegible.

"Thank you," I say, collecting the papers before trailing the Greenleys to the door. I close it behind them, watching through the blinds as Ned scurries across the lot ahead of his uncle and climbs into the passenger seat of an ancient green truck with an equally old camper top on back.

"Well, that was kind of awkward, wasn't it?" Kal asks as he comes to stand beside me.

"It was." I watch as a dark cloud of exhaust spits from the tailpipe and the truck chugs out onto the street. "You get the impression he's hiding something?"

"Oh, yeah."

"I don't suppose the name Greenley appeared anywhere on the list Jenny sent us?"

"I don't think so. But I'll check again. Not sure it'll do much good, though. Did you notice the uncle's reaction when you confirmed his name?"

"I did."

"Even I saw that, and I was in a different room," Sue says as she lines up on my other side. "Since you two have your hands full, would you mind if I did a little digging?"

I turn to face her, eyebrows raised.

"What? Is there something else you'd rather me do instead?"

I consider the question for a moment. Glance at Kal, whose face mirrors my suspicions. And, apparently, Sue's.

"Full speed ahead," I say.

My secretary is like my terriers. Once something's caught her interest, she's obsessive about it. I'm not sure if Ned Greenley's secret has anything to do with this case or not, but I have complete confidence that if it does, Sue will find out.

29

STEVE

I leave the lights off as I walk deeper into Maggie's house, on the off chance that someone driving by might see them. Wesley's footsteps echo ominously behind me as he follows. Reaching the couch, I allow myself to collapse onto it, my body feeling weak and boneless. I watch as my former friend settles onto the loveseat, spreading his arms out along the back, making himself comfortable like he doesn't have a care in the world.

If he's waiting for me to break the silence, to beg him to let me know what he wants from me, it isn't going to happen. I busy myself with looking around the room, taking in Maggie's well-worn, mismatched furniture, chosen for comfort and function, not aesthetics. Truth be told, I've always liked her place better than mine.

We made such great memories here. This is where we fell in love, me citing a number of excuses every evening for still being around when she got off work, long after I'd let the dogs out for her during the day. Plying her with late-night meals, trying my best to be interesting and charming, doing anything to make her smile.

I'd never expected to make a connection like the one I have

with her, had long abandoned the idea of ever getting married, somehow suspecting that I didn't deserve the happiness that others had. But there'd been something about Maggie, who was somehow simultaneously both the least and the most vulnerable person I'd ever met. And though she'd tried to maintain a gruff exterior, one look at how she was with her dogs was all I needed to know how lucky I'd be if she ever let me past the barbed wire that guarded her heart.

It seems an added injury, that Wesley's chosen Maggie's home as the place to do this. It makes my hatred burn a little hotter.

"I want you to get me a new identity."

I stare at Wesley, not understanding why this is something he'd need my help with, unless... "How much do you need to buy one?" Whatever the sum is, I'll gladly find a way to pay it if it means removing this thorn from my side.

"No." He shakes his head resolutely. "Not a fake one. It has to be a real one."

My frown deepens, confused.

Wesley sighs impatiently. "The name can't just be attached to some bogus Social Security number or belong to someone who died already. It needs to be able to pass an in-depth background check."

"Why?"

"You don't need to worry about that." But something about the way that he smiles suggests that I do. "All you need to concern yourself with is getting it for me. And fast, before I run out of patience. I've got big plans and I don't want to spend any more time in Hicksville than I have to. I'm giving you three days."

"I don't understand. What exactly is it that I'm supposed to do?"

"Look, it's simple. You find some guy about my age. And

make sure he looks a bit like me, too. Then you check that he has a clean record."

"And how am I supposed to do that?"

"That's where your lady comes in. Find a way to make her run the dude's prints, or break into her office and run his name yourself. I don't care. All that matters is that the guy is squeaky clean."

"And then what? You want me to steal his license and give it to you?"

Wesley laughs like I'm a child who just said something absurd. "No. Then make sure he isn't using it himself anymore. And that no one finds out who is."

I run his words through my head, trying to make sense of them. And then I do. It feels like the blood drains from my body, ice water taking its place as I realize what he's saying. What it is that he wants me to do. He doesn't just want me to take someone's identity. He wants me to take their life.

30

MAGGIE

There's nothing like running background checks on those involved in the drug trade to make a cop feel inept. I take another sip of coffee as the words blur on the computer screen, scroll down, and see more of the same. It's mind numbing, the same charges appearing over and over—possession, theft, public intoxication, burglary.

But what I'm not seeing are any violent crimes besides the occasional battery and domestic dispute. No child abuse, no manslaughter, no murder.

We need to speak with these people in person, but many are no longer at the last known address I can find for them. A few are no longer alive. And then there are those who seem to have dropped off the face of the earth completely.

I hope Kal is doing better with his half of Jenny's list. I wonder if he's feeling as overwhelmed as I am about how many criminals are lurking in our small town. It's unsettling, discovering how crowded the shadows around me are. It's my job to turn on the light, shine it into the dark places, but I feel like I've failed.

Because as small as Coyote Cove is, most of these names are

unfamiliar to me. But they're on my radar now, and when time allows, I'm going to make it my business to get to know these people a little better.

I look out through the open doorway, craning my head so I can see my lieutenant at his desk. He's on the phone, an animated look on his face. Curious, I get up, closing the distance between us until I'm near enough to eavesdrop.

Noticing, he raises his shaggy eyebrows at me and presses the button to send the call to speaker. A thick Maine accent fills the room.

"And if I do this, you'll tell them I helped you, right? See if you can't get my sentence reduced?"

Kal shoots me a questioning look and I nod. "I'll make sure that the parole board at your next hearing knows that you were cooperative in an active investigation, yes."

"Great, thanks, man. I'm not cut out to be in here. And I shouldn't be. It wasn't my fault. How was I supposed to know the drugs had been cut with rat poison. And how'd I end up serving time for manslaughter just 'cause I sold the stuff? It's not like I made her shoot up, you know?"

I pull a spare chair over and take a seat, my skin tingling. This could be the lead we're looking for. If the Warners had something to do with selling drugs laced with a lethal dose of poison, they could have made some potent enemies.

Sharing my suspicions, Kal asks, "Did Greg and Jenny Warner have anything to do with that bad batch?"

The inmate snorts. "The Warners? Is that who you're calling about?"

"We were hoping you could give us some information about them."

"Whatcha want with—? Wait a minute. You got my name from them? What are they saying about me?"

"Only that you're someone they came in contact with over the course of their dealings."

He snorts again. "They wish. We met one time at a shared acquaintance's house. Otherwise, our paths never would've crossed. I don't have time to rub elbows with wannabes. At least, I didn't."

I feel my hopes come crashing down, but Kal doesn't miss a beat. "So they didn't have anything to do with the bad batch?"

"Nah. I didn't even know they were in the game, to be honest."

Kal and I exchange disappointed looks. "If that's the case, would you mind if I ran some names by you?"

"I ain't no snitch."

"I'm not asking you to be. I already know what they're up to," he fibs. "I just want to see if you've heard of them or not."

"And you'll tell the parole board I cooperated?"

"I will."

"All right, then. Go ahead."

Kal grabs his half of Jenny's list and runs through the names.

The inmate clears his throat, the rattle thick with phlegm. "Yeah, I've heard of a few of them. None really worth knowing, though."

"What do you mean by that?" Kal asks.

"None of them are really regular users. More like dabblers. Not a lot of scratch to be made off that type."

"Any dealers in that bunch?"

"Not unless they've started since I've been in here."

I try not to feel discouraged as Kal wraps up the call, but it's hard. This could have been the break we needed.

"I'll keep digging," Kal assures me with a strained smile. "Something will turn up."

But I'm worried he's wrong.

"Aha."

I glance behind me and see Sue grinning. And maybe

gloating just a bit. I stand and hurry over, in dire need of some good news.

A search for Ned Greenley came up clean, at least with the databases the Coyote Cove Police Department has access to. It wasn't a surprise. After his Uncle Walter's reaction when I'd confirmed the name he'd given me, it seemed likely that he might not have been completely honest.

And something about the way he'd been so careful not to leave anything of himself behind, not even a fingerprint, made me suspect he had experience with the criminal justice system. That he was one of those types who had learned all their rights, and how to dance around the edges of the law, which means he would know that I couldn't demand his prints without just cause.

As such, I figured Ned must be short for his real name. That way, a lawyer could argue that he hadn't provided false information. We'd brainstormed a list of possibilities—Edward, Edmond, Edwin. But none of us thought of Dennis. Yet here he is, his doughy face recognizable in the booking photo featured in the digital issue of the *Lincoln Sun* newspaper pulled up on Sue's computer.

I read the article about Dennis Greenley for a third time. It's the break I'd been hoping for so badly only minutes before, and yet... Finally, I look up from the screen, meeting Sue's eyes. They flit over my face, searching my expression. I know what she's thinking. That this could complicate things. That it could be the straw that breaks the camel's or, in this case, *my* back.

Cases involving children are never easy, but when there's something that forges a personal connection between you and the investigation, they become even more difficult. It was hard enough when our victim was the same age and gender as my brother. When he had an uncanny resemblance. But now...

It wasn't just the loss of my brother that destroyed me. It was wondering what his last hours on earth must have been like.

Suspecting what had probably happened to him. The way he must have suffered after I discovered that the man who took him was a known pedophile.

I exhale hard, feeling a bit dizzy and weak. Grabbing the chair beside Sue's desk, I take a seat. She hops up, hurrying over to the water cooler. I hear her fill a cup. Feel her put it in my hand and lift it to my lips. I swallow, but I couldn't tell you if I actually took a sip or not.

I feel curiously numb, the sense of déjà vu back, stronger than ever.

Another little boy taken from his family. And another pedophile in the picture. Dennis—not Ned—Greenley has served time for sexual abuse of a minor.

I draw deep breaths until my pulse slows. My voice wavers as I say, "We need to get the details of his arrest record."

Kal calls from his desk, "Already on it."

"We need to get a warrant to search his uncle's house, the truck, any other space or vehicle he has access to."

Sue rubs small circles on my back. "Consider it done."

"Apply pressure, Sue. I want in there today."

"Maggie." Her voice is soft, like she's afraid I'll shatter if she talks too loud. I brace myself, knowing I'm not going to like what she has to say. "It's Sunday evening."

I wait to feel it. The darkness coming to claim me.

Because this is northern Maine. There are no judges to wake up in the middle of the night to facilitate a warrant. There's rarely even one who will answer their phone outside of business hours on a weekday.

But it doesn't happen.

I survived when it was my brother. Barely, and not without my battle wounds, but that scar tissue has made me stronger. I'll make it through this, too. And there's one very big difference between then and now.

This is my town. I'm in charge. Major crimes may fall under

state police jurisdiction, but I've never let that stop me before, and I'm not going to let it stop me now. It just means that I have to hurry.

I exhale slowly, nodding, mostly to myself. "Okay. Tomorrow, then," I say, standing. "First thing tomorrow."

"Where are you going?" Sue asks, face creased with concern. I suspect she's worried I'm going to go rogue. That I'm planning to go to the Greenley house, drag Dennis outside, and inflict some good old-fashioned vigilante justice on him.

"Home."

"Do you want one of us to drive you?"

"No."

She exchanges a frantic look with Kal, as if she expects him to stop me.

"Sue, I'm fine. Really. It was a bit of a shock at first, but... he's just another suspect. And we don't even know if foul play was involved yet. Let's just take this step by step."

And that's just what I do. I put one foot in front of the other, pull on my jacket, get in my car, and start the engine. Glancing at myself in the rearview mirror, I nod at my reflection. I look fine. Normal. Sane. That's good. Because if I didn't, there's no way I'd be able to convince the Greenleys to let me inside.

31

MAGGIE

Five years ago

Maggie is still dressed in all black when she shows up to the sheriff's department. This time, instead of ignoring her, her coworkers stare as they give her wide berth, scrambling to get out of her way as she storms to Sheriff Brewster's office.

She doesn't bother knocking as she reaches the door. Instead, she tosses it open and stands at the threshold, nostrils flaring as she glares at the men before her. Detective Hawkins glances at the sheriff, nervously moving his chair closer to the man behind the desk as Maggie approaches.

"Did he tell you?" she asks.

The sheriff steeples his fingers over his ample gut. "About?"

"About the convicted pedophile I have footage of driving by the park at the same time that my brother went missing?"

"Yes, he did. Tell me, Detective. How did you come into possession of the video?"

"I opened my eyes and looked."

"And?"

"And when I saw that one of the properties across from the park had security cameras, I knocked on the door and asked the owner for a copy."

"What part of our conversation yesterday was unclear? I told you to stay away from the case, didn't I?"

"If Hawkins was doing his job, I wouldn't have to!"

"What Hawkins is doing isn't your concern."

"Well, obviously it's not yours, either."

The sheriff shifts his girth, straightening in his seat. "Maggie, I know you're upset, but we're doing everything we can."

"Sir, with all due respect, I have to disagree."

He raises his eyebrows at her.

"Is my mom the only suspect you're investigating right now?"

"Unfortunately, the evidence—"

"What evidence?"

"Exactly," Hawkins chimes in. "Don't you think it's strange that we can't find any proof that your brother was at the park."

"Have you found any proof that he wasn't?"

Maggie looks between the two men, but neither answer.

"Then I suggest you look a little harder."

"You're too close to this case to see what's right in front of you," Hawkins says.

"Are you kidding me?" she asks from between gritted teeth. "You don't even have your eyes open. A monkey could do a better job than you have."

He glances at the sheriff for backup as she stalks forward, hands fisted, seething.

"Tell me, Detective Hawkins"—she exaggerates his title, making it a mockery—"why didn't you find the video? Do you even know if my mom walked or drove to the park? And if she went there straight from the house or if she came from somewhere else?"

Hawkins smirks nastily. "I've been doing this job long enough to know what I'm dealing with here. I realize no one wants to believe that their own family is capable of—"

"That's not what this is about!"

"Then what? Oh, I get it. It's because you're worried that the truth will get out and tarnish your shiny little record."

"Are you kidding me? We're talking about my brother here."

"Seriously, Maggie. The kid was young enough to be yours. How close could you have possibly been to him?"

She turns to the sheriff and demands, "I want him off the case. You don't want me to work it, fine, but give it to someone who doesn't have their head stuck so far up their own—"

"Riley!" Sheriff Brewster barks. "That's enough. I know that you're under a lot of stress right now. Which is why I'm telling you to take a leave of absence instead of asking for your badge."

"Excuse me?" Maggie can't believe her ears. Her head draws back over her body, like a snake preparing to strike as she stares at the sheriff. "So that's it, then? I've spent my entire career slaving away for this department, and the first time I need something in return, which is only for you to do your jobs..."

She shakes her head, looking at them both with disgust. She's not surprised that Hawkins is botching the case. He's always done the bare minimum needed to get a paycheck, and truth be told, he's never liked her, always been bitter about her success. He's probably focused his investigation on her parents as part of a personal vendetta.

But Sheriff Brewster? She'd expected more from him. As he likes to remind his officers, he's the king of this castle, and what he says goes. Which means all he'd have to do is give the word, and she'd have the entire department helping her. Instead, she's become a pariah. None of her coworkers will dare lift a finger to help her.

So why is she still here? She wants to quit on the spot. But as *she turns on her heel and leaves, she keeps her badge with her. It doesn't mean anything to her anymore, but it will to some. And if she can leverage it to open doors and force people to cooperate, well, she'll take whatever help she can get. There's no way she's dropping this. Not until it's done.*

32

MAGGIE

Walter Greenley's residence isn't at all what I was expecting. Though Walter himself seemed a little rough around the edges, and the long driveway led me past multiple leaf-shrouded trash heaps dotted along the unkempt land, the small house before me appears neat and well cared for.

I park beside Walter's beat-up pickup and climb the porch steps, noting the potted plant stationed beside the front door. The shrub is neatly shaped and pruned, certainly in much better condition than any I've ever tried to care for.

My guess would be that it's the work of the older Greenley. A part of me feels bad for him. But I can't let that detract from the reason why I'm here.

The old man answers quickly, like he's been expecting company. And the way he immediately steps back and ushers me inside, his expression more resigned than surprised, makes me suspect that he's been waiting for me in particular.

"He's in his room," Walter says, pointing to a closed door off the small main quarters. The crease between his brows deepens as he adds, "I'll feel just horrible if it turns out he was responsible for what happened to that boy, but I don't see how he could be. He never leaves the house without me by his side. That was part of the terms for his living here."

So he knows why I've come. And what I must suspect.

"Does he ever drive your truck?" I ask.

"Nope. Never." He pulls a chain from beneath his flannel shirt. A key dangles from the end. It's possible that this is a new development, solely for my benefit, but something about the man's expression, the way he doesn't shy away from looking me in the eyes, nor try to conceal the sadness in his own, makes me believe him.

"Does he ever go for walks?"

Walter grunts. "Only if it's part of one of those video games of his."

"You ever leave him home alone?"

"That I do. Didn't see the harm in it. He don't know anyone around here, and he's not exactly the outdoors type. The only time he steps outside is when we go fishing. He wouldn't even do that if he had the choice, but if he wants to eat..." Walter shrugs. "He's a grown man. Ain't my job to make his life cushy by providing for him."

"Do you always go to the same spot?"

"This time of year, conditions being what they are? Yes."

"Do you think he could have found his way there by himself?"

"He ain't stupid, just sick in the head, but if he did, I have no clue how he got there and back."

The drive to get here from town had been quite long, over thirty miles. I hadn't passed many houses over the last half of the trip.

"Where's your closest neighbor?" I ask.

"Old Ted Johnson, over to the west. He's about two miles as the crow flies, about twice that if you stick to the roads."

"Is it possible your nephew could have borrowed a vehicle from him?"

"All he's got is an old Ford. Stick shift. The boy can't drive a manual, not that Ted would let him touch it if he could."

"Do you know if your nephew ever saw PJ Warner before?"

"I can't rightly say. I don't recall ever seeing the child myself. And we don't go to town much. But it's possible."

There's a small click as a door opens. Glancing at the window, I watch Dennis Greenley approach in the reflection while I purposely keep my back to him. Shift my weight so I can feel my gun in its holster at my side.

"Where do you frequent when you do go to town?"

"Mostly just the trading post. The Loose Moose, on occasion."

Dennis stops several feet behind me, arms crossed, a glare on his face. I can feel his eyes boring into the back of my head.

"Mr. Greenley, I'd like to take a look around, if that's okay with you?"

"Don't see what choice I have."

I realize that I've put him in an awkward position. His nephew, despite what he may have done, is still family. And I don't want to risk having any evidence thrown out if this goes to court.

"You're well within your rights to decline at this time and request that I come back with a warrant."

"Yes," Dennis says.

"No." It's the first time Walter Greenley has raised his voice. The first show of any emotion other than remorse. "That won't be necessary, Chief. Not as long as this is my house."

"But Uncle Wal—"

"Enough!"

I turn to face Dennis. He's paler than I remember, and without his hat and scarf to hide behind, younger. The kind of man who you wouldn't glance at twice if you were to pass him on the street. He certainly doesn't look like a monster.

And yet we're all capable of doing monstrous things, aren't we?

"You said you had nothing to do with that boy's death," Walter says.

"I didn't."

"Then you have nothing to worry about, do you?"

Walter's head is held high, his chin lifted, as he instructs me, "Nothing is off limits. Look wherever you'd like. Take whatever you want."

I have to hand it to the man. I admire his faith in his nephew, his willingness to give him a chance and believe the best about him, despite what he'd done in his past.

Some of us hide our demons. Some of us protect them. Then there are those of us who run, hoping they never catch up.

33

MAGGIE

There are occasions when I wish the numbers of the Coyote Cove Police Department were a little larger, but times like these, I appreciate the quiet that a bigger force would never afford. Opening the door and switching on the lights, I trudge into my office and slump into the seat behind my desk, relieved to find myself alone.

I should be home right now, spending time with Steve and his family. But I can't face them, not yet.

I just feel so... I don't even know how I feel. Can't make sense of it or put it into words. But that's only part of the problem.

I never should have gone out to the Greenleys' tonight. It was unprofessional and inappropriate. But I had to do it. I had to look that man in the eye, but now that I have... I shove a stack of papers off the edge of my desk. Grab my penholder and launch it against the wall across the room, sending ballpoints flying everywhere.

My eyes sting. My jaw aches. My face feels painfully tight. I long to slam my fist into my desk, pick up my chair and smash it into my computer. I want to cry. Because my gut is telling me that Dennis Greenley isn't our man. And I don't understand how that could be.

He's a monster. He doesn't deserve the benefit of the doubt. He should be guilty until proven innocent. It's too much of a coincidence, that he was the one who found the missing boy. Yet no matter what angle I approach this from, I just don't believe he's my suspect.

It wasn't just his uncle's confidence in him, though that didn't hurt. Or even the fact that the logistics of the crime simply don't add up—without a vehicle, it would be an incredible feat for Dennis to have traveled all the way from his uncle's house to the Warners', to the lake, and back in such a short amount of time.

But what really has me convinced is that after taking Walter Greenley up on his offer, and searching his entire house, including an extensive examination of his nephew's bedroom, I didn't find one thing to suggest that Dennis was taking part in any kind of deviant behavior—and that's rare for a pedophile.

My first partner when I joined the force was an ex-sex crimes detective who had stepped down for a bit of a break. Despite that, he couldn't seem to give it up. Or maybe it was just that talking about it helped veil the images that lived inside his head. Either way, I'd spent countless hours listening to him while we drove around on patrol.

The recidivism rate for child molesters of boy victims is thirty-five percent within the first fifteen years after their initial arrest, and there's no doubt that this number is underreported. It's also not uncommon for them to engage in triggering activities before reoffending, whether that's interacting with potential victims online, possessing pornographic images, or even just owning a large amount of what would be, in the hands of a non-perpetrator, seemingly innocuous material, such as underwear ads.

I found nothing at the Greenley house.

And though I'd been concerned that Dennis may have been interacting with boys in the course of playing his video games, his gaming system is offline. They don't even have an internet connection. Of course, the absence of anything concerning doesn't mean the man is innocent. But if there's a connection between him and what happened to PJ, I'm not seeing it.

Waking my computer, I bring up my notes on the Warners' drug connections. I haven't gotten as far as I'd like with my research. But given the results Kal's obtained, I can't help wondering if it's even worth the effort.

Opening my email, I read what Kal sent me about the names on his half of the list. None of them were violent offenders. And other than the one whose call I eavesdropped on, nothing about any of them raised a red flag. Though he'd managed to track down several to talk with in person, they'd all confirmed what the inmate he'd spoken with earlier had said.

The Warners were low key. No one was aware of them having any enemies.

I skim Kal's findings again before copying and pasting it into the same document as my notes. I print the entire thing, hoping that holding the information in my hands will somehow reveal the truth, because none of these people are striking me as likely suspects. And I could desperately use one of those right about now.

Closing my eyes, I draw several deep breaths, promising myself that when this is all over, I'm going to take some time to rest. But what is *this*? The case? The wedding? Life? I laugh softly to myself at the thought of ever getting an actual break while I'm still alive. If it's not one thing, it's another, an endless chain of events, each requiring their pound of flesh and chunk of soul.

Finally, I push back from my desk. Fold the papers I printed out and shove them into my pocket as I leave the building, locking up for the night. It's time to go home.

It's been a long day. A hard one. I can't help feeling a bit defeated, my frustration like a heavy blanket wrapped tight around my body.

So many questions remain unanswered, and I suspect that discovering the truth behind some of them will cause this family more grief. I wish I could say that's what has me feeling tied up in knots, but it's not.

My job is to find out what happened to PJ Warner, no matter the outcome. I can't afford to be concerned about the consequences of that. I can't allow myself to care about the repercussions. All I care about is the truth. Someone put that little boy under the ice, and I intend to find out who.

And if my suspicions are confirmed, and the medical examiner checks the box next to homicide on the report after PJ's autopsy, the case will officially be a major crime. Once that's been determined, it becomes the territory of the state police. Not every detective is willing to work with local law enforcement, so my time to get to the bottom of this is limited.

Because it has to be me. I have to crack this. Not for myself, but for Brandon. For the family I once had, the one that was destroyed much like this one might be in the end. For the guilt I feel at the vendetta I've yet to settle, my brother's killer still walking free, the universe still waiting for me to mete out justice.

But once I do, what will that mean for my future? Once I cross that line, there may be no coming back. No happily ever after. Which was fine when I never expected that to be an option.

Now that I've had a taste of happiness, though, I want to be the woman who gets to marry her handsome prince and have her fairy tale ending, complete with two frisky terriers and the extended family Steve brings to the table. Even if I wish they weren't going to be at the table tonight.

I roll my neck, trying to relax the muscles in my shoulders.

It doesn't matter how badly I want it to be just me and Steve and the dogs when I get home. How much I long to curl up in his arms on the couch and let him soothe the stress of my day away. His family is here and that's not going to change. But maybe it's a good thing. I could definitely use the distraction.

I run over the details I've learned one last time as I drive, preparing to set them on the back burner for the night. The night before last, Jenny Warner arrived home sometime around two in the morning. After using a spare key to enter the house, which normally wasn't locked, she checked on her son on her way to bed, peeking in from the doorway so she wouldn't wake him.

The next morning, she'd gone to his room shortly after eight, surprised that he'd allowed her to sleep so late. Upon discovering that he was missing, she'd checked with her husband and her mother-in-law, and then woke her stepchildren and asked them if they'd seen PJ. No one had. She'd quickly searched the house and the yard and then driven into town in a panic.

She'd been the only one concerned that the boy was missing, which is strange. A small child had seemingly vanished from his bed. Surely, as a parent, Greg should have been worried.

Then there's the question of the locked door. Is it possible that Jenny, in her drunken state, had made a mistake? Or had someone indeed locked her out, and if so, who? Perhaps more importantly, why?

I also can't discount the possibility that the whole construct is a lie, either. Subterfuge meant to distract me from Jenny's role in what happened. As painful as it is to consider, it wouldn't be the first time that a mother has harmed her own child, whether intentionally or not.

But there's also a chance that I'm mistaken. That PJ somehow did make it out to the lake on his own. There'd been no child locks on any of the doors, like Diane had mentioned.

There'd been no child safety features of any kind in the house. It's possible that this is all just a tragic accident.

Yet, Jenny had seemed so sure that he wouldn't have left the house on his own. Even Franny had assumed that someone had taken the boy. How had she put it? That he was attached to Jenny's hip?

Then there's the possibility that PJ had been taken by someone who the Warners had bought or sold drugs to. Surely if one of these people had an issue with them serious enough to warrant killing their child, they'd know about it, but Jenny had claimed there was nothing she was aware of. I heave a heavy sigh, not sure what to believe.

As I pull in the driveway, I stare at the house a moment. Every curtain has been closed, every blind lowered, leaving the luxury cabin a dark stain against the night. It feels fitting, like it's been done purposely to keep me and the negativity I bring out.

But I need to stay positive. I tell myself I can do this. I can go in there and talk and laugh and get to know my soon-to-be in-laws. I can enjoy myself.

I can allow myself the night for the me I want to be, the future I want so badly, and not allow the face of a dead child—one that's real or imagined—to intrude upon my thoughts. But as I walk inside, a smile plastered across my tired face, I know it's a lie. Because as I cross the threshold and catch a glimpse of myself in the mirror that hangs behind the door, it's not me I see in the reflection. It's my baby brother.

34

MAGGIE

I draw a deep breath, trying to force myself to relax. Isn't this what I wanted? Haven't I longed for this all day? This closeness. This comfort. Maybe the circumstances aren't exactly what I had in mind, but after the day I've had, I should enjoy it while I can.

The weight of Steve's arm around me is like a security blanket, one I can hide under from the rest of the world. I snuggle closer, melting into him as he softly strokes my shoulder with his thumb. His other hand rests on my leg under the table. He gives it a gentle squeeze, his breath hot against my neck, sending shivers through me as he whispers in my ear.

"I told you so."

I cut my eyes toward him sharply. He gives me a grin, then presses his lips to my cheek. Jumps to his feet before I can protest, saying, "I'm going to get another drink."

I look at my own empty glass, wondering if I should ask for a refill. Knowing that it's going to take something a little stronger than wine to get me through this, but right now, I'll take whatever I can get.

"Hey," I say, trying to draw his attention. But he doesn't glance back. And he isn't even headed toward the kitchen.

"This will go quicker without him, anyways," Diane says.

I watch as Steve crosses over to the window, drawing the edge of a curtain back with one finger as he peeks outside. As he turns, I try to catch his eye, but fail. He passes by without a glance in my direction, no doubt to check the front door for the tenth time since dinner.

I get that he's worried about his Grandpa Joe, but I'm sure that he and Margot are just fine. I wish he would relax. And yeah, I understand how he might be upset that Joe is spending all his time with someone else during his visit, but his mother and sister *are* here. And now I'm alone with them.

Diane makes a noise of disapproval to herself, frowning at the clipping in her hand. She shuffles it to the bottom of a pile, nodding in satisfaction at the next picture. "Now, tell me, what do you think about this!"

I stare in horror as she uses a piece of tape to affix a cutout of a tiara to the mood board beside her. She beams at me, waiting for my reply. But there's no way I can tell her what I really think.

"It's... nice." I'm doing my best to keep a straight face, but as my eyes meet Izzy's across the table, I lose the battle. I feel my nose twitch. Then the corner of my mouth. I try to stifle the laugh that erupts as Izzy mimes putting a crown on her head with her cheeks sucked in, lips pursed, lashes fluttering like a broken doll, but the force of it is too strong. I sound like a cat trying to cough something up.

"Are you all right, dear?" Diane asks.

"Mother, that's hideous."

Diane frowns at her daughter. "Well, just because it isn't your style—"

"That 'style' doesn't appeal to anyone with working eyes over six and under sixty."

My future mother-in-law sniffs. Shifts her focus to me, and asks, "Maggie? Do you agree?"

I feel my face growing hot, know I must be blushing as red as my hair as I lie, "I think it's very pretty, but maybe it's a bit fancy."

She casts a smirk at Izzy as if to say, "See." I wonder if maybe I shouldn't have been a little more honest when she leaves it up on the board, saying, "We'll see what Steven thinks. I'm sure he'll love to see you in something like this. Where'd he run off to?"

"He said he was going to get another drink, remember?" Izzy prompts.

"Hmm. Well, he should have offered to get one for the rest of us, as well," she says, pushing back from the table. "And maybe some of the leftover cake."

Izzy gives me a wink, waits until Diane's left the room before whispering loudly, "Guess we're done for the night. That third glass will have her down for the count. Come on." She gets up, gesturing for me to follow her.

"Are you sure?" I glance guiltily at the mood board, still half empty. I appreciate all the effort Diane's put into this. I couldn't tell you the names of the half dozen types of flowers in shades of lavender and pure white that she's pinned, but they're all gorgeous. Likewise, the pewter chargers and silver linens are appealing. But the tiara, string quartet, and ice sculpture of two intertwined swans making a heart with their necks? That's what propels me out of my seat and down the hall, following Izzy into her room.

Once we're inside, she closes the door softly behind us. Holding a finger to her lips, she opens the closet and grabs a bottle of tequila and a stack of plastic shot glasses from the shelf inside.

"You come prepared," I joke.

"You have met my mother, haven't you?"

I laugh nervously, not sure how to respond. Her head tilts as she looks at me. There's something so kind about her eyes, so understanding, that I have to look away.

"Are you doing okay?" she asks.

"Yeah, why wouldn't I be?"

"I might be a bad influence, but I'm a good sister, and right now my sis sense is telling me that you need to talk. Or a drink. Probably both."

"Am I that obvious?"

She shrugs. "I'm a psychologist, remember? It's my job to pick up on these things." Arching an eyebrow, she adds, "Not that it takes a psychology degree to see that you're stressed. And not just because of all that." She waves her hand in the direction of the dining room and mood board.

The uneasiness I felt a moment ago quadruples. I feel like I'm going to be ill.

"Don't worry, I'm not trying to shrink you. I just thought maybe you could use a sympathetic ear."

My instinct is to bolt from the room. I'm not a sharer. I keep my feelings to myself, bottled up inside. Only, that hasn't exactly been doing me a lot of good. Maybe it's time to try something new.

Izzy's been so nice. And I'm marrying her brother. She's going to find out that I'm not normal like them eventually. Besides, as a psychologist, she must have encountered patients who were more damaged than me. At least, I hope she has.

Drawing a deep breath, I sink to the floor, propping my back against the edge of the bed. Izzy lowers herself beside me. Opening the bottle, she pours a shot and holds it out. When I shake my head no, she drinks it herself, then spins the empty cup in her hand, waiting patiently to see what I have to say.

Finally, I make a decision. "Has Steve told you about my brother?"

"Only that you had one and lost him when he was still little. I don't know any of the details."

I study her a moment. "There was a big age difference. I was in my late twenties when he was born. But I... I adored him. Would have done anything for him."

My voice sounds faraway as I say, "He was four when he was taken from a park. We never saw him again."

"I'm so sorry."

"Me too. It ripped my family apart. And even though I know it's ridiculous, I can't stop blaming myself, because there should have been *something* I could have done. To find him, to save him, to at least hold the rest of us together."

"But you know—"

I nod. "I know. And I'm working on it. But it's always there, just under the surface, and this case I'm working on now, it's, well, I guess it's making it all feel fresh again. Raw."

"How so?"

"That little boy who went missing the day you came to town? He was the same age. Only four years old."

That's all I get out before my throat shuts. Izzy's hand finds mine. She gives it a gentle squeeze.

"Where'd they find him?"

"In Beaverhead Lake. A couple of fishermen discovered his body under some ice off a dock."

"So this case is similar to what happened with your brother. A little boy goes missing, the same age—"

"And appearance. When I first saw him, I thought..." I shudder.

"Well, that's enough to give anyone a shock. No wonder it's bringing up all your misplaced guilt. You're blaming yourself again for not achieving a different outcome."

"Yes."

"But you realize that it's not your fault. That the child was most likely dead before you even found out he was missing?"

"You're scary good at this."

"I try. Do you have any suspects?"

I groan. "One of the men who found the body is a convicted child molester. And the parents are drug dealers. They used their son to help them make their deliveries. Put the product in his diaper so they wouldn't get caught."

Izzy doesn't try to disguise her disgust.

"But the pedophile seems to have lacked the means. And we've looked into the background of the parents' drug associates, but none of them have violent histories, and I've yet to find a motive."

There's a thought I keep circling around to. One that's been haunting me. One that I haven't wanted to acknowledge, much less say out loud, but somehow, with Izzy here, it feels like it will be all right.

"I think the hardest part is I know firsthand what a loss like this feels like, and what his family is going through right now, but I can't just leave them alone to mourn because..." I lose my nerve and chicken out. Can't make myself speak my nagging suspicion. Instead, I sidestep around it. "My responsibility is to PJ. I owe it to him to find out what happened, no matter who it might upset in the process."

Izzy nods slowly. She holds my gaze, letting me know she understands what I'm getting at. "If the killer just wanted to conceal their crime, there were easier ways, ones that would have been less likely to be discovered, weren't there?" she asks. "Likewise, if they were trying to send a message with the act..."

I nod. Silence settles between us, but it's comfortable, not awkward. Giving her a shy smile, I gesture toward the bottle. "I think maybe I'll try a sip after all."

Izzy grins as she pulls another shot glass from the stack and pours us each a drink. We clink cups before draining them. Leaning my head back against the bed, I close my eyes and focus on the burning sensation as it works its way down my throat, warming my chest. And yet, there's a chill inside me that it can't seem to reach.

I've shared some of my biggest concerns with Izzy. Should I dare to confide the thing that's bothering me the most? The one that I haven't even risked admitting to myself yet?

"Izzy?"

"Hmm?"

"Have you noticed that Steve is acting strange?"

She turns to look at me, chewing nervously on her bottom lip as she nods. Suddenly, the taste of booze is sickening sweet. It threatens to climb back up my throat.

"Do you think it's because he's changed his mind about getting married?"

"Oh, no, sweetie." She takes both my hands in hers and stares deep into my eyes. "I promise you, that's not it. I don't know what's going on with him, but it's not you. The only time he's acted even remotely normal since I've been here is when you're around."

I force a smile, doing my best to keep tears from invading my eyes. I wish I could believe her, but I can't. Because something is definitely going on with Steve, and if it's not me, what else could it be?

35
MAGGIE

Once again, the morning is overcast, the sun struggling to make an appearance through thick, steely-gray clouds. My breath forms little clouds of vapor as I hurry to my Jeep and climb inside, setting my travel mug in the drink holder. I crank the engine and blast the heat, telling myself I'll give it a few minutes to warm, though the truth is that I'm reluctant to start the day.

Last night I managed to survive family time. It makes me feel ashamed to think of it in that way—survival, as if it's something potentially harmful—but I'm sure I'm not the only person in history to feel like that. The simple fact is that the people who matter most in your life can cause damage that those who don't aren't capable of. And even the best of intentions sometimes strikes a blow.

But despite the anxiety and guardedness I went into the evening with, it turned out to be easier than I had anticipated. Even the time spent wedding planning with Diane wasn't quite as painful as I had imagined it would be. It's nice that she cares so much.

And I really enjoyed getting to know my future sister-in-law better. I feel lighter after talking to Izzy, like some of the weight of the burden I carry has been lifted. I'm fortunate to be gaining a sister like her.

Now if only Steve would tell me what's gotten under his skin. I keep asking what's wrong. He denies that anything is. But Izzy's noticed he's been acting strangely, too, so I'm not just imagining things.

He was uncharacteristically testy this morning when he found out his grandfather had already left. Admittedly, Margot might not be the best company for him to keep, but the time they're spending together seems to make Joe happy. I don't understand what the big deal is.

Though if I'm completely honest with myself, this shift in behavior started before his family came to visit. If it's gotten worse since their arrival, it's probably because all the focus on the wedding is giving him second thoughts about marrying me. Not that I can blame him. Because the deeper I get into this case, the more I'm worried that I'm not ready for that next step myself.

My phone rings, dragging me from my thoughts. I glance at the display, then answer the call, putting it on speakerphone in case I decide to actually put the car in gear and start the drive to work.

"Good morning, Dr. Ricky. To what do I owe the pleasure?"

"You know I like chocolate, right? And flowers. And cats. I have enough of those already, but they make plenty of things with cats on them. Like coffee mugs. Ooh, and socks."

"Um. What?"

"All things I'd rather you send me than a dead child."

My relief is immediate and overwhelming. "You're performing PJ Warner's postmortem."

"No."

I feel myself tighten back into a ball of nerves, the dwindling window of time I have to solve this case shutting as I stand helplessly by and watch.

"I've already performed the autopsy. Past tense. Though I'm guessing you'll want me to take my time before filing my report."

"You know that was mean, right?"

"Sorry." The apology almost sounds sincere. "But murdered kids make me cranky."

"So we're definitely dealing with a homicide, then?"

"Impossible to say."

"What do you mean?"

"Exactly that."

"Can you please elaborate?" I ask.

She releases a noisy sigh before explaining. "There were no signs of abuse. No bruises, contusions, or wounds of any kind on the child that would indicate a struggle."

Would PJ have gone with a stranger willingly? More than that, if whoever took the boy did so in retaliation against a drug deal gone wrong, would they have been so gentle as to have not left a bruise on the child?

"Any signs of molestation?"

"No."

"How about his feet?" I ask. If PJ had walked all that way, surely there'd be damage to the soles.

"Unremarkable," she says.

She'd specifically referenced the term *murdered*. There must be a reason why she feels that PJ's death was more than just an accident.

"But..." I prompt. I take a sip of my coffee as I wait, well aware that there's no rushing the good doctor.

"But he didn't drown in the lake where he was found."

I spray coffee all over my dashboard. "What!"

"You've heard of diatoms, right?"

"Yes." In Florida, it pays to be aware of what's in the water with you. Not just the sharks, alligators, and poisonous snakes that you might see, but the bacteria, viruses, and parasites that you can't. Even certain types of algae are harmful.

"Excellent," Dr. Ricky says. "Then you know that while there are certain diatoms, or microalgae, that can cause illness, in general they're an extremely important part of the ecosystem, producing twenty to thirty percent of the air we breathe."

I hadn't, but I don't interrupt as she continues.

"With an estimated twenty thousand to two million species, diatoms are found in almost every aquatic environment and can be used to not only identify a body of water, but also, in some instances, to even pinpoint the specific area where a sample of water was taken from."

I'm not entirely sure what she's getting at. I know that when a person drowns, they aspirate diatoms from the water into their lungs, which can then move to deeper organs through the bloodstream. Dr. Ricky must have discovered something odd during PJ's autopsy.

"The technician took a water sample from the lake," Dr. Ricky says, "as is customary when dealing with a drowning. The diatoms in his lungs and other tissues I sampled didn't match that of the lake water. So wherever he drowned, it wasn't there. He was put there after the fact."

"Are you sure?"

She makes a miffed sniffing noise.

"No, I mean, I know you're *sure*, but... he did drown, right?"

"Correct."

"But if not in the lake, then where?" I ask, musing out loud.

"I'm afraid that's your job. I've done mine."

"But if I get you a water sample—"

"Then we can test it against the diatoms I recovered from the boy's tissues and tell you if it's a match."

As I say goodbye, I think of the landscape surrounding the Warner house. There'd been no ponds, rivers, or streams nearby. No buckets or troughs or rain barrels. And despite being right in the thick of mud season, there hadn't even been a puddle.

I shift uncomfortably in my seat, loosening the belt across my chest. Because sometimes, the easiest solution is the obvious solution. If PJ didn't drown in water outside his home, then perhaps the water came from the inside. Which means the killer might have come from inside the house, too.

36

MAGGIE

Five years ago

The searing Florida sun shines brighter than it has a right to. The sky should be dark and gray, heavy with clouds and the threat of a storm. Instead, it's clear and blue and light. Maggie sits behind the wheel of her Jeep in the sheriff's department parking lot with the engine off. Sweat seeps from her pores, dripping down her skin. Her head feels like it's boiling.

Though she stares out the front window, she doesn't see a thing through the film of tears blurring her eyes. She's never felt so alone before. Only days ago, she had a loving family. A successful career. Colleagues who respected her.

Now what does she have?

But why is that? Where did she go so wrong? And what she doesn't understand the most is, why have her parents severed all ties?

Is it possible that Hawkins and the sheriff are right? Could her mother have had something to do with Brandon's disappearance?

As hard as it is to believe, it does happen. Mothers occasionally snap.

Maggie shakes her head, feeling horrible for even contemplating her mother's guilt. She knows in her heart that it simply isn't possible. And she has to find proof.

She turns to the mobile data terminal secured to her middle console and logs in to the MDT. Navigates her way through the department's network and accesses the case file for her brother's disappearance, downloading the information and sending a copy to her cell phone and personal email before Sheriff Brewster thinks to pull her clearance.

Her phone buzzes in her pocket as she skims through the statements. She answers it reluctantly, expecting it to be him.

"Maggie, I just heard. I'm so sorry. What can I do?"

"Linda?"

Maggie rips her eyes from the screen long enough to check the cell display, confirming the identity of the caller. Feels something inside of her crack as she realizes she's not alone after all, at least, not completely. The dam breaks and tears stream down her cheeks as she fills Linda in on what's happened—her brother's disappearance, her parents' silence, the sheriff's refusal to investigate more thoroughly and consider other suspects.

When she's done, Linda sucks in a sharp breath. Maggie tenses, dreading what her friend is going to say. Expecting to hear that she's wrong and everyone else is right.

Instead, Linda asks, "When are you going back to this Todd guy's house?"

Maggie squeezes her eyes shut. She had hoped she'd be on her way already, with a warrant and a SWAT team, but it's clear that isn't going to happen.

"Never mind," Linda says, interrupting her thoughts. "Can you hold off a couple of hours? I'm on my way."

"Linda." Maggie's throat is tight with emotion. "I can't let you do that. This isn't sanctioned."

"And I can't let you go back there alone."

"But—"

"You let me worry about any fallout on my end. Just promise me you'll wait until I get there."

The clock is ticking. Wherever he is, Brandon's time could be running out. What if she's wrong, though? She might only get one chance. Her brother is depending on her. Her gaze lands on the MDT screen.

"I promise."

"Really?"

"Text me when you get here. And Linda?"

"Yeah?"

"Thank you."

Her friend doesn't hesitate as she says, "Of course."

But Linda is a realist. A scientist. As they end the call, she doesn't promise that they'll find Maggie's brother. She doesn't tell her that everything will be all right. She doesn't lie.

For that, Maggie's grateful. Because she's a realist, too. She knows that the chances of recovering her brother are getting slimmer with every passing second.

But there's only so much she can do on her own. She needs to find a way to make the sheriff listen to her. Which means she needs proof that their suspicions about her mom are wrong. And she may have just found a lead that will help.

37

MAGGIE

Sue frowns at me from the doorway of my office. I point toward the phone, indicating I'm on a call, and wave her away, but she settles in the chair across from me instead. I do my best to ignore the concern she's eyeing me with and focus on writing down the instructions the forensic technician is giving me.

"Do you know if the sampling location is on well or city water?" she asks.

The lines from the town's water supply service a very small area, only extending through the very center of Coyote Cove. Since the Warners' house is about twenty miles from town, I say, "Let's assume well."

"Okay, then, ideally, you'll want to let the water run for several minutes before collecting the sample. Any sterile plastic container should do, but you'll want to rinse it a few times, first. Do that by filling the collection bottle about a third of the way, screw the cap on, give it a few shakes, then repeat. Three times should do. Then you'll want to fill the bottle to the very top."

"Okay."

"Well water comes out pretty cold up there, doesn't it?"

"Yes."

"Then you'll want to try and maintain that temperature. If possible, keep the sample refrigerated until you're ready to ship it, and then if you could send it in a small cooler with a couple of baggies of clean ice, that would be great."

"Do I need to take samples from multiple faucets in the home?" I ask.

"That shouldn't be necessary."

"Okay, great." I think about all the places Dennis Greenley may have had access to. His uncle's house. Public restrooms. Perhaps one of the friends or other relatives that Kal is searching for right now. "What about if I take samples from multiple locations?" I ask. "Do I need to ship the samples in separate coolers, or just label them?"

There's a pause on the other end of the line. I find my gaze drifting over to Sue without the distraction. She's still watching me, wearing *that look*. The one that lets me know she's worried about me.

And I get it, I do. I'm sure she thought I'd fall apart when I learned that one of the suspects in PJ Warner's death is a pedophile. It's just one more parallel between his case and my brother's. An almost crippling one.

The tech clears her throat, then says, "A label's fine. If you feel multiple samples are necessary." It seems a weird comment to make. Before I can question her, she adds, "I just received the report from the print lab in my inbox. I'm going to go ahead and forward that to you right now."

"Thank you, I'll look for it."

I replace the phone in its cradle and reach for the mouse on my desktop. Scroll to wake my screensaver, studiously avoiding Sue's gaze.

"How are you doing?" she asks.

"Fine," I say, keeping my eyes locked on the computer screen.

"Because it's okay if you're not. No one would blame you."

"Sue, really." I glance at her but then immediately look away. "I've got it covered."

"But you don't *have* to. Maggie." Her voice breaks. Her leg, clad in pajama pants featuring images of Snoopy and his little yellow bird friend, bounces with irritation. Or is it nerves?

"This case... the little boy, the child molester. There's no need for you to put yourself through this. Kal can handle it. You should take a break. Spend more time with Steve's family while they're in town."

The email from the state crime lab arrives with a ding. I click it open, trying to formulate my response. Sue knows me. How can I convince her that this case hasn't gotten under my skin, that it's not causing festering sores, when we both know that it is?

"Did I ever tell you about the time my kids tried to convince me that they were old enough to play on one of their friend's dirt bikes? And even though I told them no, I knew that they were going to sneak around and do it anyway, behind my back. Sometimes, children are predictable like that."

I ignore the barb. I might behave like a stubborn child sometimes, but I seriously doubt that my behavior could be described as predictable. Like what I'm looking at right now.

"And when my daughter broke two of her fingers, they tried to hide it from me. Never in their life had they worked together like they did to keep that secret. But I knew something was wrong. And I got it out of them. When you care about someone, you don't want to see them get hurt. It's not about controlling them, or thinking you know better than they do. It's not even about protecting them. It's about protecting yourself, too, because when they ache, you ache."

I know she's right, but I don't argue with her. And I don't try assuring her. Instead, I say, "All the prints they recovered from PJ's room matched those they took from the family for exclusionary purposes."

Sue sighs with irritation. She thinks I'm being difficult, but that's not true. At least, not entirely. And not intentionally.

"What's so interesting about that is, when the analyst requested to take their prints, only the child's mother and father admitted to being in the room. The rest of the family insisted that they'd never been in there."

"But?" she prompts.

"But," I say, finally able to look at her. To allow her to look at me. "Prints belonging to all three of the older kids were found in the room. Yet only a few partials were recovered in the bathroom that the family shares. It appears to have been wiped clean."

Standing, I pull on my jacket and shove one of the plastic collection bottles into my pocket. "Here." I pass my handwritten instructions to Sue and gesture toward the rest of the containers. "Have Kal go out to the Greenleys' and take samples anywhere Dennis would have access to both a bit of privacy and water."

"What if they want a warrant?"

"They won't. Walter was more than willing to cooperate when I went out there last night."

The look she gives me—I can feel it all the way to my bones, searing me with the heat of all the things she wants to say. I know that she's concerned about me not in the way an employee would worry about their boss, but in the way you'd worry about a friend. Or family. Caring about me isn't part of her job description, but she does it anyway. I'm not sure I've ever properly appreciated that.

I pause next to her on my way out the door and let my hand rest on her shoulder. "Thanks, Sue. I really do appreciate everything you do." Then I give her a cheeky grin and add, "But when your kids tell the dirt bike story? They say they only told you about your daughter's broken fingers so you would never find out about your son's broken ribs, because they cared about you and didn't want you to worry. So I guess that it goes both ways, huh?"

Her expression is priceless. And I'm hoping that, since they're both grown with children of their own now, I didn't just get them in trouble. I'm also hoping that she gets why I told her. Yes, it's only natural to want to protect the people you love. But sometimes, the best way to do that is to deny them the very thing that they think they want to know.

38
STEVE

I wipe the back of my wrist along my forehead. The cuff of my sleeve is damp when I'm done. I swear I must be the only person who can sweat when it's below freezing out. But that's not why this is a horrible idea.

We're too exposed out here. Danger could come from too many angles.

But Izzy had wanted to walk the dogs, and I couldn't refuse. If I had, she'd know that something is wrong, and I can't let that happen. She'd kill me if I ever said it out loud, but she takes after our mother. If she thought I was keeping something from her, she'd never let it rest until she found out what it was.

I feel like my head's on a swivel as I scan the tree line to either side, checking to make sure there's no one lurking in the woods, anxious to check every small noise that I hear as we stop for the dogs to sniff a sapling. Holding still seems dangerous. It makes us easier targets.

I swallow hard at the thought and lower the zipper on my jacket, hoping the frigid air will help cool me off before I overheat. My sister gives me side-eye, bouncing in place to keep warm. I force a tight smile before I check the source of a creaking sound to my left.

"Hoo," she says, finally breaking the silence.

"What?" I jerk to face Izzy. "No one, why?"

"No, not *who*," she says. "*Hoo*. Like an owl. I thought you wanted me to guess what you were doing an impression of." She grins, giving me a playful elbow to the side. "Geez. You used to have a sense of humor. What's going on with you?"

"Nothing," I say, taking a step away like I've been pulled forward by the dogs.

"Yeah, right."

"What do you mean?"

"I mean, you've been acting really strange since we got here," she says.

"No, I haven't."

"Fine, you haven't."

We pause again while Sully sniffs a broken pine bough. Laurel squats. Tempe looks over her shoulder and smiles at us like this is the best adventure ever.

"*They're* enjoying my company," she mutters.

"Listen, Iz, it's not that. I just have a lot on my mind, okay?"

"The wedding?" she asks.

I shrug.

"Is everything okay between you and Maggie?"

"Of course."

"You're not feeling any regrets? Not overwhelmed by all the planning?"

"What's with all the shrink questions?"

"What's with all the attitude? Seriously, Steve. If being around me makes you so miserable—?"

"It's not you."

Izzy does her best impersonation of our mother and stares me down. I sigh, shaking my head as we move forward several feet before stopping again. Swab the perspiration on my neck with the arm of my jacket before looking at her.

"I'm just worried, okay?"

"About what?"

We're tugged back into motion. This time the dogs keep moving, which is fortunate. It allows me to avoid eye contact without seeming like I'm trying to. Which I am, but still.

"I'm worried..." I speak slowly, carefully. "That Maggie might get cold feet."

"You don't have to worry about that," she assures me. "I talked to her, and she's fine. No Popsicle toes at all."

"Are you sure?"

"One hundred percent."

I release a loud mouthful of air. "Shoo. That's a relief. Thanks, Iz."

"What else are little sisters for?"

"Giving noogies?"

"Try it, mister." She raises a fist and mock scowls, issuing the challenge. And though I grin and feign an attack, I'm still on high alert. My chest tightens, heart spasming. My pulse pounds in my ears. The tendons in my neck feel stretched so tight they might snap, like guitar strings.

I just lied to my baby sister. I can count on one hand the number of times I've done that before, and every single one of them has been for a catastrophic reason. The kind that changes lives. Only this time, it could end them, too.

39

MAGGIE

From the outside, the Warners' house looks no different, but on the inside, it's hard to believe it's the same place that I've found myself over the last few days. Dark-clad mourners crowd the living room, squeezed into the corners. A bottleneck jams up the narrow hall as visitors wait to use the restroom. Home-cooked meals brought by neighbors cover every surface of the kitchen, stacked two deep in places.

I do a quick lap around the rooms, looking for any members of the family, but only manage to find Franny, sitting on the steps outside the back door chain-smoking. The crease between her eyebrows deepens as I approach, her cheeks sinking deep as she takes a drag off her cigarette.

"Do you know where Greg and Jenny are? I need to speak with them."

She stares at me for a long moment, as if debating whether to answer. Gets to her feet, still without saying a word. I've never noticed before what a big woman she is. I'm not exactly petite, but she has to be almost as tall as her son and just as broad shouldered. She flicks her cigarette into the yard, where it lands in the mud with a hiss, then gestures for me to follow her as she leads the way back into the house.

The crowd parts, making room for her to pass, bodies pressing against the walls in the hall as she strides to the very end, stopping before a closed door. She takes a ragged breath, as if bracing herself, before tapping gently. When there's no answer, she darts a quick glance in my direction before opening it a crack and sticking her head inside. I look past her and see Greg Warner sitting on the edge of a bed, elbows on his knees, face cradled in his hands.

"Greg."

He ignores her.

"You have a visitor."

Still nothing.

"It's Chief Riley again."

At that he looks up. He pins me with a look that could hammer a nail through a tree. His eyes are red and swollen, bloodshot.

"You find out who hurt my boy yet?"

"I'm working on it."

He snorts.

"That's why I'm here, Mr. Warner. I'm sorry to disturb you, today of all days, but I'm afraid I need to ask you a few questions that can't wait."

He lifts a hand in the air, shakes his head, and rolls his eyes. "Go ahead then."

"Where's your wife?"

"She's left."

"Where to?"

"Don't know, don't care, but I assume her mother's. No reason for her to stick around now that the kid's gone."

"I'm sorry to hear that."

He shrugs. "Never should have gotten married in the first place."

"Mr. Warner, I wanted to ask a bit more about the relationship between PJ and the children from your first marriage."

"What about it?"

"Did they ever play with PJ?"

"Sure."

"I've been told that Jenny discouraged that."

"Best way to make sure a kid does something is to tell them not to."

"Where did this playing take place?"

"What do you mean?"

"Did they play in the living room? In the yard? In PJ's bedroom?"

His eyes narrow. "What's this all about? Why are you asking this?"

"Mr. Warner, prints from all three of your older children were found in PJ's bedroom."

"Well, he's their brother. They've got a right to go in there, don't they?"

"They do."

"There's nothing abnormal about that."

"There's not," I agree.

"Then why are you wasting time asking stupid questions?"

"Because, sir, when the forensic analyst asked to take their prints yesterday for exclusionary purposes, all three of them denied having ever been in PJ's room before."

"Well, so what? They lied. Maybe they were just scared."

"Of what?" I ask.

A muscle in his jaw tics. His Adam's apple bobs as he swallows. He rises from his seat on the bed, hands balled into fists by his sides. His voice is low and thready as he says, "I've had enough of your questions. What's wrong with you, that you can't let a man grieve in peace? Do you really have nothing better to do than to try to turn this into something it's not?"

"And what's that, exactly? Mr. Warner, I'm sorry if my

questions upset you, but I'm just trying to figure out what happened to your son. Don't you want that?"

"What I want is for you to get out of my house and leave me and my family alone. Go on. Get out."

I nod and start to turn around. Pausing halfway, I say, "I'm aware that you and Jenny deal drugs, but I believe we've been able to rule out any connection between that and what happened to your son. I'm not sure if that will be of any comfort to you or not."

"What?" Greg's eyes are wide, his mouth hanging open. He takes a step back, collapsing heavily on the edge of the bed. Stares at me with disbelief, like he wishes he could beg for me to tell him I lied.

"I thought you'd want to know. It's an avenue we'll no longer be pursuing in our investigation." His mouth snaps shut and I turn and retreat back through the door out into the hallway.

"You don't have a clue what happened, do you?" he calls after me, his volume rising with each word, drawing stares from the mourners clustered nearby. "Here, you want some help? You want to know what happened to PJ? You need to find that soon-to-be ex-wife of mine and get her to confess. I know what she's done even if you're choosing to ignore it. And I'm not going to let her get away with it. One way or another, she's gonna pay."

I hear several gasps at the accusation. Can feel the eyes of the crowd drilling into me, searching my face for answers as he gets up and slams the door shut. Whispers fill my ears as I make my way toward the front of the house, but instead of leaving, I duck into the kitchen, checking the time as I turn on the faucet.

Letting the water flow at full blast, I remove the plastic collection bottle from my jacket pocket and begin rinsing the container as I'd been instructed, though at this point, it almost seems unnecessary. I'm confident that whatever happened to PJ Warner, it happened in this house. And every member of his family is a suspect.

Belinda James answers the door, her eyes widening as they land on me. Her expression is a mix of shock and fear. One hand rises to the base of her throat, the other clutching at the casing beside her as she leans heavily against it, as if not trusting her legs for support.

"Chief Riley."

"Mrs. James."

Her voice trembles as she asks, "Why are you here?"

"I need to speak with Jenny."

She frowns as if confused. "Did you need me to come with you? You don't have more bad news, do you? You can't possibly."

Now I'm the one feeling confused. "Isn't Jenny here?" I ask.

Her head shakes from side to side. "Why would she be?"

"Greg said that she'd left."

"The house? Or him?"

"I believe he meant both."

She exhales as her eyes roll toward the ceiling. "Well, if there's one thing to come out of this tragedy, at least there's that."

"You're not a big fan of his, I take it?"

"Greg and I were classmates. We attended our junior prom together. I can't imagine many mothers would want to be able to say that about their daughter's husband, would they?"

"No, probably not."

"I told her they didn't have to get married just because she got pregnant. Offered to let her stay here. I would have gladly helped her out. But she's seen how much I've had to struggle over the years as a single mom. I don't think she wanted that."

She pinches the bridge of her nose, squeezing her eyes shut. "You have to let them make their own mistakes, you know." It sounds like she's trying to convince herself. "I tried to be supportive. And after they made it through the first year, I'd hoped that maybe I was wrong, that they'd be happy together, but all you had to do was look at her to see that she was miserable."

"Why do you think that was?"

"Jenny was so young. And Greg was absolutely no help with the baby. Not to mention that his other kids were always giving Jenny a hard time, making noise to wake PJ when he was sleeping, sneaking him sugar so he'd get hyper and cranky."

"I was under the impression that Jenny got along well with her stepchildren."

"Well, I don't know who told you that, but I do know it wasn't Jenny. Those kids did their best to antagonize her. And then when Greg's mother moved in—" Belinda shudders. "Have you met Franny Warner?"

"I have."

"Then you know what I'm talking about. Greg tried to sell the arrangement as some live-in help for Jenny, but there's no way she'd let that woman touch PJ. Franny's a complete lush. Always has been. Drinks her breakfast and lunch, then takes a nap so she can drink more for dinner."

She makes a doubtful face as she says, "I have no idea where she finds the money for all that booze. And Jenny was constantly having to clean up after her. She'd find cigarette burns all over the furniture despite telling Franny not to smoke in the house. Honestly, I don't know how my daughter did it. She should have left him years ago."

"But Jenny's not here now?"

"No."

I'm starting to get a bad feeling about this. From what I saw yesterday, Jenny's in no condition to be alone right now.

"When was the last time you saw her?"

"Last night, when I left to come home."

"Did she give you any indication that she intended to leave Greg at that time?"

"None at all. I wish she had. I would have brought her with me right then."

"The vehicle she shares with Greg was still at their house. Do you know of another she could have borrowed?"

"No. She knows she's always welcome to use mine, but she didn't ask."

"Do you have any idea where she might have gone?"

"Honestly, I haven't a clue. She hasn't worked since before PJ was born. And I think she fell out of touch with most of her friends from school."

But that's not entirely true, I think to myself. She'd been out with friends the night PJ went missing. At least, that's what I'd been told. I try to recall the names Jenny had given me, but I'm drawing a blank. I'm going to have to look at my report.

"Mrs. James, would you say that Jenny's the type to withdraw and want to be by herself in a situation like this?"

Her head shakes slowly from side to side. "No. I mean, I don't know. She's never had anything really bad like this happen in her life before. I have no idea how she'll react. Why? You don't think—" As if realizing the answer to her own question, her face contorts into the same look of terror she'd worn when she first opened the door and saw me on her doorstep.

Why had she looked so scared to see me? What had she thought I was here to tell her?

I try to put myself in Jenny's shoes. Being so young. Having just lost my child. No, not lost. PJ's body was hidden, disposed of, to conceal what had happened to him. There's a difference. Life and circumstances didn't just throw a tragedy into Jenny's life. Someone caused it.

Greg's accusation echoes in my mind. What if he was right? What if Jenny's the one who had hurt her son? Is it possible she's left town, taken off before it could be proven?

"Chief Riley?"

I look into Belinda James's face, feeling the sadness in her eyes tugging at me like a riptide, threatening to pull me out to sea.

"Yes?" My voice is barely above a whisper.

"Will you please find my daughter for me?"

Backing away from the door, I nod as she closes it. I will find Jenny Warner. Just like I'll find out the truth about what happened to PJ. But something tells me that when I do, it might cause more pain and heartache, not less.

41

MAGGIE

I turn into the dirt parking lot of the scenic vista outside of town and pull up along the guardrail behind Kal's cruiser. He gets out of the vehicle, and I grab the small Styrofoam cooler off the passenger seat as he comes around and gets inside.

"That for the samples?" he asks. "Here."

He hands me a white paper bag and takes the box from me. Removing the lid, he places the water he'd collected from the Greenleys' next to the bottle I'd taken from the Warners' house. I stare down at the two containers, hoping that one of them holds the secret to the mystery of what happened to PJ.

"We've got to overnight it," I say as he redistributes the ice and places the cooler on the floor between his feet.

"I'll take care of it."

He gestures to the bag he'd handed me.

"What's in it?" I ask.

"Just open it."

I do so reluctantly, almost afraid to see what's inside. Looking up from the two sandwiches, I try to hand them back, even though my stomach growls at the sight.

"I can't... This is your lunch."

"I made extra."

He grins, dimples showing, as I take the one on top and hand the bag back to him.

"Thank you."

It's late. I wonder if he waited for me to eat, hoping that he didn't but, as I take a bite and realize how famished I am, grateful if he did.

I look out the window at the view beyond as we chew in silence. Mountains stretch into the distance as far as the eye can see, trees shrouding any sign of man all the way to the horizon. It reminds me of how remote I am, not just literally, as a resident of Coyote Cove, but as a person who's done her best to sequester herself from the rest of humanity.

I glance at my lieutenant. We've been working together almost six months, and the only thing I've learned about him is that he's almost as private as I am. And that his jaw clicks when he chews. I consider asking him about it in an attempt to get to know him better. Maybe it's an old sports injury. Or he could have always had it.

But before I can speak, he says, "Walter Greenley told me you paid them a visit last night."

My gaze drops to my lap. "I did."

"You know, I should be going with you in situations like that. That's what I'm here for. Day or night."

"I know."

"I just wanted to make sure that you did."

I nod, feeling my cheeks heat, because it's true. I do know. And I should have brought him with me. Things could have gone much differently. I got lucky they went so well. But maybe a part of me wanted them to go poorly. And that's not something I can explain, because I don't quite understand it myself.

"For what it's worth," Kal says, his voice gentle, "I don't think Dennis did it."

"Neither do I." I can't believe I finally admitted it. I felt like a traitor just thinking it, but now that it's out, it feels like a huge weight has been lifted from my chest. The interior of the Jeep goes quiet again as what we've left unsaid lingers loudly between us. Finally, I say, "Jenny Warner is missing. When I went over there today, Greg said that she had left."

Kal turns toward me, one eyebrow raised, and I realize I probably should have led the conversation with this.

"Is that right?"

I nod. "Her mom says she has no idea where she is, and I believe her."

He leans forward in his seat, giving me his full attention, the remainder of his sandwich forgotten in his lap. I chew on my lip, trying to soften a rough edge. Even though it feels like a betrayal, I know I have to say it. It's my job.

"Greg also said that he thinks Jenny was the one who drowned PJ."

"And what do you think?"

"I'm not sure what to think, to be honest. I don't want to believe it, but is it possible? Yes."

"So what now?"

I look back out the window again. Rays of light streak the sky, the sun trying to peek through the clouds.

"I'm going to go speak with her friends, the ones she was out with the night PJ went missing. See if anyone knows where she is, or if she said something to one of them that might clue us in to her state of mind, what she was thinking."

"Do you want me to go with you?"

I know he wants to come, but, "Next time. I think they'll be more likely to open up if a man's not around. And I need you to overnight the water samples. Right now, that's the most important thing we can do."

He gives me a wistful smile. Gathers his trash and stuffs it in the bag. As he opens the door to return to his car I put a hand on his arm, stopping him.

"Kal? Thank you. Really. For everything."

"Just, be careful, okay?"

"Of course."

But the look he gives me says that he knows it isn't a given. That he understands what it's like to have your toes curled over the brink of self-destruction, staring at the drop below. Which makes me wonder how close he's been to the edge himself.

42

MAGGIE

Coyote Cove is a small town, but it's rural. It's not the kind of place you can get away from without a vehicle, which means that Jenny Warner is either still in the area, or someone helped her escape.

If not her mother, then maybe one of her friends. Perhaps even one of the women she was out with the night PJ was taken. I need to speak with them anyway, even if it doesn't lead me to Jenny, because I can't shake the feeling that there's something I'm missing. There has to be.

I need to go back to the start of this, to that night, to the hours before PJ was discovered gone, and go over the details with a fine-toothed comb because someone knows something. I just need to find out who.

Though I recognize the pretty woman in her mid-twenties sitting before me, I don't think we've ever spoken before now. And there's no denying that she's nervous. But is it because I'm a cop? Or is there another reason?

Trish Sims smooths the front of her jean skirt over her thighs on the couch across from me, then jumps up and paces behind the sofa. "Are you sure I can't get you something to drink? Or eat? I could throw something together real quick? Do you like grilled cheese?"

I do, but I smile and say, "No, thank you. I'm fine."

"Everyone likes grilled cheese," she babbles. "I always add some of every cheese I've got in the fridge. It's impossible to get it to cook through, though. I always have to microwave it once the bread's done cooking to get it to melt properly." She laughs nervously.

"Trish, why don't you come sit back down?" I suggest.

She busies herself straightening a picture on the wall, instead. "You know, some people use oil to toast the bread? I've even heard that some people use mayonnaise. But not me. I use butter, just like my mom did and her mom before her."

Trish is smiling when she turns back to face me, but it doesn't reach her eyes, which are welling with tears. Her lips tremble. A whimper escapes. She bites the knuckles of her clenched fist, trying to steel herself, but it doesn't work. She collapses onto the couch, sobbing.

"I'm sorry. I just keep wondering if this is all my fault."

The words freeze me where I am, halfway across the room on my way to comfort her.

"What makes you say that?" I ask, approaching cautiously.

A long silence stretches between us before she answers. Finally, she says meekly, "Because I'm the one who invited Jenny to come out with us that night. Maybe if I hadn't..."

I wait for her to continue. When she doesn't, I lower myself to the couch beside her. What could she possibly think would have been different if Jenny had stayed home? According to Jenny's statement, PJ had been in bed when she returned and checked on him. It wasn't until morning that she'd discovered he was missing. What does Trish know that I don't?

"What happened that night? When you all went out for drinks?"

She sniffs, lifting teary eyes to my own. "Nothing. I mean, we were all just catching up."

"And what was that like?"

"A bit awkward, I guess. We hadn't hung out with Jenny in years, you know. Not since she got pregnant."

"Had she changed much?"

Staring down at her hands, she says, "She just seemed really sad, I guess. And she used to be so happy."

"Did she say why that was?"

Trish shrugs. "Not really. But she didn't really have to."

"And why's that?"

"We've all seen Greg out and about, on the prowl."

"What's that mean?" I ask.

She looks at me, eyebrows raised. "You know."

"Greg was cheating on Jenny?"

Her eyes drop to her lap, her face coloring like she regrets saying anything. "Well, I can't say for sure if he was or not, but he sure did like to flirt."

"And Jenny knew this?"

"We wouldn't have— I mean, we thought that's why she—" Her voice cracks and a fresh wave of tears spills down her cheeks.

"She didn't know," I say. "But someone told her."

She bites her lip as she nods.

"And how did Jenny handle the news?"

"She tried to play it off like she didn't care, but I know it had to have been a shock. How could it not be? That was the first time she'd been out with us since before PJ was born, which was, like, over four years ago. To find out that she's been stuck at home taking care of their kid all that time while he's been out playing around. I mean, how could you not be seriously pissed about that?"

"Did she say she was upset with Greg?"

"Not at first, no. But the more she had to drink, the more you could tell that, yeah, there was some trouble brewing."

"Did she say what she was going to do?"

"Not exactly. She said something about teaching him a lesson, but I just thought she meant she was going to leave him. I had no idea, I mean, if I thought for even a second she'd do something to hurt their child..." Her voice chokes off into a whimper.

A surge of heat sweeps over me. Sweat bubbles to the surface of my skin, dampening the roots of my hair and making my scalp itch. I pull at the collar of my shirt, struggling to get air.

"You think she's the one who put PJ in the lake?" I ask quietly, seeking confirmation.

"Isn't that why you're here?"

I don't answer because, although it should be, it's not. I don't know Jenny Warner well enough to judge her character or to say what she is or isn't capable of, and given what those who do know her are saying, she should probably be my main suspect right now.

But I just can't believe that she'd been the one to hurt her child. Her grief had been too real, too raw, too like my own. Or am I just seeing what I want to see?

I'd come here looking for confirmation that my gut was right when it told me that Greg Warner was wrong. Instead, I've found the opposite.

Ignoring her question, I ask, "Do you know where Jenny is now?"

She wraps her arms tight around herself as she shakes her head. Whispers, "What's going to happen to her?"

"I don't know yet, but I need to find her. If you hear from Jenny, will you let me know?"

Trish reaches for my card seemingly on autopilot, as if she's too stunned by our discussion to focus. She remains seated, puddled against the couch cushions as I show myself out. But as I'm closing the door, her eyes flash, tracking my departure, still very much aware.

I slide behind the wheel of my Jeep, buckle my seatbelt, and take a moment to collect my thoughts. When Greg had accused Jenny, I thought he'd been trying to shift my focus from his children. But what if that wasn't it? What if he'd known that Jenny had a motive to hurt her own child—one that he'd given her? A motive that they may have shared.

Because it sounds like Jenny wasn't the only one who wanted out of their marriage. Hadn't Greg told me that she was too young, that they never should have married? I'd assumed at the time it was his grief talking, but maybe he had felt that way even before what happened to PJ.

I think back to what she told me that first morning, about Greg not wanting nice things after losing his house in his divorce from his first wife. Is it possible that he'd take desperate measures to avoid a second one? A grim picture is starting to emerge, and it doesn't look good for Greg Warner.

43

MAGGIE

Five years ago

Maggie pulls into the parking lot, flips down her visor, and checks her reflection in the vanity mirror. She looks rough, like she hasn't slept in days. Her face has grown gaunt, deep hollows under her cheeks and eyes. Her skin is sallow and her hair is greasy. But she doesn't have to pass for a beauty queen, only a professional.

She finger-combs her hair into a ponytail and exits the vehicle. Halfheartedly brushes at a streak of dried mud on her pants as she crosses the blacktop and enters the store. Keeping her spine straight and her head held high, she strides up to the customer service desk with an air of authority.

Flashing her badge at the woman behind the counter, she says, "I need to speak with your head of security, please."

The woman's eyes widen and she nods, picking up the phone before her and placing a call. Long minutes pass by. Maggie feigns nonchalance as her skin ripples with the sensation of being watched. She studiously avoids glaring at the black globe mounted to the ceiling above her.

Finally. a giant of a man wearing a black t-shirt with the word SECURITY *spelled in yellow letters ambles toward her. He approaches until he's well within her space, forcing her to take a step back and tilt her head to look up at him.*

Taking in his aggressive stance, hands fisted on his hips, an expression of derision etched across his beefy face, Maggie feels a twinge in her gut, instinct telling her to tread carefully. Forcing a friendly smile, she holds out her hand.

"Detective Maggie Riley, Wakefield County Sheriff's Department."

The man makes no attempt to return her greeting.

"You're the head of security, I presume?"

"I am."

"Great. I'd like to see your security footage from the day before yesterday, if I may. Between the hours of nine and eleven should do."

"You got a warrant?"

Maggie's eyes narrow. Her jaw tightens. "Is that your company's protocol?"

The man shrugs.

"So then you can give me the footage?"

When he doesn't reply, she takes a step forward, reclaiming the space he'd taken from her. Mirrors his posture. She's met people like this before, the miserable sort who delight in making things as difficult as possible.

"A four-year-old boy is missing," she says, barely managing to keep her tone civil. "Time is of the essence. If I don't have that footage in my hands within the next five minutes, I'm going to call a press conference and hold it in your parking lot. Make sure consumers know that this store is unwilling to help in an active investigation of such a sensitive nature."

"You can't do that."

Arching an auburn eyebrow, Maggie continues. "I'll also issue a warning to all the parents watching that they should keep your refusal to assist in mind before they chance bringing their children to this business."

"You can't do that," he repeats.

Dropping her voice low, she says, "By the time I'm through with you, your employers will be begging for us to press charges against you just to save face."

The man sneers. "You can't do any of that."

"Watch me," Maggie hisses. She holds his gaze as she pulls her phone from her pocket. Gives him her meanest smile as she turns away.

"Wait."

Maggie glances at him over her shoulder.

"Which camera feed did you need?"

"All of them?"

"But that'll take hours."

"Then we better get started."

He sighs wearily, gesturing for her to follow him. But it doesn't take hours. Twenty minutes later, as they sit before a bank of monitors, rewinding the video recorded by the camera mounted over the exit, she sees what she needs.

"There. Stop."

The image freezes.

"Can you zoom in?"

The picture enlarges, and there, plain as day, is Maggie's mother, a plastic shopping bag in one hand, her son's tiny palm in the other. The timestamp on the lower right-hand side places the footage as being recorded less than twenty minutes before Brenda Riley called 911 to report her son missing from a park that's a twelve-minute drive away.

"Trace them out to the parking lot," Maggie says, already standing. She grabs a business card from her wallet and sets it on the desk before the man. "Then email a copy of both to this address."

Whatever had happened to her baby brother, it had taken just minutes, which fits with the statement her mom had given. That when they'd gotten to the park, Brandon had run toward the swings while Brenda had headed for one of the benches to watch. After taking a seat, she'd looked for her son, but couldn't find him. He was already gone.

All it takes is seconds. But sometimes, the consequences last forever. Maggie prays that this isn't one of those times as she races back to her car.

I shiver against a bitter chill as I linger outside of CeCe's House of Hair. I check the time, then shove my fists deep into my pockets, moving to the side as a customer exits, her hands rising automatically to her freshly tended tresses as the wind threatens to disturb them.

Inside, the lights flick off, leaving only the dim glow of LED rope lighting that runs along the backs of the counters that line the room. A moment later, a young woman steps through the door. She *brrs* against the cold, then makes a small exclamation of shock as she notices me standing there.

"Chief Riley! Sorry, I didn't see you. CeCe's still inside. Do you want me to go get her for you?"

"Thanks, Olivia, but actually, I'm here to speak with you."

"Speak with me," she repeats dazedly. Shaking herself from her stupor, she gives a nervous laugh. "There aren't any parking tickets that I've forgotten to pay, are there?"

"Not that I'm aware of." I give her a friendly smile, trying to reassure her and get her to lower her guard. I don't think it works.

"Whatever would you want to speak with me about?"

"I was hoping I could ask you some questions about your friend Jenny Warner."

"Jenny? I don't think I'd be a good person to ask about her."

"Why not?"

"Because I don't really know her, not anymore."

"But you did go out for drinks with her the other night, didn't you?"

"Yeah, but that was the first time I'd talked to her in years. I couldn't believe it when Trish told me Jenny was going to meet us."

"Because it had been so long since the last time you hung out?" I ask, trying to understand.

Olivia's gaze drops to her feet, her mouth pursing into a knot. "I've always liked Jenny."

I give her side-eye while I wait for her to continue.

She sighs, checks over her shoulder like she's making sure she won't be overheard. "But, I mean, Trish never really did. Like Jenny, I mean. Yeah, we all hung out together when we were in school, but Trish kind of, I don't know... almost saw Jenny as competition, maybe? So I was surprised when she asked Jenny to come."

"And how did Jenny feel about Trish?" I ask, wondering why she had accepted the invitation.

"If Jenny noticed, she didn't seem to care. She wasn't catty like that. She's always just been a nice, sweet girl."

The door opens behind her and CeCe steps out, jiggling a ring of keys in her hand. She stops short when she sees me. Covers her surprise with one of her famous red-lipsticked smiles.

"Well, as I live and breathe! Chief Riley! What brings you around? Please tell me that tonight's the night you finally let me get my hands on that hair of yours."

I laugh, raising a hand self-consciously to the lank ponytail that's fallen over my shoulder. The ponytail that I've allowed to get too long while I work up my nerve to visit CeCe's salon.

"No, not tonight. But soon," I promise.

Her eyes sparkle as she claps her hands together. Then they narrow as she realizes her question hasn't been answered. "Then why are you here?"

"I have a few questions that I need to ask Olivia."

"Well, not out here in the cold, you don't. Come on inside." I try to protest, but the tiny woman has already looped one of her freakishly strong hands around my arm, her pale blonde waves bouncing as she tugs me into the building. "There now. Why don't I make us something to drink? Tea? Or whiskey?"

She sighs at my expression. "Tea it is. But one day. You mark my words."

I don't have many friends in the Cove. And I can't remember the last time I had a girls' night. Like Jenny Warner, it's been years.

I allow myself to briefly consider the idea of tossing back a few shots with CeCe at some later date and am surprised to find myself warming to the notion. But not here. Not now. Not while a child's been killed and his mother's gone missing. I need to find Jenny Warner first.

A faucet runs in the background as CeCe fills a kettle and I take a seat in one of the salon chairs, across from Olivia. I keep my voice low as I say, "This competitiveness that Trish had toward Jenny. Is that why she told Jenny about Greg?"

A cup clatters against the counter. CeCe hurries over and sits beside me, spins my chair to face her, forgetting about the tea. Leaning close, she studies my face, her eyes intent on mine as she asks, "Why are you asking her about Jenny Warner?"

Something in my expression must give me away. She withdraws back from me, covering her cherry-stained lips with her hands as she gasps. "What happened to that poor child wasn't an accident, was it?"

"I'm not sure what it was yet," I say, realizing it's the truth. "Accusations have been made. And it appears as if Jenny may have found out her husband was unfaithful the same night PJ went missing. Now she's gone, and no one knows where she is. There's a lot that doesn't add up right now."

"Please don't tell me that girl went and did something stupid. Not over some man who didn't deserve her in the first place."

My spit thins. Everyone seems to be making the leap that Jenny may have hurt her son. I'm supposed to remain impartial as I collect evidence, to let the facts speak for themselves, but I'm starting to doubt that's what I'm doing. Am I letting my own biases cloud my judgment?

"I hope not," I whisper.

CeCe closes her eyes and mutters a prayer. When she's done, she says, "I don't have to imagine what she felt. Being so young and vulnerable with a kid to raise, scared to do it on your own. I've been there myself. But surely she wouldn't have hurt her own child. And she must have known what she was getting into. It's no secret how she and Greg got together. I always tell the girls here, 'If he'll cheat with you, he'll cheat on you.'"

"So it was common knowledge? That Greg and Jenny had an affair?"

"Boy, was it. I still remember the first time Loraine came in to get her hair done after Greg left her. That woman was mad enough to spit hornets."

"Seems to me like she's still pretty upset about what happened," I say.

"Can you blame her?" CeCe asks.

I shake my head no. "Do you think she's still angry enough to have done something about it?"

CeCe's eyes roll up as she thinks about the question. "Possibly. But to have hurt a child? Never. She's a momma herself, and a good one at that. Besides. I think she considered that poor girl being stuck with a husband who was chasing half the women in town revenge enough to even the score."

"Is he that obvious about it?"

CeCe laughs. "Oh, yeah. That man must think discreet is a kind of deodorant."

"Did Jenny seem surprised?" I ask Olivia. "When Trish told her?"

She looks reluctant to be drawn back into the conversation. "I can't say for sure. Some of the comments she made before Trish told her... Well, I kind of got the impression that she wasn't very happy. Like maybe she regretted getting married."

"Do you think she was resentful of her son?"

Olivia shakes her head with absolute conviction. "She adored PJ. Really. She couldn't stop talking about him, showing us pictures. And she was so excited to be hanging out. I mean, as far as I know, she hasn't spent any time with friends in years. But it seemed like it also kind of made her a little sad, maybe. Like she was just realizing everything she had missed out on by becoming a mom so young."

"Did you get the impression that she was enjoying the night out?"

"Oh, yeah. She really seemed to be having fun. At least until Trish decided to tell her about Greg."

"And would you say that was typical behavior for Trish?"

"Actually, not really. I mean, something about Jenny has always seemed to rub Trish the wrong way, but she used to just make snarky comments, you know? A little jab here and there. Jenny never even seemed to notice. And Trish has always had a bit of a witchy streak, that's just been her personality for as long as I can remember. You have to take her with a grain of salt."

Olivia frowns as she says, "But that night, it was like Trish had an agenda. I mean, we've been friends practically forever, but that was the first time I've seen her act like that. Honestly, I felt bad for Jenny. She didn't do anything to deserve it. I have no idea what Trish was thinking."

"So you think she was being cruel on purpose?" I ask.

"Yeah. I hate to say it, but I do."

"One last thing," I say, rising to my feet. "Do you have any idea where Jenny might go if she needed to lay low for a while, clear her head? Maybe a mutual friend's house, or a spot you frequented as teenagers?"

"There was a time I would have said my house. But now?" Olivia shrugs her shoulders, shaking her head. "I have no clue. I don't think she really has anyone she can rely on besides her mom anymore."

I wait for CeCe to lock up the shop and for the two women to get into their cars and drive off before climbing into my own vehicle. The more I learn, the more my heart goes out to the young mother. Why *did* Trish antagonize Jenny that night? Was it just a case of evening the score between an old frenemy? Or was there something else at play?

When I woke up this morning, during those first few foggy moments between being asleep and fully alert, everything seemed normal. It was just another day, sure to be a good one. But as the haze of slumber burned off and the memories of my recent encounter with my old friend sharpened into focus, reality slammed into me with the force of a train.

Everyone I care about is in danger, and I am the one who put them there.

The anxiety that's become my norm returned in an instant. So, too, did the jumpiness I've been trying so hard to conceal. But as Maggie turned in bed beside me and I flinched into an upright position, it became clear what a poor job of it I've been doing.

A crease formed between Maggie's brows as the sleepy smile slipped from her face, replaced by a frown. "Are you okay?" she asked, propping herself up on an arm.

"Yeah. Why?"

I could feel the heat of her gaze as she studied me. I kept my eyes averted as I hurried out of bed, busying myself with getting dressed.

"I don't know. You've just seemed... distracted lately. Stressed."

"Nope." I tried to make myself look at her as I lied, but I couldn't.

"Is it your family being here?"

"Of course not."

"Is it..." I could hear her swallow hard, the uncharacteristic timidity in her tone as she said, "Me?"

"Don't be ridiculous."

Because it wasn't her. It could never be her. And yet, as much as I wanted to confide in Maggie at that moment, as much as I knew she needed to hear the truth, that she would find a way to blame herself for whatever she thinks is going on with me if I didn't come clean, I kept my mouth shut. I hurt the woman I love for my own selfish reasons.

She slipped silently from between the sheets and crossed the room without a sound. Which made the hard click as she shut the bathroom door firmly behind her seem like a sonic boom.

I have to end this before I ruin everything. I need to find a way to get Wesley out of Coyote Cove, for good.

So when I started searching the internet this afternoon, it was to see what else I could find out about my former friend. Surely if he'd only recently been released from prison, there must be someone checking up on him. But I couldn't find a single thing I didn't already know about Wesley or his crime.

And as the hours passed and my frustration grew, my attention turned to researching local disappearances in the area. I felt horrified when I realized what I was doing. Because there's no way I can actually consider trying to find a new identity for Wesley.

Yet, there's no denying that's exactly what I was looking to do. And that I'd felt an overwhelming disappointment when a likely candidate didn't immediately appear.

What might happen if I did as he asked? Would he kill again? I couldn't know that for sure, could I? I mean, you can't actually predict someone else's behavior, right? He could just want a fresh start.

But if that was true, why did I feel so guilty? Or like I was doing something wrong, slamming the lid of my computer down when Izzy came into the kitchen to get a snack? Why had my cheeks burned with shame and my eyes been unable to meet my sister's?

Now here I am, wearing a ditch into the floor with my pacing, desperate to see Maggie's headlights pulling into the driveway. My Grandpa Joe walk through the door. A news broadcast that there's been an avalanche and a man named Wesley Banks, the only victim buried beneath the rubble, has perished.

I check my watch, then lift the corner of a curtain to peer out into the night. Still nothing. No one's out there. At least not that I can see. It's this thought that strengthens my resolve.

There's only one option, and that's to find a way to send Wesley back to prison. It's the only way to keep everyone protected. Given Wesley's past, setting him up should be as simple as having a woman make an accusation against him. Surely no one would believe his word over theirs. But who can I get to help me?

Turning away from the window, I find Izzy standing there, watching me with an unreadable expression on her face. Not my little sister. There's no way I could bring her into this, use her like that. I have to keep her as far away from this mess as possible.

My face twitches as I struggle to give her a smile. The one she returns mine with is equally tense.

This is all my fault. I'm the one Wesley hates. The one he wants revenge against, restitution from, the one against whom he feels the need to even the score. The only one who should have to pay the consequences, no matter what they might be.

46
MAGGIE

I should go home. Steve and his family are waiting for me. But I can't bring myself to join them just yet. There's too much I shouldn't bring with me still weighing heavily on my shoulders.

I know Steve was lying this morning when he told me nothing was bothering him. Which means he could have been lying when he said that it wasn't me. And every time my mind drifts to trying to figure out what's wrong, I get overwhelmed by guilt. Because I have more important things to worry about right now.

Like a little boy whose body was slipped through a hole in the ice after he drowned somewhere else. A father who was unconcerned by his disappearance, who is now blaming his wife for the child's murder. A wife who had just discovered her husband was cheating on her. Who had said she'd make him pay. Who is now nowhere to be found.

I need to speak with Jenny Warner.

I'd been so sure I'd find her at her mother's or a friend's, but no one's seen her. She couldn't have gone far without a car. I make a note to check and see if the subpoena's come in yet granting access to the Warners' financials. Maybe I can find some clue on their bank statement or credit card history and locate her that way.

In the meantime, I can't help expecting the worst. I need to find out more about the people I'm dealing with here. I need to figure out who's most likely to be a killer.

I pull into the parking lot of Margot's Motel, shivering against the cold—and my suspicions—as I leave the warmth of my Jeep and slip inside. The bell on the door rings, announcing my arrival. A moment later, Margot emerges from the back room, straightening her shirt. I can hear Steve's grandfather urging her to hurry back as she shuts the door.

Her weathered cheeks color when she spots me. She gives me something between a grin and a grimace, her tiny eyes staring hard into mine, daring me to challenge her as she says, "What? Don't judge me."

"Oh, I wasn't," I hurry to say, feeling my own cheeks heat.

"Good. When you get to be my age, you don't have time to fuss around with any games. You've got to get straight to the good stuff and hope you both survive it."

All the thoughts that had been circling around inside my head like hungry sharks suddenly go still. I want to laugh, but I kind of also want to cry. I settle on retreating.

Taking a step backward, toward my escape, I say, "Sorry for disturbing you."

Margot waves off the apology. "Go ahead. Tell me why you're here."

"It's nothing that can't wait. I'll stop by tomorrow."

"You're here now. I can tell you need to talk, so out with it already."

I'm about to insist that I let her return to her date, but the words won't come out. Instead, I close the distance between us. Beckon her forward and keep my voice low as I say, "When you first heard PJ Warner had gone missing, you came to me to say I should look at his father, Greg. I need to know why."

"Because he's scum."

I nod, hoping she'll elaborate. When she doesn't, I prod, "What made you feel strongly enough to point a finger?"

Margot's withered lips press into a stern line. "Honestly? There's nothing in particular. Just a feeling."

I can't tell her about Greg and Jenny dealing drugs. It's part of an open investigation, and until I find out what happened to their son, so I can shift my focus to confirming what Jenny told me, it's still just hearsay. Because I don't have any actual proof, do I?

For the first time I realize that all I have is Jenny's word. Greg never confirmed nor denied the accusation. Even the convicted felon who had been on the list of their supposed drug associates that Jenny had given me couldn't confirm that they'd been dealers when Kal spoke with him.

Could Jenny have told me that just to divert my attention away from her? To keep me busy looking at suspects who had no connection to the case while she figured out her next step?

But I'm here already, and Margot is a shrewd judge of character. I want details about what's formed her poor opinion of Greg Warner. So I grasp at a straw she's already aware of, and ask, "Because of the time he forgot about his son in the car while he was in the Loose Moose drinking?"

"Not entirely. You ask me, there's just something that's not quite right about him, is all. Look him hard in the eyes and tell me you don't see it."

"Do you think he killed PJ?" I ask.

"Do you?" she fires back.

"I'm not sure. Right now, he seems awfully intent on pointing the finger at Jenny."

Margot nods. "That's possible, too."

I feel myself wince. "Really? You think?"

"You don't?"

"Him? Yeah, I can buy it, but Jenny? I just don't see—"

"Of course you don't."

"What's that supposed to mean?" I ask, feeling slightly wounded.

Margot gives me a look that tells me I'm being difficult.

"No offense..." Margot's voice softens, which is never a good sign. If you've earned her pity, you're either already drowning or drawing your last breath. I prepare myself for the sting of whatever she's going to say. "But you've got a certain blindness where mothers are concerned. You'd think any mother who didn't abandon her young is a good one."

"That's not true," I rush to say. But is it? It just might be.

Do we ever really see ourselves as we actually are? It's so easy to assume that others' perceptions of us are incorrect, that only we truly know ourselves, but maybe that's inaccurate. Maybe we only know the lies we want to believe are true.

"But I appreciate your honesty," I add. "And you're right. I should consider Jenny a little more strongly as a suspect. Thanks, Margot. I'll let you get back to your date now."

"Are you sure?"

I nod, pushing my lips into a smile.

"'Kay. But don't you hesitate to stop by if you need to talk. About anything."

Ignoring the offer, I cross the room quickly to the exit as she returns to the back. A cackle of a giggle hits my ears a second later. It's so disconcerting, especially from someone like Margot, that I pause. My gaze lands on a framed map of the valley hung next to the door.

The paper is old and yellow and cracked along the edges. In the very center sits an artist's rendition of Beaverhead Lake. Locating the area where the Warners' house would be, I track the distance between the two with my eyes.

There are dozens of places that would have been both easier and better spots to hide a body. Whoever took the time and added risk to transport PJ's remains must have done so because they had cared about the little boy. I can't deny it's possible that Jenny was responsible for her child's death.

I push my way dazedly out to the parking lot. Climb into my Jeep and steer home on autopilot, completely lost in my own thoughts. Despite all the evidence and opinions that support a conclusion to the contrary, my gut is still telling me that Jenny Warner is innocent. But it's entirely possible my desperation to believe that Jenny didn't hurt her son could have something to do with my own mother.

And yet, there's a growing sensation that I can't shake off, one that tells me that Jenny's in trouble, but whether from herself or someone else I couldn't say. If her husband really believes she's responsible for what happened to their son, there's no telling what he might do to her. Then again, if he's correct, there's no telling what she might do to herself.

47

MAGGIE

My stomach growls as I pull up to the house. I glance at the clock and feel a wave of guilt crash over me. It's late, almost nine o'clock. I've missed dinner. More than that, I've missed yet another opportunity to spend time with my future in-laws. No wonder Steve's been acting so distant. Why wouldn't he, with the way I've allowed this case to take precedence over everything else?

I vow to myself to make more of an effort to prioritize family for the rest of their visit, even though I have no idea how I'll manage it with this current investigation. Maybe I should have Dr. Ricky file her report, let the state police take over. Even as I think it, though, I know that I'm incapable of making that decision.

I can't just turn my back and wash my hands of this. I have to uncover the truth about what happened to PJ Warner and make sure the culprit pays for their crime. And I have to take an active part in this family. I'll just have to find a way to handle both.

The dogs greet me as I walk through the front door, jumping up for attention. I shed my jacket, hang it on a hook, then take a seat on the floor. They vie against each other for the prized spot of my lap, their furry bodies wiggling as I wrap them in my arms and give them cuddles. Their tongues lick away the stress of my day, erasing my frown lines, covering me in love. It makes me crave Steve.

Getting to my feet, I wander deeper into the house. Diane glances up from the couch, smiling over the top of her reading glasses and taking a sip from the wineglass in her hand before returning to her book. I find Izzy in the kitchen, pulling a tray of freshly baked cookies from the oven.

They smell amazing, the tantalizing aroma teasing my empty belly. I'm famished. But as much as I want to fill my belly with sugar and chat with my future sister-in-law, I'm a woman on a mission.

Steve looks up as I enter our bedroom, his eyes wide and frantic. His hair sticks up in clumps where he's run his hands through it. He leaves his post by the window and hurries toward me.

"Where the hell have you been?"

I step back, shocked by his outburst. Glancing over my shoulder, I ease the door shut. Draw a deep breath as I take in his harried appearance.

"Is everything all right?" I ask, reaching a hand tentatively forward before letting it settle on his arm. I've never seen him like this before. It worries me.

"No, everything isn't all right. Do you know what time it is?"

"It's no later than I usually get in when I'm working a case. In fact, it's quite a bit earlier."

"Yeah, well, that doesn't make it right. You think it's fair to just leave me here without a word, not knowing where you are or if you're okay? You think I like that?"

My throat tightens and a part of me wants to cry from the shock of his anger. He's never spoken to me like this before. But the other part wants to hold my ground and thunder back. I've done nothing to deserve this. It's not my fault if he's feeling stressed. He shouldn't be taking it out on me.

I don't know what has him so worked up, but I realize that I should. Whatever he's going through right now, he's dealing with it on his own because I haven't been there for him. I swallow my temper.

"Steve, what's really going on here?"

"It's just—" His eyes flash and he tugs at his hair again. "It's nothing."

"Maybe so, but I'd like you to tell me anyway." Closing the distance between us, I place my hands against his chest and brush a kiss against his lips. His heart kicks against my palm.

I kiss him again, tenderly, soothingly, my arms sliding around his waist until our bodies are pressed close. I feel some of the tension drain from him, the nervous energy that has him jumping like a live wire easing.

"I'm sorry." He returns my embrace, tucking my head under his chin. "I was just worried. Sometimes it's hard, not knowing where you are. If you're safe. And now with Grandpa Joe off galivanting around—"

"Galivanting?" I tease, chuckling.

"Well, you know. Chasing after Margot like a lovesick teenager."

"Is that what has you so upset?"

"No."

"Then what does?"

I feel him shrug against me.

"You know, I think your grandpa and Margot have the right idea. I bet they're a lot more relaxed right now than you and I are."

He laughs. "Yeah, because they're—"

I let my fingers play over the button on his jeans. "They don't have to be the only ones."

"Ew. I mean, not you ew, but the whole idea of them..."

"Yeah, I realized the comparison might have been a bit yuck after I said it. But the offer still stands."

I lean back so I can see his face and give him a smile. Wiggle my eyebrows suggestively.

He glances at the door behind me, unbuttoning my shirt. "Why do I feel like we're doing something illegal right now?"

"Because your mom's in the house?" I suggest.

"You know, I totally would have snuck you into my bedroom when I was a teenager," he says.

"I would have let you," I joke as we shuffle a few steps closer to the bed.

He stops, pulling back to look at me. "Promise me something. Promise me it will always be like this. That we won't ever let anything come between us."

I do. I promise. But as we sink onto the bed, I can't help but wonder what he was referring to. Because Steve is not a *what if* kind of guy. Not the type to imagine alternate realities. Which means he definitely has something specific in mind. And whatever it is, he thinks it's possible that it could tear us apart.

48

STEVE

The house is too silent. And my racing thoughts are too loud.

I crane my ears, listening for the barely audible sound of Maggie's breathing as she sleeps. Needing something, anything, to fill the space inside my head. But the soft sounds of her slumber do nothing but remind me of what I stand to lose.

I want to cuddle up beside her, take her in my arms, hold her while I still can, but I can't bring myself to do it. Just the idea feels like some kind of violation, because if she knew the truth, I'm not sure she'd be beside me right now. I've got to find some way to make this right.

I wish I could stay here, in this moment, safe and sound beside the woman I love, forever. But that sense of safety is false. The narrative I'm spinning is a lie.

What's worse, I can tell by the look in her eyes that she suspects something is wrong. And knowing Maggie, she's probably convinced it's because of her. Yet every time she asks, I deny there's a problem. I don't deserve her. Not her love, and certainly not her trust. Not now.

The first time I saw her was the day I moved in here. She'd been walking the dogs, her auburn hair loose in the wind, sparking like flames as it caught the sun. And fire seemed the perfect description for her, wild and alive, bringing both protection and danger.

It had quickly become clear that she'd been hurt--badly--that trust wasn't something that came easily to her. Yet I pursued her tirelessly, willing to do whatever it took to scale the barrier that surrounded her heart. And though I've been grateful for each day I've spent with her in my life, I realize now that I should have walked away.

Because I've always known that something like this could happen. If not Wesley coming back to haunt me, and in turn, us, then some other event that would lead to me disappointing her. I don't have the best track record when it comes to women, and now that I've finally found one that means the world to me, I've been careless... My own selfishness astounds me, because even now, I want to hold her close when I know I should be letting her go.

Slipping from beneath the sheets, I force myself away from the warmth and comfort I don't deserve, and creep out into the hall. The sound of nails clicking across the hardwood floors carries as the dogs come to join me. They follow at my heels as I tiptoe to the next room, holding my breath as I turn the knob and peer inside. I can just barely make out my sister's sleeping form through the gloom.

I was six when Izzy was born. I still remember the day my parents brought her home from the hospital. And though I was upset because I'd told them I wanted a pet hippopotamus, and they'd brought me a baby sister instead, from that first moment I saw her, I was filled with a strange mix of awe and pride. I was a big brother. This little creature was mine to protect.

And I've always done my best to do so. When she was five and afraid to go to school by herself, I walked her to class every day, even holding her hand, until she had the confidence to go alone. When she was seven and our dad died, I slept on the floor of her room for almost half a year until she stopped waking up every night in tears, not wanting her to feel like she was alone with her grief. When she was twenty-four and broke up with her live-in boyfriend at one in the morning, I was there by two to help her pack up her things.

From the big things to the small, I've always tried to keep Izzy safe. Always. It's destroying me to know that I've put her in harm's way now.

I retreat, closing the door noiselessly behind me, and shuffle through the dark to the next room, repeating the process until I'm sure that my mother is okay. She sighs softly, a sleep mask drawn tight over her eyes.

I'll be the first to admit that my mother is not an easy woman to get along with. Growing up, free will was for other children, not hers. We were expected to follow her formula and her rules and achieve success. At the same time, she always tried to conceal the sacrifices she made for us.

I caught her once, in the kitchen at 3 a.m. when I went to get a glass of water, sitting at the table with a mountain of paperwork in front of her. Had been shocked to see the name of a local law firm on some of the documents. I still remember the fluttery feeling I'd had in my stomach as I'd asked her if we were being sued, dreading the answer.

Pushing her reading glasses up onto her head, she had laughed and patted my hand. Assured me that everything was fine. But I hadn't believed her.

"Then what are you doing?" I pried, insisting that she tell me.

Leaning back in her chair, she confessed that she'd taken some freelance accounting work to help make ends meet. Thinking about the expensive shoes in my closet I didn't really need, the braces I wore to correct a barely noticeable overbite, I apologized and confessed that I never thought about how we afforded so much, told her that I could get by with much less and was old enough to get part-time work to help out.

She gave me a sad smile as she told me what a wonderful man I was becoming, but that school was my job, everything else was hers. Then she swore me to secrecy, making me promise to never tell Izzy or Grandpa Joe, as if she was ashamed of any of us knowing how hard she was working on our behalf.

How do you ever repay that? Not like this.

The dogs trail behind me as I shuffle to the room Grandpa Joe is staying in. The shut door barely muffles the sound of his snoring, and I can't help but smile.

Not many men would give up the rent-controlled condo in Miami they'd managed to nab for their retirement, making a return to harsh New England winters so they could move in with their widowed daughter-in-law to help with his grandchildren, but he hadn't hesitated for a second. He'd been the one to teach me how to drive. How to shave. And how to be a man.

I feel like I've failed him. First, all those years ago when I took the cowardly way out and helped bury that girl under a tree on a lonely country road, and again now, in the present. I know he'd be disappointed in me if he ever found out the truth.

My head hangs low as I make my way out to the rest of the house, systematically checking that every door and window is locked.

This is no way to live.

I've put my loved ones at risk. What's worse, they don't even know it because I've been too chicken to tell them, afraid to see them look at me the same way I've been looking at myself in the mirror. There's no excuse. It's despicable.

But there's another reason I can't tell them the truth, a reason that's even worse than my shame. Because if they knew what was going on, they'd try to help. And I can't let that happen.

I would do anything for Maggie. For my family. For the

dogs keeping me company as I patrol the house while my loved ones sleep peacefully. I'll do whatever it takes to keep them safe.

Even kill for them, if it comes down to it. Which is exactly what Wesley wants, isn't it? What he's counting on me to do?

But there's got to be a better way out of this. I need to buy more time.

49

MAGGIE

We sit at the kitchen table after breakfast, Steve's mother nursing a cup of coffee as she shows me pictures on her iPad of wedding dresses that she thinks I might like. I smile and nod, but I'm absolutely clueless. To be honest, it's not something I've ever really thought about before—I wasn't one of those little girls who dreamed about her big day.

I have no idea what I want, and just the idea of all the big decisions that lie ahead makes me feel a bit nauseous. I glance toward Steve and catch him watching me. A rush of heat spreads up my neck and into my cheeks as memories of last night fill me with a curious mix of elation and anxiety. I've found a man who I connect with, one who I want to spend the rest of my days with. For the first time in forever, I feel like I have so much good in my life.

But that just means there's more to lose.

I try not to let the dark thoughts in. I'm trying to focus on the positive. But what he said set off alarm bells in my head.

Is it possible that I'm blowing a simple comment out of proportion? There's no denying that I have a history of living my life with one foot out the door, always looking for a reason why a situation, a plan, a relationship won't work. Trying to jump ship before I could possibly fail.

Because love is messy and chaotic and uncontrollable. It makes you vulnerable. All things I detest. But sitting here across the table from him, there's no denying the way he makes me feel. I want to marry this man.

It's enough to make me lower my guard, to make me actually *like* looking at the wedding dresses on the screen before me, though the dresses themselves don't appeal to me at all. As Diane scrolls to another page, I have to fight the urge to comment. *Too itchy looking, too revealing, too heavy, too formal.*

And then my eyes land on one that doesn't make me squirm. It's simple, pretty, elegant yet understated. It looks comfortable. It looks like the kind of dress I could wear. It looks perfect.

"That one's nice," I say, trying to sound casual as I point.

Steve leans across the table to see, but his mother bats him away. "Uh-uh. The groom isn't supposed to see the dress."

"I thought it was that he wasn't supposed to see the bride in the dress," Izzy says.

"Same thing." Diane's head tilts to the side as she squints at the screen. Her gaze moves to me, shifting back and forth. Slowly, she begins to nod.

"Here, let me see." Izzy gets up and moves behind her mother. "That one?"

I nod.

"It's gorgeous. I love it."

Steve finishes his coffee, slips nonchalantly behind our chairs on his way to the kitchen for a refill.

"Steven!" Diane sounds like she's scolding a young child and not a man in his forties. "That's enough. Go find something else to do."

"But I—"

"Shoo!"

He feigns a mock-annoyed look, fails when he can't keep the grin off his face. It's a relief to finally see him smile. But it also makes that little unsettled feeling I've been carrying around inside me grow into something bigger and more worrisome.

He used to smile so freely. When did he stop? More importantly, why? If the problem isn't me, which last night seems to support, then what's going on with him?

"Fine," he says. "I'm gonna go wake Grandpa Joe so I won't be so outnumbered."

"You still won't get to see this dress," Diane calls after him as he disappears down the hall. To me, she says, "This shop's not that far away. It's over in Lincoln. We can get there and back before noon if you can take the morning off."

I'm surprised to discover that I want to do it. That I'm considering letting Kal take the reins for the morning, have him check Jenny Warner's bank account and credit cards while I go try on a wedding dress. And why shouldn't I?

Don't I deserve to live my life? To carve out a little time for myself? The thought immediately fills me with shame as the image of a tiny frozen body fills my mind.

Under the table, one of the dogs leans against my leg. I look down to see Sullivan staring up at me, his eyes bright, his mouth open in a smile. It's enough to banish the visions I haunt myself with. How can I expect to stay positive and find happiness if I keep myself mired in a constant pit of grief?

"You know what?" I say quickly, before I can change my mind. "Let's do it."

"Excellent!" Diane bounces up from her seat, clapping her hands together.

"Do you have any idea what you're getting yourself into?" Izzy stage whispers.

"Oh, hush." Diane shoots her daughter a threatening look. It instantly vanishes as she turns back to me. "This is going to be so much fun! Now, hurry, both of you. Let's get—"

"Grandpa Joe is gone." Steve bursts into the room frantically, eyes wild, the whites showing.

Diane frowns "What do you mean gone?"

"He's not here. The car is missing, too."

"Well, maybe he just ran up to the store to grab something."

Izzy smirks. "More like he went to visit his new girlfriend."

"Then why wouldn't he have told anyone?"

"Because he's an adult. He isn't used to checking in before he goes somewhere," Izzy says, giving her brother a funny look.

"We need to find him. Now."

"Relax, will you? What's gotten into you?"

Before he can answer, Diane holds up her phone. "Izzy's right. He texted that he was driving into town to see Margot. Mystery solved."

Steve rubs a palm over his suddenly exhausted-looking face as he releases a sigh that's pure stress, sinking into a chair. "Okay. Good. That's good."

"Now that that's settled, time to get the show back on the road," Diane says, ushering me and Izzy out the door without delay.

As I'm hustled toward the car, I glance over my shoulder at Steve, still slumped in his seat, and I know—this worry that's been niggling at me is not me searching the shadows for boogiemen that don't exist. It's not just my normal inclination to imagine the worst. It's instinct.

I can't stick my head in the sand anymore. The secret Steve's hiding is serious. Whatever it is, it's got him scared.

Anxiety tightens my chest as I drive away from town, trying to pretend like everything is all right. Adrenaline crashes against me in sickening waves, and yet, I do my best to pretend that everything is okay despite the way my pulse races as I chat with Diane. Joke with Izzy. Go through the motions of what I imagine a girls' day might be, gleaned from TV and movies.

Because I really don't know, do I? The last time I went

shopping with friends I was in high school, girls I fell out of touch with decades ago. I feel like I'm treading water in the middle of the ocean by myself, with no land in sight. I need someone I can talk to. Confide in. Beg for advice. I need a sounding board.

I need Linda.

She's the closest friend I have, one of the only ones, if I'm telling the truth. And while we've never tried on outfits together or done spa days or mani-pedis or whatever it is that most female friends do, we've faced demons with the other by our side. I should call her the first chance I get.

But what will I say? My throat tightens as I try to form my suspicions into words. Because the truth is, despite how good I am at burrowing under the dirt that most people use to keep their secrets buried, at knowing which shadowy corners I need to dig deep in to find the answers I'm after, for once in my life, I haven't a clue where to look. And that terrifies me.

"Your phone."

"Huh?" I glance away from the road, over at Diane in the passenger seat beside me.

"Your phone," she says again, gesturing to the device buzzing away in the cup holder.

"Oh. Thanks." I pin the cell between my ear and my shoulder as I answer the call. "Chief Riley."

"It's Kal."

I know instantly from his tone that something is wrong.

"Where are you right now?"

"On Route 3, about twenty-five miles outside town. Why?"

"I'm so sorry to have to do this, but I need you to come back."

The cold hand of fear wraps around my throat. A litany of the worst things that could have possibly happened runs through my mind. We've only been gone twenty minutes. But a lot can happen in that time. All it takes is a second for a life to be lost, for another to be changed forever.

"What is it?"

I'm all too aware of my companions listening in to my side of the conversation. I ignore their questioning looks as I check my surroundings before slowing the car and making a U-turn. Because the truth is, somehow, I already know.

50

MAGGIE

Five years ago

Navigating through traffic, Maggie allows herself to feel the first smidge of hope since she learned of her brother's disappearance. She can do this. She can bring him back. She can reunite her family.

Todd's arrest record included a prior kidnapping charge. The little boy had been in his possession for over a week. He hadn't killed the child. He'd done other horrible, despicable things, but the kid was still alive, that's what mattered. She and her parents would help Brandon through this, get him any help he needed.

Her phone rings and she glances down, checking the display. It's the sheriff. Signaling, she pulls off the side of the road. She tries to check her email, to make sure she's received the footage from the security guard and can forward it to her boss, but her screen is too sensitive and she answers the call by mistake instead.

She wants to hang up but knows she can't. She needs to keep the sheriff onside. Needs his support. The larger the team he sends out to Todd's to help her, the better. Cursing silently, she brings the phone to her ear. "Hello?"

"What the hell are you doing?"

"Sir?"

"I just received a complaint that you used extortion to obtain access to video surveillance. Is that true?"

Maggie debates her response. Decides to go with the truth. "Yes, but—"

"Did you not understand what I said earlier?"

"But, sir, did you see the video? It shows Brandon with my mom less than twenty minutes before she called to report him missing."

"That has absolutely no bearing on this case."

Maggie's eyes feel like they're about to bulge out of her head. "Of course it does! It proves he was alive!"

"Not when the call was made. Or that he ever made it to the park."

"The park is twelve minutes from that location. Twelve minutes! Do you really believe that my mom—what?—killed my brother and managed to hide his body so well it still hasn't been recovered and did it all in less than five minutes? There's no way."

The sheriff sighs loudly on his end of the line. "Have you ever considered that maybe she had help?"

"Like who?"

"Your father?"

"That's absurd!"

"Is it?"

"Yes!"

"Maggie, think about it for a moment."

"I have. And it sounds an awful lot like you're suggesting that my parents had some kind of premeditated plan to murder my brother."

Maggie's pulse races, her heart beating against the walls of her chest.

"I can't even begin to imagine what you're going through right now, Maggie, and my heart goes out to you, it really does. The department will get you the help you need to get you through this. But I'm going to need your badge."

"You're kidding."

"I did warn you. Hopefully, this will only be temporary."

Maggie laughs bitterly.

"You need to rein yourself in or you'll be facing charges."

"Such as?"

"Obstruction of justice. Tampering with evidence. And as of this moment, if you cease to comply, impersonating a law enforcement officer."

Tears sting her eyes. She punches her steering wheel. Her phone pings, and she almost throws it. Instead, she pulls it away from her head, the sheriff's voice growing faint as she reads the text from Linda.

I'm driving into town now. Where do you want to meet?

Maggie considers for only a second.

The place with the best milkshakes. See you soon.

She looks at her phone. Can still hear the sheriff talking. Lowering her window, she extends her arm outside, and gives her phone a toss. Rolls forward until her front tire rolls over the device with a satisfying crunch. Then she waits for a break in traffic and pulls a U-turn.

As she drives away, she leaves the glimmer of hope she'd felt only moments before behind her. She knows that there's no coming back from this. The thing she'd sacrificed everything in her adult life for, the career she'd worked at so hard for so long, is over.

But that doesn't matter, the only thing that does is Brandon. Without him, she has no family. She has nothing. And if that turns out to be the case, she might as well be the one to light the match before watching it all burn to the ground.

51

STEVE

Maggie's on her way to look at a wedding dress right now. I almost can't believe it. Part of me is absolutely ecstatic—we're actually moving forward with our wedding plans. Our future is starting to feel real.

The other part of me is in sheer panic because there's just so much for me to lose. So much that Wesley could take away. I can't let that happen. But I can't give him what he wants, either.

I've got to think of a way out of this. I have to come up with a plan. But for that, I need more time, which isn't going to make Wesley happy.

As much as I dread it, I'm going to have to meet with him again so I can try to convince him that I intend to do what he's asked of me. But I need to make sure that my loved ones are protected in case he doesn't buy it. I might not get a better opportunity than this.

As soon as Maggie, Izzy, and my mom are on the road, I text Wesley telling him we need to meet. Then I call Grandpa Joe to make sure that he'll be spending the day with Margot. If there's one positive to come from their relationship, it's that he's probably safer with her than he'd be here. But maybe that's just wishful thinking.

By the time the call with Grandpa Joe ends, I have my response. Wesley will meet me at Maggie's in ten minutes. The fact that he can be there that quickly, that wherever he is, he's that close, has me clenching my jaw so hard my teeth ache and I get a sharp pain behind my left eye.

I pull on my jacket with sweaty hands and step outside into the cold. Barely feel the bite of the wind as I hurry down the driveway and across the street. I want to get there first, and I want to get there quietly. I need to see which direction he comes from.

Jogging up the front steps to Maggie's place, I keep my eyes peeled and my ears open, straining to listen for the sounds of an engine. I hadn't seen a vehicle last time we met, but I know he has to have one. Getting around the valley would be impossible, otherwise.

I climb the steps to the front door, then start a slow scan of the woods, looking for flashes of color or movement. Maybe he's using an ATV. Maybe he's renting one of the vacation rentals nearby.

"Gotta say, I thought I'd have to chase you down when it was time to collect, but look at you, making the first move."

I jump, start coughing on the gasp that strangled in my throat.

"You okay, man?" Wesley slaps me on the back. Even through the layers I'm wearing, the contact makes my skin crawl, the hair on the back of my neck bristle.

"Fine," I manage, blinking back the tears brought about by the coughing fit.

"So." Wesley rubs his gloved hands together. "How'd you do it?"

"Do what?"

Wesley's eyes narrow. "Whack the oaf whose identity I'm taking. What else would I be talking about?"

"About that."

"Don't tell me you're backing out."

He takes a step toward me, the air between us crackling with menace. I hold my hands up, preparing to ward off an attack.

"No. No, I'm going to do it. It's just, these things take time. Planning."

"Like you know."

"I know I don't want to get caught afterward. And I know that neither of us wants me to screw up and choose poorly."

"That better not happen."

"And it won't," I say, feigning confidence that I don't feel. "Believe me, the last thing I want is you showing up again, unhappy. But that's why I need more time. You want me to find you a new identity. I want to make sure it's a good one."

Wesley gives me a doubtful look. I need to find a way to sell this.

"What's a bit longer if it means the difference between being a doctor or a janitor?"

His eyes stay on me as he scratches his chin, the stubble rasping loudly.

"Two more days," he says finally. Holds up his fingers in a peace sign so there are no mistakes. "Two. That's all you're getting, so it better be enough."

"It will be."

"Yeah, well, we'll see. You better go get started. Before I change my mind."

My muscles tighten into knots as I force myself to turn my back on him. Fight to keep my legs steady as I walk down the porch stairs.

"Oh, and Steve-o?"

I freeze.

"You don't want to disappoint me on this. Trust me on that."

I nod, concentrating on making myself walk, not run, away from him. This might have been a mistake. I may have made this a million times worse. And I still don't even have an idea what direction he came from. I turn and look back, over my shoulder, but Maggie's front porch is empty. He's already gone.

52

MAGGIE

Unseeing eyes stare blankly at the gray sky. Pale skin resembles the frigid lake it was so recently pulled from. Long hair curls into tendrils resembling the tentacles of a sea creature.

I swallow down a bubble of emotion as I squat beside Jenny Warner and take a closer look at her body, though I can't say exactly what it is that I'm feeling. Grief? Regret? Anger? None of them seems quite right.

"We were hiking around the lake when we found her."

I glance up at the couple clinging to each other a dozen feet away. A pair of tourists who I bet are wishing they'd planned their vacation somewhere tropical right now instead of a muddy mountain valley.

"We thought maybe she might need help," the woman says. "But once we reached the edge of the water, well..."

She doesn't need to say it. It's obvious to even an untrained eye that Jenny Warner is beyond help.

"Are you the ones who fished her out?" I ask.

The man nods. "She was right at the edge. All I did was grab her by the shoulder and flip her over."

"That's when we called 911," the woman explains.

Turning back to the body, I let my gaze drift over the scene. I can't even see the corner of the lake where PJ Warner was found. So why here? I study the landscape around me, hoping for a clue.

A jumble of footprints has churned the mud along the shore. The two sets approaching from the south belong to the couple. The two leading down the embankment from above can be explained by me and Kal. But where's the path that Jenny would have made?

The surface of the lake is smooth as glass right now, but it was breezy when I took the dogs out last night. It's possible that Jenny's body drifted. Beaverhead Lake has hundreds of miles of shoreline. She could have gone in anywhere. I stand, closing the distance between me and Kal.

"Let's check which direction the wind's been blowing from over the last twenty-four hours."

"You think she went in somewhere else?"

"I think it's a possibility."

He nods, typing a note into his phone.

Keeping my voice low, so the couple can't hear, I ask. "What'd you tell the staties when you called it in?"

"That we had an unattended death, undetermined circumstances," he says.

Undetermined would cover both natural causes and suspicious ones, such as suicide and homicide. The question is, which are we dealing with here? Jenny Warner lost her son, was even, perhaps, the cause of his death, and now she turns up dead in the same body of water where PJ's body was left.

It paints a very obvious picture, one that speaks of guilt. One that would wrap up this investigation in a nice, tidy little package with no loose ends. Jenny wouldn't be the first mother to commit suicide after losing a child. But is that what really happened?

My gaze drifts to Jenny's body, wondering if she really had

something to do with her son's death. And suspecting that whatever the answer is, it's the reason she's in the condition that she's in now.

I finish taking a full statement from the unfortunate couple who made the grisly discovery, then leave Kal with Jenny's body to wait for the state police to respond to the scene. I need to make a phone call. Bringing up my contacts list, I stare at the name for a moment before pressing the button to dial.

I may have been wrong about Jenny Warner. It's not an easy thing for me to admit, even to myself. All the evidence was there, and still I ignored it, despite numerous people trying to convince me otherwise. My gut failed me. I shouldn't allow what happened in my past to keep me from properly doing my job. I need to speak with the one person who won't make excuses for me.

The ringing stops, replaced by Dr. Ricky's familiar voice. "I was just about to call you."

"You were?" I ask, surprised.

"Uh-huh. We got the results of the water diatom analysis back. That's why you're calling, right?"

"Actually, it's not."

"This isn't a social call, is it?" she asks warily, and I find myself wondering what has her more concerned: the prospect that it could be or that it probably isn't.

"No."

Dr. Ricky sighs deeply into the phone, though with relief or disappointment I couldn't say. "I see. Well, which of us gets to go first?"

"Why don't you."

"Okay. Well, the water in the boy's lungs matches the sample you took from the faucet at his family's residence."

Maybe it should feel like a victory, but it doesn't, because it means that what happened to PJ was most likely done to him by someone he was supposed to be able to trust. A lump fills my throat as I think about what the poor child went through, what he must have felt. Even if it was an accident, he must have been terrified. Although, if that were the case, why did someone go to such lengths to hide what happened?

After a moment of silence, Dr. Ricky clears her throat. "You okay?"

"Yeah, I'm fine. Why wouldn't I be?"

"I don't know, I just thought maybe... never mind. Why were you calling?" she asks.

Was Dr. Ricky going to point out the errors I've made? Was she going to suggest that I've allowed this case to be personal? I shake my head, trying to clear my thoughts and find my focus. "We recovered another body. From the same lake."

"Are you serious?"

"Unfortunately, yes."

"Does it appear as if it's another drowning?"

"I don't know. Possibly."

She sounds frustrated as she asks, "Why do I get the feeling that there's more to this story?"

"The body belongs to the boy's mother."

I hold the phone away from my ear until the barrage of cursing is done.

"Are you thinking suicide? Does that mean she's the one who killed him?" she asks.

"That's why I'm calling," I say softly. "I know that I should, but I just—" I take a deep breath before releasing my confession. "I just can't believe that Jenny Warner killed her son. And I'm worried that I'm allowing... a personal experience to influence me on this case. I need a reality check. Is there anything we might have missed? Anything at all about PJ that was out of the norm that might clue us in to what happened?"

"There was nothing. I'm sorry."

"If she took her own life..."

A long moment of silence lingers between us as I think of

the young mother in mourning who'd been found floating at the edge of the same lake where her son's body had been discovered. Had Jenny wanted to join him? Had her intention been to disappear?

If so, was she punishing herself or simply putting an end to her sorrow? It hurts my heart to think of the pain she must have been in.

Clearing my throat, I say what I've been avoiding. "If Jenny Warner was responsible for her son's death, we might never be able to prove it without a confession. And since that's no longer possible, this case might never be closed conclusively."

"Does this mean you want me to file my report, then? Alert the state police to the suspicious element, that the boy drowned somewhere other than where he was found?"

"I don't think we have a choice."

It's never easy to admit defeat, but I don't want Dr. Ricky to get in trouble for delaying her findings, and if I can't resolve this investigation, then we have no choice but to proceed. Yet, even though we both know it's for the best, there's no denying that we're both decidedly somber as we end the call.

As I pocket my phone, I find myself looking around, searching the nearby shadows. This loss feels personal, and I can't help but wonder—if I was so far off base in my assessment of Jenny Warner, what else have I missed? A shiver runs down my spine. I tell myself that it's the cold.

53

MAGGIE

I keep my gaze averted away from Jenny Warner's body as I rejoin Kal along the bank of the lake. The sky overhead mirrors its surface, dull and steely. It feels like the temperature has dropped. Everything is silent and still. If I had to guess, we're in for some late-season snow.

That's the last thing we need. I feel like I'd sell my soul for a little bit of sunshine. For spring to finally arrive. To not be surrounded by an environment that's the epitome of the way I feel inside, gloomy and hopeless.

A heavy sigh escapes from deep within me, drawing an odd look from my lieutenant. His mouth opens, then shuts. It's obvious there's something he wants to say. I can only imagine what it is.

"What?"

"Nothing."

"No, seriously. What?"

Kal presses his lips together and gives me a tight smile. "I just wanted to say that I'm sorry."

"I don't see how it's your fault."

"I should have handled this on my own."

"Are you suggesting that I'm not capable of doing my job on this case?" I've been accusing myself of that exact thing, but the fact that my lieutenant has been wondering the same, well, it hurts.

"What? No! I'd never—"

"Then what?"

"It's just, you never take any time off for yourself. And I know your wedding's getting closer. You should be getting your dress right now, not standing out here with me waiting for the staties. I ought to have handled this myself so you could go shopping."

The urge to laugh battles my overwhelming desire to cry. "Is that what you're worried about? That I had to cancel a shopping trip?"

He shrugs, looking embarrassed. "It's not like there's anything we can do for her."

"We can investigate. Ask questions. Find out what happened to her and not make assumptions."

"Well, yeah, that goes without saying. But whether we started now, or this afternoon..."

"You did the right thing. I'm glad I got the chance to see the scene before the state police stomped all over it."

Kal's voice sounds distant as he asks, "What do you think happened? Really?"

I keep my back to him, unable to meet his eyes as I say, "The diatom analysis of the samples we submitted concluded that PJ Warner drowned in water that came from his own home."

A full minute of silence passes before he responds. "Does that mean we're clearing Dennis Greenley?"

"Yeah, I think it does."

"What about the Warners' drug connections?"

Turning to face him, I say, "Honestly? I think it's highly

unlikely that if someone snuck into the Warner house to kill their child, for whatever reason, that they'd stick around long enough to drown the boy there instead of doing it elsewhere if they planned to take the body with them."

"You're right," he says, squinting in the direction of Jenny's body. "But that still doesn't leave Jenny as our only suspect. Anyone with access to that home could have done it."

I nod, grateful that he's said it. It would be so easy to jump to conclusions, but all we know for sure is that something happened in that house, behind closed doors, and whatever it was, two people are dead now because of it. And chances are good that one of their remaining family members was responsible. I stare out over the lake, wondering what secrets it has to tell.

Before I know it, the sun, though hidden by the clouds, is directly overhead, and a convoy of vehicles has pulled up at the curb above us. Doors slam and voices shatter the peaceful quietude. Kal jogs up the incline and returns leading a half dozen state police officers and the retrieval team from the medical examiner's office down the incline.

A young man breaks free from the pack, shaking my hand and introducing himself as the medicolegal death investigator who'll be assisting with the case. As I suspected, the state is treating this as it appears—as either a suicide or an accident, which means there'll be no detective to contend with.

"Is the identity of the decedent known?" he asks.

"It is," I say. "Her name is Jennifer Warner."

He nods, making a notation on the clipboard he carries. "Has the family been notified yet?"

"No."

"Would you like us to handle that?"

It's a generous offer. No one enjoys breaking someone's heart with the news that their loved one is dead. Only, in this case, I can't help wondering if there might be less heartbreak and more a sense of relief.

"Thank you, but I'll do it. I feel I owe it to the family."

Kal catches my eye as I turn to leave. We exchange a knowing look as he gives me a barely perceptible nod. Because my visit to the Warner household is not motivated by kindness, but by determination. This isn't over yet.

54

MAGGIE

Five years ago

Maggie finds a parking spot around the rear of the building where her Jeep can't be seen from the road, then backs in, sandwiching her license plate tight between her bumper and the brick exterior. Searching her back seat, she finds a baseball cap, which she tugs low. Keeping her head down, she walks into the building, relieved to pass Linda's ancient Honda on the way.

Spotting her friend immediately, she hurries toward the booth in the corner. Pinches the inside of her cheek between her teeth, biting down hard to keep herself from crying as Linda jumps up and wraps her in a tight embrace.

"Oh, Maggie. I'm so sorry."

Maggie nods, not daring to speak. Pulling away, she sits quickly with her back to the door. Avoids her friend's eyes as they study her.

"Here. Medicine," Linda says, pushing a drink in a Styrofoam cup into Maggie's hands.

Maggie obediently puts the straw between her lips and sips.

Knows that it's a triple-chocolate milkshake, though she can't taste a thing.

"So, what's the plan?" Linda asks.

Maggie shakes her head, staring at a sticky smear on the tabletop.

"Come on, I want to help. What can I do?"

Maggie's throat is too tight to speak, she's afraid that if she tries, only a squeak will come out.

"I can join the search crew, or hand out fliers, or help answer hotline calls. There has to be something."

Linda isn't a cop. She works closely with law enforcement, but as a forensic anthropologist, by the time she's assisting on a case, it's too late for the victim. Yet even she knows the things that are supposed to be happening right now.

"Maggie?" Linda dips her head low, tilting it until Maggie has no choice but to look at her. "Come on, talk to me."

"Brewster fired me."

"What?"

"They're convinced my parents had something to do with Brandon's disappearance."

"Has he lost his mind?"

Maggie gives Linda a grateful look, appreciative of her friend's outrage on her behalf.

"They're barely investigating. I found footage that proves my brother was alive less than twenty minutes before my mom reported him missing. Between the drive from the store they were at to the park and the time my mom placed the call, we're talking less than a five-minute window. You'd think between that and the video of a known child predator driving by the park during the time Brandon went missing, that would be enough..."

"But they still...?"

When Maggie nods, Linda curses.

"But it has to be this Todd guy, right?"

"I don't see who else it could be."

"*Then what are we waiting for?*" Linda slides to the end of her booth and stands in one fluid movement. "*I'll drive.*"

"*Linda.*"

Her friend pauses to look at her. There are so many things that Maggie wants to say: That it's dangerous. That it might be too late. That it's possible everyone else is right and she's wrong about this. But she can see in Linda's eyes that she already knows all that.

"*Thank you,*" she whispers.

55
MAGGIE

I stand on the front porch of the Warner residence, preparing to knock. I can't believe that I was here just twenty-four hours ago. It seems like so much longer. Such a short amount of time, yet so much has changed. The place even looks different somehow. Less lived-in. More neglected.

Drawing a deep breath, I knock on the door. I feel the approach of footsteps through the boards under my feet. Can sense the eye scrutinizing me through the peephole. Fighting the urge to fidget, I force myself to remain still, confident, patient as I wait.

Finally, with a creak, a gap appears before me. Franny stares out at me with a wary gaze. "What do you want?"

"Is your son home? I need to speak with him."

"He doesn't have anything left to say to you."

"That's fine. But I need to talk to him all the same."

With a tortured sigh, she opens the door wider. "Wipe your feet. I just got done cleaning."

I obediently scrape the bottom of my boots on the mat before stepping inside. The interior is darker than it's been on my previous visits. Quieter. It has the vacant feel of an empty house.

Nodding toward the couch, she says, "Take a seat."

On my other visits, she'd been more of a casual observer. Now that she believes her daughter-in-law has left, it appears Franny has taken charge.

"Greg?" Her voice fills the room, echoes off the yellowing walls. "Come on out here, will you? The chief is here to talk to you again."

She settles in the armchair across from me, taps a cigarette out of the pack sitting on the end table beside it, and lights up before jerking the recliner lever. The seat tilts back with a croak of gears.

"If the children are here—"

Franny interrupts, barking out a cloud of smoke. "They're with their momma. Why?"

Before I can reply, Greg shuffles from the hallway, yawning. He stares at me bleary eyed, hair standing on end. It appears as if I've interrupted a nap.

"What now?" he asks.

"Mr. Warner, can you take a seat for me, please?"

I pat the cushion beside me and nod encouragingly. He squints at me suspiciously as he takes the long way across the room, keeping his distance from me, before dropping heavily onto the opposite corner of the couch.

I wait until he's settled, then lean forward, closer to him. "Mr. Warner, I regret to inform you that we've found your wife."

He sneers, and mumbles, "Yeah, I regret ever finding her, too."

I clear my throat. Take a breath. And pin him with a look that could bore a hole through a redwood as I say, "Her body was discovered this morning in Beaverhead Lake. I'm afraid it was too late for any resuscitative efforts. She had already passed away."

The color drains from his face. A sheen of sweat springs from his pasty skin. "What'd you say?"

"She said that Jenny's dead, Greg." Franny speaks loudly from her place on the recliner, as if Greg's problem is a hearing issue.

He stares at me wide eyed and slack jawed, but is he waiting for confirmation or something else? Like for me to tell him he's under arrest?

"I'm afraid it's true. I'm sorry for your loss."

He rubs a hand over his face. "So she did it. She killed PJ and then she offed herself."

"I'm afraid I can neither confirm nor deny that statement," I say.

"But that has to be it, right? It's the only explanation that makes sense."

It's not, but I don't share my thoughts. Or my suspicions. Despite his seemingly genuine reaction, I can't forget that this man is a suspect. But for one death, or two?

"Grief can affect people in funny ways, Mr. Warner."

He snorts. "Don't give me that BS."

"Sir—"

He jumps to his feet, hands balled into fists at his sides. "No. Whatever it is, I don't want to hear it, so don't waste your breath."

Franny leans forward, her recliner locking back upright with a bang. "It's fine, Greg. Calm down."

But he doesn't calm down. Instead, he rounds the couch, storming from the room.

"Before you go? Just one more thing, Mr. Warner."

He stops mid-retreat at the entrance to the hallway. His expression contorts into one of pure hatred as he spins to face me, snarling, "What?"

"The medical examiner has completed her report. Your son didn't die in Beaverhead Lake. The water in PJ's lungs matched that from a sample I overnighted her yesterday. One that I took from your kitchen faucet. Your son drowned here, in your house."

Greg slumps like a puppet with its strings cut. I can hear the air whoosh from his lungs. His mouth hangs open, eyes blinking rapidly as he stares at me. But does his shock stem from the fact that someone took his son's life while he was asleep in the next room? Or because I'm that much closer to discovering his own guilt?

Franny points at me. "It's time for you to leave."

Standing, I allow her to escort me from the house. Closing the door behind her, she glances over her shoulder before hissing, "This is over now, do you hear me? My son's been through enough without you making him rehash his child's death every five minutes."

"And I'm sorry for that, Franny, I truly am. But I'm just doing my job. Now, if you'll excuse me, I have to go break the news to Belinda James that she's now lost her grandson and her daughter to suspicious circumstances."

Franny reels back away from me like I gave her a shove. I see something flash in her eyes in the seconds before she turns away, as she gropes behind her back for the door handle. Was it sympathy? Could the woman have developed an ounce of empathy for another mother's loss?

Or was it something else? Something more basic and primal? Something like fear? Does Franny suspect her son is capable of murder?

56

MAGGIE

Belinda James takes one look at me standing on her doorstep and knows why I'm there. A noise starts deep in her chest, an inhuman sound that builds as it rises until it parts her lips in a mournful wail. She slumps against the wall as her legs give out, knocking a mirror from its hook, sending it crashing to the floor. It shatters into sharp, shiny pieces, as irreparably broken as the woman who wrecked it.

"Mrs. James." I rush forward, grabbing her under the elbow, looping my other arm behind her back to keep her from falling on the broken glass. "I'm so, so sorry." My voice chokes in my throat as I half drag her to the living room. Trish Sims stands frozen in place by the kitchen breezeway, gawking as I rush Jenny's mother past her and onto the couch.

"How?" It's part gasp, part sob as the grieving woman struggles for breath.

"She was found this morning in the lake."

Her hands clutch at her face as she repeats the word *no* over and over. Is it denial? Disbelief? Or—

"She wouldn't have done that!" The way she screams the

words makes the hair on my arms rise, the skin on the back of my neck prickle.

"I'm sorry, ma'am."

"No. It's not true. It can't be."

"Mrs. James." Trish gives me a withering look as she rushes to the grieving mother's side. "She must have had an accident, that's all." Her eyes dare me to challenge what she's said. "But... maybe it's for the best. PJ was her whole world. And Greg was moving on."

A hard knot forms in my stomach. The sensation makes me stand up straighter and take notice. Because I can't help thinking that it's an odd comment to make.

Greg had said that Jenny had left him. And when I spoke to Trish before, she'd led me to believe that Jenny hadn't made a decision about the fate of her marriage the last time they had talked. She also maintained that she hadn't seen Jenny, had no idea where she was or where she'd go. So how had she found out Jenny and Greg had separated?

"Did you speak with her?" I ask Trish.

"What? No. Not since the other night."

"How'd you hear that she and Greg had split?"

She gapes at me a moment. I can practically see the gears turning in her head as she struggles to formulate a lie. Which means she can't tell me the truth.

"I... I didn't. I just assumed. I mean, it seemed pretty obvious it was going to happen."

"From your conversation the other night?" I ask.

"Yes, that's right."

"You told me that Jenny was unhappy with the relationship."

"She was."

"But just now, you said that Greg was the one who was moving on."

I can see the instant when she realizes her mistake. But she doesn't seem embarrassed or ashamed. And she doesn't seem sad that her so-called friend is dead. Now that I think about it, she hadn't seemed too surprised, either.

I recall what Olivia had told me, about how Trish always seemed in competition with Jenny. Is that why she had invited Jenny out for drinks? Why she had told her about Greg? Did she want him for herself? Or did she already have him?

"How well do you know Greg Warner?" I ask her.

She sputters, trying to decide on an answer.

"What are you doing here?" I add. Because now that I think about it, it seems awfully suspicious, Trish visiting Jenny's mother while Jenny's body was being fished from the lake.

"I... I was worried about Jenny after you came to talk to me yesterday. I thought I'd stop by and see if her mom had heard from her yet. Is there something wrong with that?"

We stare at each other. The exchange is silent, but plenty is said.

Belinda lifts her head, her teary gaze bouncing back and forth between us. "I don't understand. What's going on?"

I force a sad smile as I settle beside her on the couch and take her hand in mine. "Nothing for you to worry about, Mrs. James. Is there someone I can call to come stay with you?"

"My sister. She should know. She, oh, she'll be heartbroken. She loved Jenny like her own. I can't believe I let this happen."

I give her hand a squeeze, briefly debating telling her this isn't her fault. It's mine. I let this happen. But it's a confession I can't quite bring myself to make.

Instead, I accept her phone and make the call. Explain the situation. Promise to stay with her while her sister makes the drive over from the nearby town of Lincoln. The entire time, I don't take my eyes off Trish. Even more telling, she doesn't take hers off of me.

I can see it all too clear, the picture as sharp as a photograph taken on a bright sunny day. A young woman. A married man.

A vendetta, even if just an imaginary one. What better way to settle an old score than to take what isn't yours?

But how far would the woman before me have taken it?

Far enough to sleep with the married man? Yes. Far enough to have invited her old acquaintance out for a drink just to spill the news that her husband was unfaithful? Certainly. But would she have killed a child? Of that, I'm not so sure. Yet I can't deny that the motive is there.

I put myself in Trish's shoes. If she had decided that she was in love with Greg, that she wanted him to herself, full time, what was standing in her way? Obviously not Greg's moral compass. But perhaps the small child that had caused him to marry Jenny in the first place.

Had she decided to remove the child from the equation? Had that been her plan all along?

She got Jenny drunk that night. Too drunk, by Jenny's own admission. Purposely drunk, according to their friend Olivia.

Had that been so she could follow Jenny home? Had she waited in the dark for her chance? Slipped into the house under the cloak of night, lifted the young boy from the bed, drowned him in his very own tub? Had she then secreted his body away, slipping it through a hole in the ice to further Jenny's torment? Or to cast suspicion on her?

I have to play this carefully. As much as I want to interrogate Trish Sims, she has her guard up now. She's not likely to let anything incriminating slip.

"Let me go make you a cup of tea," I offer, squeezing Belinda's hand. If she hears me, she doesn't acknowledge it. And I doubt she'll drink it even if I do. Still, I stand, vowing silently that I'll get this mother some answers as I retreat to the kitchen.

I understand firsthand what not knowing can do to a person, a parent especially. I recently had the chance to see with my own eyes how my mother had become a shell of her former self, her sole mission in life to uncover the truth about what happened to my baby brother. And though I tried to help, to share what I discovered, I think maybe now, for the first time, I can grasp why she never listened.

This case has made me see in a new light what happened when Brandon went missing. My mom was the one who brought him to the park that day. My mom was the one who took her eyes off him. My mom blames herself.

I never realized that before. Not until I listened to the guilt in Jenny's voice as she explained the details about the night her son went missing, how she hadn't been there when he'd needed her. And the way everyone is all too ready to believe that she killed herself, even if she wasn't behind the child's death, because it was her job as his mother to keep him safe, and she'd failed. The same way Belinda James blamed herself for her daughter's death just moments ago.

Maybe by some twisted train of thought my mom believes that the only way to forgive herself is to be the one to find the answers about what happened. And to think, I've spent all these years thinking I was the only one playing that game.

The kettle sings, letting me know it's come to a boil. I turn the burner off, opening cabinets until I find the coffee mugs and an ancient-looking box of chamomile tea. I pour the water, then remove my phone from my pocket, typing out a message.

I'm not going to let this rest. If Jenny's innocent, I have to clear her name.

My cell buzzes with an incoming text. I glance at the reply, then tuck the device away. Grabbing the mug of tea, I carry it back into the living room.

Trish knows I suspect her. She'll watch what she says from now on.

But with an ounce of luck, once I'm out of sight, I'll also be out of mind. When she leaves here, I have no idea where she'll go. But Kal will be waiting for her. He'll follow along behind her. And hopefully, she'll lead us straight to the truth.

For the first time since PJ went missing, I finally have the feeling that we're on the scent of a trail. I check my phone anxiously, even though I know it's too early for an update from Kal about Trish. Is she the one we're looking for? The one who put this whole chain of events in motion? It's possible.

But she's not the only one with an axe to grind against Jenny. In fact, it seems like most of the people in Jenny's life harbored ill will toward her. Some of them have just been more transparent about it than others.

Then there's the thing that's been bothering me this whole time, something that hasn't made sense, and that's the locked door Jenny encountered when she came home from the bar the night PJ went missing. Had someone done it intentionally? Was it related to what happened to PJ or just a coincidence? I need to find out who locked that door and what their connection is to my case.

I stand on the front porch, waiting. It sounds like there's a war going on inside. Shouting. A dog barking. An explosion and a scream, both of which I hope come from a blaring TV. I'm a little surprised when the door opens, shocked that anyone could hear my knock over the chaos within.

Loraine Garner stands on the threshold facing the other direction, yelling over her shoulder. She turns forward, the exasperation on her face turning to annoyance when she sees me standing there. "Listen, I feel really bad for Greg and Jenny, I do, but I don't have time to be dragged into whatever drama they've got going on right now. I have my hands full enough as it is."

There's a loud crash, followed by cries of "Mom!"

"I've got to go." She starts shutting the door. I step forward, preventing her from closing it completely.

"I'm really sorry, Loraine, but I need to speak with you. You and your kids."

"We've got nothing to say to you. The kids won't even be going over there anymore for a while. Not until things die down."

She pushes the door against my foot.

"I'm afraid I'm going to have to insist."

The look on her face is pure outrage. Before she says something we both might regret, I hurry to add, "Jenny Warner is dead."

"Jenny... what?"

"She was found this morning by a couple of tourists. Floating in Beaverhead Lake."

Loraine gives me a hard stare for a long minute, like she's trying to gauge whether I might be lying. Finally, she takes a step back. "Come on, then. Let's get this over with."

Her shoulders are rigid, high beneath her ears as I follow her inside. She snatches a backpack from the floor, kicks a lone shoe to the side as she marches into the living room.

Jamie, the youngest, immediately runs to her side and starts pulling on her arm, pointing at his brother as he tattles about some transgression. Dylan rolls his eyes, a smirk perched cockily on his face.

"Where's your sister?" she asks, ignoring them both. Grabbing the remote, she mutes the TV. "Amanda? Can you come down here?"

"Hey, I was watching that," Dylan complains.

"Enough." She jerks her head toward me. "We have company." Freeing herself from her youngest's grasp, the ten-year-old already taller than her, his weight pulling her down in a way that looks exhausting, she says, "Go sit. Amanda!"

"Take a chill pill." Amanda shuffles into the room, a pair of earbuds dangling from a cord around her neck. Her eyes widen when they spot me. "What's going on?"

"Sit." Once the girl has taken a seat, Loraine gestures to me. "Go ahead. Tell them."

Three spooked gazes follow me as I step farther into the room. I take a breath, organize my thoughts, and say, "I regret to inform you that your stepmother was found dead this morning."

"Jenny?" Amanda asks. "Jenny's dead?"

"Yes."

The girl pales before my eyes. She speaks with a trembling voice from around the thumbnail pinned between her teeth. "How?"

"We're not sure yet."

She watches me closely as she asks, "Is Dad all right?"

"He's understandably upset, but other than that, he appears fine. But there are some questions I was hoping to ask you."

Amanda shoots a worried look at her brothers, who stare at me open-mouthed. "We don't know anything."

"There may be something you're aware of that you don't realize is helpful. I'd like to ask again about the night Jenny went out with her friends. The night PJ went missing. Are you sure that none of you heard anything that night?"

Three heads nod an affirmative.

"What about that morning? Is there a chance that one of you noticed something odd, anything out of place that might suggest that someone else had come into the house that night?"

Dylan frowns. "I'm not a cop, but it seems like that would be an easy enough mystery to solve."

"And how's that?" I ask.

"Well, were the doors still locked in the morning?" he asks, the entire sentence spoken with the inflection of *duh*.

Amanda cuts her eyes toward him sharply. I make a note to follow up with her. But first, "I was told that it wasn't customary that the doors were kept locked at your dad's house."

Dylan snorts. "Everyone locks their doors at night."

"You'd think," I say. "But I was told that isn't the case over there. In fact, Jenny had mentioned how strange it was that when she came home that night, she found the front door locked. She thought your grandmother had done it on purpose, but your grandmother denies knowing anything about how the door got locked."

I give the kids a sympathetic look. "Jenny's mom told me that you guys weren't her biggest fans. And I get that, I really do. But if one of you locked her out, whether purposely or accidentally, I need to know."

Both Amanda and Jamie glance at their brother. The one who supposedly wasn't there the night PJ disappeared. I take a step closer to the teenager. Stare down the bridge of my slightly crooked nose at him.

"I need you to think carefully about what I'm about to ask you, Dylan. And before you answer, I'd like to inform you that lying to a police officer during an investigation is a Class D crime. You had previously told me that you spent the night in question at a friend's house. Did you at any time go to your father's house that night?"

Loraine's gaze flits between me and her son. I can feel the concern radiating off her.

Dylan shrugs. "I mean, maybe. But why shouldn't I?" His mother releases a strangled gasp beside me. He gives her an annoyed look. "What? Larry was being a dick, so I decided to go crash at Dad's. What's the big deal?"

"The big deal is that you lied about where you were." His mother sighs.

He crosses his arms. "Seriously? Yeah, I was there. That doesn't mean I grabbed the kid out of his bed and what? Drowned him in the tub?"

"PJ's body was found in Beaverhead Lake," I say, staring hard into the boy's eyes. "What would make you suggest that he was drowned elsewhere?"

Maybe it's the way my body tenses, like a predator tracking its prey. Maybe it's mother's intuition. Whatever it is, Loraine hurries forward, moving her tiny body between me and her son.

"That's it. This talk is over." I open my mouth to respond, but she shuts me down. "You won't be getting another word out of any of us. If you have a problem with that, you can talk to my lawyer. Do you hear me?" she asks her children, pointing to them one by one. "Not a single syllable. Not a peep."

Turning toward me, she says, "You can see yourself out."

As I head for the door, I realize that I never got the chance to ask them if they knew Trish Sims. But I'm not so sure it matters now. It isn't so much that Dylan Warner purposely lied about being in the house the night his half-brother drowned that has my adrenaline pumping. It's that he somehow knew that was where the little boy had died.

58
MAGGIE

I'm exhausted. My bones ache with a weariness I can't shake off. One that comes from a case involving a dead child. One made worse by another child becoming my lead suspect. One exasperated by the knowledge that my fiancé is hiding something important, and I have no choice but to go home and pretend nothing's wrong while I make nice with his family.

But how can I when my brain feels like it's ready to explode?

I need to speak to someone, try to offload some of my angst and confusion before I can look Steve's family, or even Steve, in the eye. Because I just have so many doubts right now.

I select Linda's name from my contacts list, push dial, and put the call on speakerphone. The sound of ring after ring fills my car. Mocking me. Tears burn my eyes, threatening to spill as her voicemail picks up. I blink them away, ashamed of myself. I'm being a baby.

The beep sounds and I force a brightness I don't feel into my voice. "Hey, it's Maggie."

That's all I've got. At least, all I can offer with fake cheer. Sighing, I confess, "I'm having a really hard time here. I'm working a case involving a little boy, and I just, I mean, he looked so much like Brandon. Same age, same hair color... And it's just, it's stirring up so much that I need to keep buried."

I imagine what she'd say to me if she was on the line right now. What she'd tell me to do.

"And I can't talk to Steve about it. Something strange is going on with him. At first I thought it was because his family's here, staying with us. I mean, that's enough to make anyone act weird, right?"

I laugh nervously. My voice trembles as I continue.

"But it's more than that. He's hiding something, and judging from the way he's acting, it's serious. And I'm worried that whatever it is, it'll mean the end. And then I do the me thing and tell myself that of course it's the end and I was an idiot for even thinking for a second that I could be normal or happy or even just loved and—"

The mailbox cuts me off with a shrill beep. I feel like I've been running a race. My heart is beating too fast, and I can't catch my breath. I tighten my hands on the steering wheel until my knuckles hurt, use the pain to center myself. I can't leave it like this.

I hit redial and wait for her voicemail to pick up again. "Sorry for filling up your message box like this. I'm fine. Really. Just blowing everything out of proportion, expecting the worst and imagining dragons. You know me. But still... when you get this, call me, okay? I miss you."

As I hang up, I find that I'm feeling even lower than I did before. I wish I had someone else who I could call. But I don't. Not friends, not family... and though I've always been okay with that before, I now realize that needs to change. Steve can't be my only sounding board anymore.

We've become too dependent on each other. It's not like he has his own circle of friends—he's just as lacking on that front as I am—but he has his family. I need a tribe of my own, and as soon as this case is over, I'm going to find one. The decision makes me feel calmer. More focused and centered, like I can play at being human again, which is a good thing, because I'm almost home.

I think of puppy kisses and food, because once again I've failed to feed myself during the day. It's no wonder I'm having a meltdown. I turn into the driveway, thinking about dinner, hoping that whatever it is, it contains a great deal of melted cheese, when I have to stop short to avoid hitting an unexpected car parked in front of me.

Turning the engine off, I study the silhouette visible through the back window of the vehicle. Swallow down a pill of unease because we don't get many unexpected visitors out here. I unsnap the latch securing the firearm in the holster strapped to my hip before exiting my Jeep. A man gets out at the same time I do, smiling and giving me a friendly wave.

"May I help you?" I ask, mustering an authority I'm too tired and hungry to actually feel.

"You must be Maggie."

I don't like it when people I don't know presume to know me. I give him a once-over, looking for hints as to who he is and why he's here, but there are none. Not the clipboard of a census taker, the pamphlet of a door knocker, the black tie and slacks of a Mormon missionary, nothing.

"And you are?" I ask bluntly.

He chuckles. "I'm Wesley. Wesley Banks. Steve's best man for your wedding."

My voice gets lost on the way to my mouth, but it doesn't really matter because I have no words. Steve hasn't mentioned this man to me, not once. I can't recall ever hearing his name before.

"Are you surprised?" he asks. "Steve really wanted to keep me a surprise."

"Yeah, you could say that."

But Steve is not a surprise kind of guy, and even if he were, he knows that I'm not a surprise kind of girl. You don't try to shock a woman who wears a gun.

The hunger pains in my stomach are replaced by a hard knot of anxiety as I realize that the man is lying. But why? More importantly, to what end? Something tells me that this man is not Steve's friend.

59
STEVE

Tempest's head jerks up. Sullivan jumps off the couch and races for the front door, his companion right on his heels. I know immediately what it means. I hop to my feet and hurry after them.

Rounding the corner, I smile to myself as Maggie's voice fills the hall. Feel myself hesitate as I realize that it's not the dogs that she's talking to. Nerves seize my muscles, making them twitch. My feet seem rooted to the floor. I force myself forward like I'm moving through quicksand, each step a Herculean effort.

She probably just ran into Grandpa Joe. Or maybe she brought Kal home for dinner. But despite what I tell myself, somehow, I know exactly what I'm going to see when I reach the foyer.

"Oh, hey," Maggie says, looking up from where she's crouched on the floor with the dogs. "Look who I found."

Wesley smirks over her shoulder. "Hey, Steve-o." He holds my eyes as he squats close beside her and reaches out to pet Sully. "Hey there, little buddy."

Sully takes a step back, his fur bristling, teeth showing as he growls. Maggie grabs him, gathers both dogs to her quickly, guarding them from Wesley's touch.

"Sorry, they don't like strangers much. It takes them a while to warm up," she says as she scoops them up. "I'll just put them in the bedroom."

She doesn't look at me as she passes by, and it's not just because she's focused on juggling fifty pounds of terrier. She just flat out, bald-faced lied to Wesley. Both dogs love everyone, new friends and old. I've never heard either of them growl at a person before.

But then again, they have good instincts. And so does Maggie. I wait until her steps fade, then round on Wesley.

"What the hell do you think you're doing?" I hiss, stepping sideways to block the hall with my body.

"Chill. I'm sure it won't cause too much of a hardship to have one more for dinner."

"What? No. I want you out of my house."

"And I want to make sure you stay motivated."

I glance over my shoulder, swallowing hard. "I will. I am. But you have to go."

"And disappoint Maggie? I wouldn't dream of it."

"We had a deal."

Wesley shrugs. "As long as you keep your end of it, I'll keep mine."

"You promised you'd leave them alone."

"I will."

"Then what do you call this?

"Insurance," he answers, his voice a low snarl as his hand curls painfully tight around my arm. "Now, be smart and play nice. We wouldn't want anyone to get confused and think that something was wrong, now, would we?"

As Maggie reappears at the end of the hall, I don't dare tell him it's already too late for that. Because although her smile appears genuine and her tone of voice is friendly, there's one very obvious clue that Maggie knows something is amiss. And that's even though we're about to settle down to a family dinner, she's still wearing her gun.

She hurries to the table and takes a seat before anyone else can notice. Not that, with our guest, anyone would.

My mother looks up at our arrival, the serving spoon dropping from her hand and clattering to the table, mashed potatoes spattering the tablecloth as her gaze lands on Wesley. She gives a hard blink, as if not believing her eyes, a hand rising to her collarbone.

"Mrs. W. Long time no see."

She gives a stiff nod. "Wesley. How nice to see you. Have you been doing well?"

"Good enough, I suppose."

"And your mother?"

I can't help noticing the intensity with which Maggie is watching the interaction. The way she studies my mother's face, focus shifting to Wesley as he replies, "A bit lonely, I'm afraid. She would have loved to be here to join us."

Mother gives a tight smile, obviously uncomfortable.

"Is Grandpa Joe with his friend?" I ask, trying to change the subject.

"Where else?" Izzy asks, emerging from the kitchen with a plated roast in hand.

"Hey, Iz." Wesley doesn't even try to conceal his leer as he eyes my sister up and down. "Looking good."

Her head cocks to the side. "Wesley Banks? Is that you?"

"In the flesh."

"What rock have you been hiding under? I haven't seen you in forever."

"Oh, I've been here and there. Keeping busy. But when I heard my best bud was getting married, of course I had to drop everything to come meet the bride."

The smile frozen on Maggie's face grows a little more strained.

"How long are you staying?" Izzy asks.

Wesley turns to look at me. What I see in his eyes sends an electric shock down my spine, sweat beading to the surface of my skin.

"That remains to be seen," he says, grinning at me. I've never noticed before how sharp and dangerous his incisors look, more fangs than teeth. "Turns out that there's a lot more around here to occupy my time with than I had initially thought. Might have to stick around for a bit longer to play. What do you think about that, Steve-o?"

I struggle to find my voice, but it fails me. I need to find a way to end this fast, before it's too late. But as I sit, trapped by my traitorous body, unable to take action, I realize that it already is. The clock's run out.

The sound of their conversation fades into the distance. I strain to catch the words, but can't hear them above the buzzing in my ears as my heart pounds spastically against the walls of my chest. I've missed my chance. And I'm the only one who knows what a deadly mistake I've made.

By all rights, Wesley Banks should be a likable guest. He's polite. Charming. Intelligent. Attentive. But here's the thing about being a cop that ruins you for normal company—the same could be said about a number of serial killers, too. Ted Bundy, Charles Manson, and Paul John Knowles were all known for their charisma.

There's no denying that Wesley has plenty of that. But there's something about him that makes me uncomfortable. His rapt attention, his probing questions, it's more than just a casual getting-to-know-you conversation. It's like he's trying to burrow inside your head, searching for a weakness, a crack he can use to break you.

And there's something intense about his gaze, something *hungry* in his eyes. It makes me feel like he's imagining me without my clothes on. Or worse, without my skin.

According to what's been said so far, Steve and Wesley were inseparable growing up. But it's obvious that Steve is not happy to see him. In fact, it doesn't seem like anyone here is too thrilled to see Steve's old friend.

Are they, though? Still friends, I mean. I can't recall Steve ever mentioning his name before. Which means they went from being joined at the hip to, what? Strangers?

Enemies, a little voice in my head whispers.

Something must have happened between them. Whatever it was, it must have been bad. And Steve's been acting so odd lately. Now I can't help wondering if it has something to do with the man before me. Did he know Wesley was in town?

Behind a closed door down the hall, I hear the dogs fussing, making low moans and growls. Beside me, Steve grinds his teeth. The sound of it makes me cringe, and instinctively I turn to him, wanting to tell him to relax, but I'm too shocked by what I see to speak.

He sits in his chair like a vulture, hunched and rigid, his jaw clenched tight and jutted slightly forward. A vein I've never noticed before is visible on his forehead. His hands are clenched into fists. He tenses, looking like he's getting ready to spring up and jump across the table. I track his gaze to Wesley, now leaning closer to Izzy, who looks like she'd rather be anywhere but here.

"You know, Iz, you were such a pretty little girl. And I know you always had a bit of a crush on me when we were growing up. If you hadn't been my man Steve's little sister... But now, I mean, look at you. Wow. If I'd known you were going to grow up into all this, I wouldn't have let that stop me. I'd have locked you down back when you were still a kid."

She laughs nervously. "Well, a lot of time's passed."

"So, what, then?" His voice sounds strangely aggressive, challenging, almost, as he says, "You saying I missed my chance?"

Diane makes a noise and shifts in her seat. She seems stiffer and more uptight than usual as she stares at Wesley like he's some kind of fungus that she's trying to identify. Not that I can blame her.

"And Mrs. W," he says, turning his attention to her. "Let me just say, you've aged like a fine wine." He picks up his glass, staring at her while he sips his merlot, not stopping until the cup is empty. He licks his lips and moans. "Mmm. Guess I'm thirsty."

Diane looks away, her face flushed a deep shade of red. I look at Steve, wondering why he'd ever be friends with someone like this.

"Yep. Steve-o is a lucky man to have himself such a gorgeous collection of women. Still, I thought I must have heard wrong when I first found out he was getting married. But Maggie."

I want to tell him that it's Police Chief Riley.

"Now that I've seen you, believe me, I get it."

I want to tell him to get out of the house, my town, this state.

"Men must be lining up to get handcuffed by you."

"I've been told it's not a pleasant experience," I say in my frostiest tone.

"Oh, I have a hard time believing that." His eyes drop to my chest as he says, "You know, you and I should get together."

There's no mistaking that the proposition is sexual. He reaches out and strokes the back of my hand. His fingertips feel coarse and intrusive. They make my skin crawl. I snatch my hand away, suspecting that I'll feel the touch for long after, like when a bug grabs at your skin with its prickly little legs.

The grin he gives me is predatory. He's feeding off my discomfort. Off all of our discomfort.

"Man, the things I'd like to say to you. What do you think, Steve-o?"

All eyes shift to my fiancé. I'm sure I'm not the only one wondering why he hasn't put a stop to this yet.

"Do you think I should tell Maggie here all your dirty little secrets?"

Steve flinches as if he's been struck, his skin blanching white. His eyes flash with panic. Suddenly, it's clear. This man is dangerous. He knows something about Steve, and whatever it is, Steve doesn't want me to find out.

That's why Wesley is here. Why Steve hasn't shown him the door. And why I can't, either. Because you have to know your enemy before you can defeat them. Whatever's going on, I have to wait for Steve to tell me before I can act. I can't risk making it worse.

61

MAGGIE

Unbuckling my utility belt, I drape it over my nightstand, careful to keep the act casual. To not draw attention to my break from routine. To not betray the fact that I feel the need to keep my firearm a little closer than usual.

"So. Wesley seems nice," I say, watching Steve in the mirror as I unbutton my shirt.

His body stiffens. His gaze meets my reflection, then quickly flits away. I swallow down the urge to scream, to yell, to do whatever it takes to make him disagree with me and tell me the truth about his old friend, why the man is here, and how long it will be until he's gone.

"It sounded like you two used to be pretty close once." When Steve doesn't reply, I add, "But I can't remember you ever mentioning him before. Is there a reason for that? Did something happen between the two of you?"

He shrugs. "People grow apart. You know how it is."

"So there was no specific reason why you two stopped talking?"

He ignores the question and busies himself with checking that the pockets of his jeans are empty, treating it like an important task. The act causes a surge of anger to heat my skin because it's not. What's important is that there's something he's keeping from me. Something he's so desperate to keep secret that he let us share a table with a predator to keep it quiet.

And I have no doubt that's exactly what Wesley is. From the moment I met the man, my senses have been on high alert, the primitive part of my brain whispering *danger*. Judging from the way the dogs reacted to him, I'm not mistaken. That man is not someone I want in our home, much less our lives.

I wish I were the type of woman who could just let it go, put the whole thing out of mind until it actually becomes a problem, but I'm not. I can't let this rest. I need to find out what Steve is hiding from me, and what Wesley has to do with it.

"Guess we'll probably be seeing a lot more of him from now on, huh? Maybe we should invite him to stay here at the house."

"No." Steve takes me by the shoulders and spins me to face him. Opens and shuts his mouth like he's struggling with the words he wants to say. Searching his expression, I see a great deal of sadness and regret mixed with the fear I find there. "Just, if you see Wesley, stay away."

"Why?" My tone is sharper than I intended, but I'm out of patience. "What aren't you telling me?"

"Nothing."

And this is it. The moment I draw my line in the sand. The reason I've never made it this far into a relationship before. Because as much as I love Steve, there's a broken part of me that won't let me trust him, at least not completely.

"Why is he really here?"

"Maggie."

"I know you're hiding something. You need to tell me what it is, Steve. Right now."

He tries to put his arms around me, to draw me into a hug, but I pull away. Sighing, he takes my hand and sits on the edge of the bed. Stares up at me with the mournful eyes of a dog who knows he's been bad.

"I love you. You know that, right?"

I give him a stony look.

"I would never, ever do anything to hurt you. But Wesley... You have to stay away from him. You can't listen to a word he says. If you see him coming, go the other way. Please. Promise me?"

"Why?"

"I... I can't tell you. Not yet. Just, please. Trust me."

I lift a shoulder and let it drop. I'm not sure I do trust him anymore. Because I fully intend to run a background check on his friend the first chance I get.

Tugging my hand free from his, I walk to the bathroom, shutting the door behind me. Squeeze my eyes shut against the sting of tears as I replay the conversation in my mind.

Steve said he'd never hurt me, but it's obvious he's concerned that something might. And he doesn't want me to listen to anything his old friend has to say. Is there some ugly truth about Steve that he's afraid will injure me? Or am I in actual physical danger?

62

MAGGIE

I wake feeling stiff and groggy, muscles aching from a restless night. Something's really wrong, even worse than I suspected. After seeing Steve's reaction to his old friend Wesley, and the evasive conversation we had last night, I'm not sure I can trust him anymore.

Because he's worried that whatever he's hiding might hurt me, and yet he still won't tell me what it is. Now my brain is running rampant with all the possibilities of what he's keeping secret.

Maybe he owes someone money. Or somehow got mixed up with the mob. Maybe he has a child somewhere that I don't know about. Or even an entire other life, a wife he's still married to. But wouldn't his family know about that? Maybe not. I mean, it's possible. Entire TV shows have been formed around such secrets.

I try to ignore the little whisper coming from the darkest corner of my mind that's telling me it's none of those things. That it's something even worse. Because the truth is, most of those secrets would have shown up when I performed a background search on Steve when we first started getting serious.

That's right. I did a deep dive into Steve's past, looking for reasons to reject him, and I'm not making any apologies about it.

You've got to be careful, protect yourself. I've seen too many women meet a violent end because they were too trusting. I've always told myself I wouldn't be one of them, but here I am, making excuses, being the dumb girl in a horror movie who goes to investigate a strange noise wearing nothing but a towel when my instincts are telling me to keep my clothes on, grab a weapon, and run.

Which is why I've got to get to the bottom of this. I can't let it rest. I have to find out what it is that Steve's hiding. But what if it turns out to be something trivial and I destroy our relationship with my lack of trust?

I've worked myself up into such a basket case of nerves that I jump when my phone starts buzzing. "Oh, thank God," I mutter, reaching for the cell and blindly stabbing at the screen to answer the call.

Linda returned my call last night, but I missed it because I was so wrapped up in the tension fizzling between Steve and Wesley, unwilling to take my eyes off their interaction for even a second until Wesley left. I tried calling her back when I took the dogs out before bed, but she must have already been asleep. The relief I feel is overwhelming, almost enough to make me burst into tears, because I need to talk to her now more than ever.

"Hey!"

"Hello."

"Dr. Ricky?"

"You sound disappointed. Is now a bad time?"

"No, sorry. Now's perfect." I draw a deep breath and switch from Maggie mode into Chief Riley gear. "What have you got for me?"

"I completed the postmortem on the latest decedent you sent me, the boy's mother."

I'm only half listening, still preoccupied by my own thoughts. Not wanting a fresh reminder of a tragedy that might have been avoided if only I hadn't been so distracted.

"Do you know if she had a prescription for Ambien?"

"That's a sleeping pill, isn't it?"

"It is."

"Not that I'm aware of, but I'll check. I'm assuming you found some in her system?" I ask. It wouldn't be abnormal. Occasionally, people who commit suicide utilize more than one method to make sure that their goal is achieved.

"I did. Enough to have knocked out a horse, given the amount left undigested. But despite that, it looks like she put up a good fight."

"Are you saying that she changed her mind?" I ask. It feels like my heart's being squeezed like a stress ball.

"No, I'm saying that there were signs of a struggle. Bruising would indicate that someone held her under the water until she drowned."

"Wait? What!"

"There was a contusion on the back of her skull, as well as multiple bruises along the back of her neck and shoulders. Is this a surprise?"

"Not entirely," I manage to choke out. A list of possible suspects stampedes through my head as I add, "But also yes. I guess a part of me believed that her grief may have driven her to take her own life."

"Well, I suppose that could still be a possibility, albeit a quite unlikely one," Dr. Ricky says. "Especially given that one of the bruises looks remarkably like a handprint."

"What size?" I ask.

"What do you mean?"

"Would the hand-shaped bruise be more likely to belong to a man, woman, or child?"

"I'm uncomfortable making that inference. I will say that

it's larger than my own, but not as large as Harold's, my new assistant."

Dr. Ricky is a petite woman, so it could be an older child, but just as likely a woman or smaller-sized man, which would rule Greg Warner out. But that doesn't mean he didn't help.

"I'll email you the pictures I took to document the injuries. The alternative light photographs are especially telling."

"Thank you."

"Also, you'll see it in my report, but based on the conditions recorded by the technician, the liver temperature taken at time of recovery, and the fact that rigor was dispersing, I'd place time of death a minimum of twenty-four hours before she was discovered."

Which means that it's quite likely that Jenny was already dead when her husband told me that she'd left him. I search my memory but can't recall whether he had said she had told him directly, or if he had just assumed. Or is it possible that what he gave me was a cover story because he knew she was another kind of gone?

"And oh, this time? The diatoms recovered from the lung tissue were a match to the profile of the lake water."

"So she was drowned where we found her."

"Or very nearabout."

But she didn't do it herself. Her death was murder, not suicide. My mind is reeling, the beginnings of a headache tightening my temples. I failed her. Not only have I not discovered the truth about what happened to her son yet, I also allowed the same fate to happen to her. I didn't protect her.

I feel like I should have known, should have somehow been able to foresee this happening. My stomach churns as I ask, "Is there anything else?"

"Yes. Given the circumstances, I had to file my report."

I know what she's telling me. This case has officially become property of the state police.

"Also, I released the boy's body yesterday. He and his personal effects should have arrived at the requested funeral home by now."

"Thank you."

"Chief Riley?"

"Yes?"

"You know you can talk to me, right? If you need someone to listen? I know I'm not the best sounding board there is out there, but I do consider us friends."

I'm stunned. I thought I'd been putting up a good front, but if Dr. Ricky, who isn't the most emotionally astute person, was able to detect that something was wrong just from speaking to me over the phone, then it must be pretty obvious how much I've let this case and my personal life upset me.

"Thank you," I say. "I appreciate it. And likewise. Friend."

She snorts a laugh. "Yes, well. If the two most socially awkward people on the planet don't have each other's backs, then who will?"

I chuckle as we exchange pleasantries and end the call, but something about what she said has gotten under my skin, where it pricks and stabs like a sandspur, feeding my insecurities. Because what if she's right? What if normal people will never understand us, are incapable of giving us what we need?

Maybe I should put an end to things before I get hurt. Stop wasting my time on a mystery that Steve obviously wants to keep secret. Maybe I should be preparing myself to walk away instead of down the aisle.

63

MAGGIE

I feel like everything is spiraling out of control. My personal life. My emotions. This case. I've lost my grip. I need to do something to get everything back in hand. Changing course, I steer away from the police department, unable to face Sue and Kal just yet. I need time to wrap my brain around this new information first.

I know that I can count on them, trust them, that they'll do their best to help me, but I don't deserve it. Where was I when Jenny Warner was fighting for her life? Or PJ? My brother, for that matter? There's no making this right. The only thing I can do now is try and bring Jenny and her son justice.

Turning into a parking lot, I pull into the space next to the only other car there. Hurry across the blacktop before I can think twice about this decision. A bell jingles on the door as I push through into the lobby.

My eyes immediately focus on the small white coffin tucked against the far wall as I wait, but no one comes. I find myself inexplicably drawn closer, my feet carrying me across the room as if they have a will of their own, because I don't want to look down inside that tiny box.

I don't want to imagine PJ—or any other child's head—resting on the pillow within. But at the same time, I can't help wondering what it would be like to have a chance to say good-bye. If it makes the wounds of loss ache any less.

Somewhere behind me a throat clears, and I realize that I'm no longer alone. I spin quickly, find Chris Hensley, the funeral home director, staring at me with a curious look. "Everything all right, Chief Riley?"

"Yeah, fine. Sorry. You've received PJ Warner's remains?"

"I have. Did you want to see them?" he asks, raising an eyebrow.

"No." I say the word too loud, too fast, but the very idea unsettles me. I'd be more than happy if I never had to see a life-less body again. Enough so that it makes me wish I had taken the time over the years to develop another talent besides law enforcement. As much as I love my job, there are days when I'd rather do anything else. Maybe I could learn to knit dog sweaters.

He laces his fingers, hands clasped in front of him while he waits for me to disclose why I'm here if it's not to view the body. Obviously he's not the type who feels the need to fill an uncomfortable silence. He'd probably make an excellent detective.

"I'm here to collect his personal effects," I say. "So I can return them to the family."

"I can give them to Mr. Warner when he comes in to make arrangements, save you a trip."

"No, I think I'd like to deliver them myself, if you don't mind."

He shrugs as if to say it doesn't matter to him either way. "Then I'll go get them for you. I'll just be a moment."

I step away from the tiny coffin while I wait, though I can feel it like a hot ember behind my back, burning with the injus-tice of the death of someone small enough to use it. I focus my attention on a pamphlet about final expense insurance, staring at the words until they blur before my eyes.

"Here you go." Chris returns from the back, a sealed plastic bag in his hand. I thank him as I take it, struck for the first time by how cold and impersonal it is to return a family member's items to their loved ones in the same type of container as you'd pack a sandwich. I'm not sure I can do it this time.

Returning to my car, I place the package on the passenger seat and start the engine. Debate whether to stop by the trading post to buy a different container, but what? A box? Tissue paper? Handing Greg his dead son's things to him wrapped like a present seems even worse.

I pull into the Warners' driveway and park. Stare at the parcel beside me. The oversized eyes of the cartoon dog wearing a police cap seem to stare back. Finally, I make a decision. Breaking the seal on the bag, I slip PJ's pajamas free and carry the neatly folded bundle up to the house.

The door opens almost immediately after I knock. Greg Warner stands in the gap looking ten years older than he had at the beginning of the week.

"What do you want?"

"I'm here to return these to you. They're what PJ was wearing when he was found. I thought that maybe you might want them back."

He looks down at the pajamas in my hands, his irritated expression slowly morphing to one of confusion. He takes a step back, staring at the outfit like it's a snake that might strike.

His voice breaks as he asks, "That's what he was wearing?"

"Yes."

He shakes his head as if to deny my answer. "That's impossible."

"These weren't the pajamas you put him in?" I ask, needing clarification, mind already racing with the possibilities of why someone might have changed the boy that night.

"I didn't put him in any pajamas at all. Didn't want to risk waking him. I knew Jenny would be pissed when she got home and saw. She made me swear to give him a bath before bed, so he'd sleep well, but she doesn't understand. Or didn't understand, I guess."

"Didn't understand what?"

"How much harder it is for a dad to get his children to behave. Women have it easy. Kids want to behave for them."

It sounds like a cheap excuse to me, and a pretty inaccurate one at that, but I keep my opinion to myself, because a picture's beginning to emerge.

"You didn't bathe PJ before bed that night?"

"I just said so, didn't I? Even though I knew Jenny would read me the riot act."

"And why's that?"

"The kid had sensitive skin. He'd get itchy and uncomfortable without one, would wake up fussing."

"Fussing for a bath?"

"Well, not exactly. Just fussing. He'd come wake Jenny up whenever it happened."

"Did PJ wake you up that night?" I ask.

"Don't know. I'm a pretty deep sleeper. There's no guarantee I would have woken even if he tried."

Thinking about the Ambien Dr. Ricky found in Jenny's bloodwork, I ask, "Do you ever use a prescription sleep aid?"

"No."

"What about Jenny?"

He shrugs. "If she did, I never saw her take it."

But she wouldn't have needed a prescription that night to make her difficult to rouse. By her own admission, she'd had enough alcohol to do that.

"Mr. Warner, is there anyone else who PJ might have gone to in the event that he tried and was unable to wake you?"

"It's possible."

"Who?"

His eyes narrow as he sees what I'm getting at. "Chances are he just waited for Jenny to get home. She was probably so drunk that she passed out while he was in the tub and this whole thing was all just a desperate coverup on her part 'cause she couldn't face what she had done."

It's a plausible scenario, one that's crossed my own mind a time or two. But there's one thing wrong with the theory. Jenny didn't kill herself. She was murdered. Was it in retaliation or because she had discovered who had really been responsible for PJ's death?

Studying Greg's expression closely, I ask, "Do you really believe that?"

"Doesn't really matter what I think, does it? It's not my job to try and figure out what happened. It's yours. Or have you forgotten?"

His words sink deep. I can't help biting back.

"Believe me, Mr. Warner, I haven't forgotten. But if you don't want to cooperate, I suppose I'll just have to go speak with your surviving children again. And Trish Sims. I suspect she might have some interesting things to say."

The blood seeps from his face, leaving him the color of oatmeal.

"Oh, and another thing? We've received the preliminary results of your wife's autopsy, not that you cared enough to ask. I thought it might interest you to know that we'll be pursuing her case as a homicide."

His mouth rounds in surprise and he grabs on to the doorframe, knuckles going white as he holds on to keep himself upright. It's not clear yet whether or not Greg Warner murdered his wife. But if he didn't, I think he suspects he knows who did.

64

MAGGIE

Sitting behind my desk, staring at the computer screen, I study the photographs of the bruising taken during Jenny Warner's autopsy, looking for answers. Whoever killed Jenny left us this clue. I just have to figure out how to use it to narrow down my suspect pool.

But I have to work fast. I'm running out of time. I'm sure the state police have a detective already on the way to Coyote Cove this very moment.

I wrap my own palm around the back of my neck, trying to match up the placement, but I can't get the correct angle. The thumb is on the left side, the smallest bruise, from the little finger, is the lowest mark on the right, indicating that the right hand was used.

"Sue?"

My secretary stretches her neck so she can see me from above her own computer.

"Can you come here for a moment, please? I need your help with something."

Joining me, she glances at my screen and quickly looks away. "What's up?"

"Grab me."

She arches an eyebrow, looking at me from over the top of her glasses.

"Put the thumb of your right hand here." I point to a spot directly in line with and several inches below my left ear, matching the mark left on Jenny's neck.

"Do I get to squeeze?" she jokes, wrapping her warm soft hand around the back of my neck.

Sue is petite. Her hands are small. Her fingertips fail to stretch far enough to match Jenny's bruising. This finding excludes Greg's youngest from his first marriage, Jamie, though I hadn't really considered him a suspect. But it also excludes his ex-wife, Loraine.

"No, you get to sit."

I stand and gesture for her to take the seat. She eyes me suspiciously but settles into the chair, muttering about a raise under her breath. I align my thumb and stretch my hand around Sue's nape. Hers is slightly smaller than Jenny's, yet my grip is almost an exact match.

Closing my eyes, I try to picture the people involved in this case. Trish Sims is about my size. So is Amanda Warner. And Dylan is only sixteen...

The phone on my desk rings, disturbing my thoughts. Sue leans forward, giving me side-eye, obviously relieved to escape guinea pig duty as she answers the call.

"It's Kal. He says to watch the video he just texted you."

Sue puts the phone on speaker as I pat my pockets, locate my cell, and thumb the screen to life. Opening the video file Kal sent, I press play.

"What's this I'm looking at?" I ask. Sue pulls on my wrist, lowering the screen so she can see, too. We watch as a woman exits a vehicle pulled along the side of a street, head swiveling around like she's checking to make sure she's alone. "Is that Trish Sims?"

"You told me to keep an eye on her," he says, a note of satisfaction in his voice.

The woman hurries forward, slipping into a side yard and creeping her way around back. The picture jostles as Kal follows. He ducks behind a shrub and zooms in as Trish continues on to the next property and knocks on the rear door of the abutting house.

The image is grainy, but you can still clearly see that it's Greg Warner who answers, and judging from his expression, he's absolutely livid. Angry hisses carry through to the recording like the whisper of grass in the wind. Trish gestures wildly with her hands, signaling how she parked down his street and crept through his neighbor's yard to make her approach, but it does little to appease the man before her.

He points, one foot stomping to accentuate the directive. But apparently, Trish Sims is not a woman who will leave before she's good and ready. Her eyes narrow as she crosses her arms over her chest. She leans forward at the waist. And if I had one wish, it would be to hear what she just said. Because whatever it was? It's shut Greg Warner right up.

Even from the distance the video was taken you can see that the man is cowed. His jaw is slack, eyes drawn and haunted as Trish spins on her heels and storms away. Whatever information this woman has on him, I want to know it, too.

"Where are you now?" I ask, adrenaline surging through me as I grab my jacket.

"Tailing her. If I had to guess, I'd say she's heading back to her place. What do you want me to do?"

"Confront her with the video when you get there, find out what her connection is to Greg Warner. Text me when you find out."

"You want me to wait for you?" he asks.

I'm torn. I'd love nothing more than to sink my teeth into

Trish Sims right now. The woman's been lying to me. But she's not the only one.

"No. I've got to get back to the Warner house."

"Shouldn't we stick together?"

I don't answer because we both know we should.

"You want me to meet you there? We can circle back to Trish after?"

"If we give them too much time, someone's going to disappear on us."

Kal sounds reluctant as he asks, "You sure?"

"Maggie," Sue says softly. She's looking at me disapprovingly. I give her a smile.

"It'll be fine. I'm sure."

Sue shakes her head and sighs as I end the call with Kal. I know they're both upset with my decision, but I'll make it up to them later. I have to do this. It can't wait. I'm so close to getting answers. To finding out who's responsible for a young boy's needless death. And this time, they're not getting away with it. Someone is going to pay.

65
STEVE

I don't have a choice. I'm in over my head. Wesley crossed a line when he came to the house and disrespected the women I care about most in this world right in front of me, knowing I'd be helpless to intervene, and now my back is pinned against the wall. The only way to protect the people I love is to come clean and risk losing them.

Maggie knows I'm keeping a secret from her. I have to tell her everything, from the horrible atrocity of that night almost twenty years ago to Wesley's reappearance in my life, his threat to expose what I helped him do if I don't give him what he wants: a new identity. One he expects me to kill to get.

If she leaves me, I deserve it. If she decides to arrest me, I deserve that, too. I've lived the last two decades of my life with this hanging over my head like a dark shadow, stalking me wherever I went, but I was alive to live them. That girl was not.

Georgia Pierce.

That was her name. I didn't even know that until now. All these years I did my best to avoid finding out, as if that was what would make it real.

But it was real for her family. When their daughter never

came home. When they never heard from their sister again. The pain of not knowing, the heartache I prolonged by being too selfish to give them the answers they sought. To provide them with a body to lay to rest with their grief.

Just like Maggie wanted for her brother.

And just like Brandon, Georgia's family still hasn't stopped thinking about what happened to the girl with the large brown eyes and friendly smile. They've fought to keep her case alive, still searching for the answers that I can give them. My shame is overwhelming as I read an article in which Georgia's older brother describes a strong, confident young woman as he shares a story from their childhood.

The tale strikes too close to home. It could be me and Izzy. My heart spasms at the thought of how I'd feel if I were the one who had suffered the loss instead of the one who caused it. There's no way to make this right, I know that. But I also know that I have to do whatever I can to try and give Georgia's family some closure.

I close the lid on my laptop, Georgia's smiling face as immortalized on a missing person poster still on the screen. I'd like to think that I'm a better person now, but I know that's a lie. Because a better person wouldn't have endangered the people he loves like I've done.

I was a fool to think that I could handle Wesley on my own. But what's worse is that I was going to allow Maggie and myself to start our marriage on a lie. I love her too much for that. Respect her, even though I haven't done a very good job of showing it through my actions.

Cracking the door open, I listen for sounds of my family. I can't face them. Can't risk a distraction or getting waylaid. If I don't do this now, I might lose my nerve.

When I'm sure the coast is clear, I sneak through the house and slip outside. Get into my car, close the door as quietly as I can and start the engine.

On the drive to town, I think of the look on Maggie's face when she saw the wedding dress she liked. The way her eyes lit up when they landed on *the one*. I pray I get a chance to see that expression on her face again. That I haven't ruined our future together. But I can't live beside the woman I love knowing I don't deserve her, and that every day together is built upon deception. I have to confess.

I'm relieved to see Maggie's Jeep as I pull into the police department lot. Parking beside her, I draw several deep breaths, staring at the building, gathering my nerve. I can't put it off any longer. I have to do this. I force myself from the vehicle before I can change my mind.

"Do you think I'm stupid?"

I freeze, mid-step. An army of spiders crawls across my skin as I slowly turn around to face the voice. Wesley stands behind me, glowering. He jerks his right hand, drawing my attention, but doesn't remove it from his pocket. I have no doubts about what he has clenched in his fist.

"Get back in the car."

"Wesley."

"Shut up." Spittle flies from his mouth. A fleck lands on my cheek, though I don't dare move to wipe it away. "Do you really think I bought your little act? That I really believed that the sanctimonious Steve Winters was going to pay his debts?"

"What debts?" I ask, unable to control myself.

It's the wrong move. Wesley's face purples, his expression absolutely livid, eyes burning with rage.

"You've lived all these years free, while I was caged like some animal."

"You killed—"

"So did you!" He shouts. He checks over my shoulder, lowering his voice as he says, "You think I didn't hear about your self-defense case? But your record is still clean, isn't it?" Smirking, he says, "I mean, you're no doctor, but still a step above a janitor, huh?"

Ice shoots through my veins. Nausea seizes my body in a firm grip. I've been a fool. Was this his intention the whole time? To kill me and take my identity? Was he just toying with me, making me think that I might find a way out of this mess?

"Now. I'm going to tell you one last time. Get in the car. Unless you want to do this right here, which is fine with me. But if that's the game we're going to play, I'm just going to wound you first, so you can count how many shots I get off before your fiancée has a chance to even pull her gun."

I can tell by his expression that he means it. My time is up. There's only one thing I can do now to atone for my wrongs, and I'm more than willing to do it. I'll gladly sacrifice myself if it will keep Maggie out of his crosshairs.

66

MAGGIE

Five years ago

Maggie stares out the passenger window, watching but not seeing the blur of the landscape as they speed by. They pass an unmarked side road. A guardrail, twisted and dented by decades of impacts. Two weathered pieces of wood nailed into a cross, the name on the memorial too faded to read. They're almost there.

She swallows hard, trying to push down the strange feeling growing inside her. It isn't nerves, or excitement, or even fear. It's something she's not quite sure she's ever experienced before. Desperation.

Because so much is riding on this.

"Pull over here," she says, gesturing to the same stretch of shoulder along the road where she'd parked the night before.

Linda obeys, glancing at her nervously as she puts the vehicle in park. The tick of the hazard lights fills the silence between them. Outside, the double yellow lines of the no passing zone waver, blurred by the waves of heat rising up from the asphalt. Maggie imagines her friend is probably regretting her decision right about now.

"Listen. You don't have to do this. You should stay in the car."

"What? No. I'm going with you."

"It might not be safe."

Linda gives her a look from under raised brows, then opens the door and exits the vehicle. Maggie hesitates a moment before joining her, wondering if she's making a huge mistake. There's no way to predict what's about to happen. She might get the one person who's bothered to stick by her hurt.

And yet, it's a chance she'll have to take. She has to go. Now. She can't wait any longer.

The area looks no less menacing in broad daylight than it had last night. Shadows dart at the edge of her vision, playing tag among the trunks of the half-dead pines towering over them. Saw palmettos whisper threats into the wind. The overgrown grass grabs at her legs as she hurries to catch up with Linda, the mosquitoes so thick she can feel their bodies knocking against her hands as she walks. The thick humid air is ripe with the stench of swamp and decay.

Catching Linda's eye, she gives her friend one last chance to back out. Linda gives her a single curt nod, her hardened expression matching Maggie's own as she steps forward, leaving the pavement. Their feet kick up a cloud of dust as they walk down the dirt driveway. A trio of vultures turns in their direction, watching calmly with beady eyes as the two women approach. One goes back to picking at a flattened patch of fur with its beak.

They round a bend, and Todd's house appears before them. Maggie scans the scrubby yard, but his car isn't parked where it had been last night. It's nowhere in sight.

She quickens her pace, breaking into a jog. She can hear Linda panting behind her, knows they should stick together, but her legs aren't listening, they have a mind of their own as they race forward.

"Maggie, wait."

But she can't. Brandon might be inside the house alone. Or he might not be there at all. She has to find out.

And yet, as she reaches the dwelling, she draws to a sudden stop. A wave of apprehension ripples beneath the surface of her skin. The hair on the back of her neck rises.

The place is even uglier now that she can see it clearly. The rotting wood panels and peeling roof shingles are a blight on the earth around it, a dark festering sore. To call this place a home would be generous.

There's something menacing about it. She has to force herself to creep the last few feet forward, wincing as she knocks.

"Hello?"

She tilts her head, listening for any sounds coming from inside. Knocks again, then sidesteps to the window, cupping her hands together against the glass as she looks in.

Maggie had imagined this moment so many times, but none of her versions went like this. She had expected Todd to be here. Maybe he'd slam the door in her face or he'd take off running, but it always started with the two of them facing off.

"What now?" Linda asks from behind her, breathing heavily.

She turns to face her friend. Wishes she could give her a smile, but her lips are pressed into a grim line and won't bend. "Wait here."

Cautiously, Maggie loops around the house, circling to the backside, eyes peeled, ears straining. She eyes the back door warily.

Pulling her sleeve down over her hand, she tries the handle. It's locked. But like the rest of the place, it looks half decomposed and decrepit. And this time, she doesn't have to worry about waking Todd. Taking a step back, she plants her foot, steadies her balance, and kicks. The frame cracks and splinters and the door slams open, juddering on its hinges.

She draws a deep breath, half shocked by her actions,

acknowledging that there's no going back from this moment. Then she hurries forward.

"Brandon?" she calls.

The air inside is stale and reeks of mold and overripe trash. Scant sunlight filters in through the filthy windows. Her eyes brush over the framed photos on the walls, all hunting shots, a younger, skinnier Todd posed with other rough-looking men and their prized carcasses.

She scans the sparse furniture in the living room, a coffee table piled high with junk mail and dirty plates, an entertainment center with an ancient TV, a tower of unlabeled VHS movies, a fabric couch shiny in places from wear and body grease, on her way to the bedroom.

"Brandon?"

Would he answer, or would he be too scared? Or even gagged? The thought makes her teeth grit together. She pauses to push open the bathroom door, almost retches at the sights and smells. Cranes her head around a shower curtain that was once probably white but is now a dingy yellow, the orange film of mildew along the edge starting to curl and peel. Other than a gray ring around the tub and a rat-sized clump of hair, there's nothing.

She pauses in front of the bedroom door, afraid of what she'll find on the other side. Drawing a deep breath, she steels herself.

"Brandon?"

Still nothing. Nudging the hollow panel open with the toe of her boot, she steps inside. Finds a full-sized bed with only a top sheet. An open closet filled with camouflaged gear. A stack of shoes in one corner, a pile of clothes in another. A nightstand topped with empty beer cans and a deer antler lamp with no shade. And there, on the floor at her feet, a tiny t-shirt that she recognizes.

Bending, she scoops it up and stares at it, not wanting to believe what she's seeing. But there, on the front, is a cartoon image of her brother, one that's been added to join the rest of the Scooby Gang. It's a one of a kind, something she'd had made just for him.

Pressing the fabric to her face, she inhales, and her brother's familiar graham cracker scent fills her nose. It feels like her heart's been ripped from her chest and pulled up into her throat. He was here. He was here and now he's...

She flies forward, knocked off her feet. Lands hard on her face, jamming her wrist. Feels her insides fold around a boot as it jabs into her stomach. She tries to push up, coughing and choking, when a knee gouges against her spine between her shoulder blades, pinning her, the laminate floor gritty and sticky beneath her.

Struggling to catch her breath, she manages to gasp, "Where's Brandon?"

"Gone."

"Gone," Maggie whispers to herself. He didn't ask who she was talking about. He didn't deny that the little boy had ever been there. She's too late.

How late? If she'd been an hour sooner? Two? If she hadn't lived in a world where people were so quick to believe the worst about a mother...

Todd wraps one hand around the back of her head, slamming her face into the floor. The room spins as he shouts at her. "Who are you? What are you doing here?"

Maggie doesn't answer. She doesn't fight back. It's all over, anyway.

"No matter. You're gonna regret you ever came."

There's a hiss of metal, then his other hand appears, a knife clenched in his fist. She watches it numbly, as if from a distance, as it gets closer to her face. Imagines what a relief it will be to have this all over.

"Oof."

Todd grunts and tips to the side, off her back.

"*Maggie, get up.*"

Linda sounds frantic. Her hands shake spastically as she reaches for Maggie. Maggie lifts her gaze until she can see Linda's face, her features tight with terror.

"*Come on, we've got to—*"

Her friend's eyes go wide. Her head jerks back violently. Todd's brown teeth appear in a sneer as he uses the hand he's wrapped Linda's long black braid around to drag her across the room.

Linda.

Maggie curls onto her side. Draws her limbs to her. If it were just her, she wouldn't care. But she can't let him hurt her friend.

She pushes silently to her feet. Looks around. Snatches the lamp from the table, the cord yanking free from the outlet. And slams it with everything she has left against the side of Todd's skull. It collides with a meaty thwack, the man instantly releasing his grip on Linda as he sinks to his knees.

Maggie drops the weapon and curls her hand into a fist. Feels a satisfying crunch as it meets with Todd's nose. And then she can't stop, she's pummeling the man, all her hurt and anger and grief and rage pouring out of her in a shocking display of violence, and it feels good, better than giving up. It might not bring her brother back, but there's a certain satisfaction in the thought of vengeance, of taking an eye for an eye, a life for a life.

"*Maggie.*"

Now Todd's the one curled on the floor. She hovers over him, driving the toe of her boot into his soft belly.

"*Maggie. We need to go.*"

Linda grabs her by the arm as she's drawing back for another hit.

"*I panicked when he came home. I called the cops. They're on their way.*"

She doesn't care about being caught.

"If you kill me," Todd croaks, "you'll never find out what I've done with him."

Maggie freezes. Stares down at the man at her feet, his face broken, bloody, bruised.

"Where is he?"

Todd's eyes flutter, then roll back in his head. She grabs him by his shirt, knotting her hands in the fabric by his collar and shakes him. His head lolls limply. He's unconscious. Cursing, she releases him.

"Maggie," Linda begs.

She looks at her friend. Nods her head slowly. Todd's days are numbered, but today is not his last.

67

MAGGIE

A strange prickling sensation spreads through me as I read the text from Kal relaying his conversation with Trish Sims. Anger flushes hot beneath my skin. It feels like I'm shaking.

Trish is not in a relationship with Greg Warner.

She initially denied even knowing the man when Kal first questioned her, but when confronted with the video he took of her on the Warners' back doorstep, she confessed her involvement. She was there to collect the money Greg owed his supplier, who just happens to be her boyfriend.

I could kick myself for dropping the drug angle so readily. I should have taken a closer look at who the Warners were involved with. But even if I had, I still wouldn't have the answers I seek.

Because Greg's supplier couldn't have been the one to hurt either PJ or Jenny. He was arrested for possession with intent to distribute in Lincoln the night Jenny and Trish were at the Loose Moose. He was—and still is—in jail. That's why Trish was pressing Greg for the money he owed earlier today, so she could afford to bail him out.

And though Trish admitted the whole reason she invited Jenny out that night was to make Greg sweat, she'd gone straight to Lincoln from the bar after listening to the voicemail her boyfriend had left her after being booked. When Kal called to confirm, he'd been told that she'd been there for hours raising a fuss, trying to get her boyfriend released.

Owing money to his drug supplier—which Trish was told Jenny wasn't aware of—is just one more bit of information that Greg Warner failed to provide. He couldn't have known it had nothing to do with his son's and, later, his wife's, murders. Not unless he knew what really happened.

The man has done nothing but lie to me, and I've had enough.

Slamming my car door, I march to the house and up the front steps, yanking off my glove before knocking, not wanting the authoritative rap of my knuckles muffled by the wool. It might seem petty, but I don't care. I want him to know I'm serious. This time, I'm not leaving without answers.

My irritation grows as I hear someone moving around behind the door, yet not answering it. I knock again, hard enough to make my fist hurt, the fiberglass slab rattling on its hinges. Finally, there's the click of a deadbolt turning. Have they changed their stance about locks because of what's happened? Or is it because of why?

Did Greg and Jenny Warner cross the wrong people? Did I stop pursuing their drug connections too soon? Is Jenny Warner's death all my fault?

A moment later, Franny's scowling face appears. "What do you want now?"

"I need to speak with your son."

"He's not here."

"When will he be back?"

Her eyes dart around my face as she studies me. My determination must be clear, because she steps back with a weary sigh and waves me inside. "He shouldn't be long. You can come on in and wait, I guess."

I walk into a house that's been transformed. Every surface is clear and clean. Though still dark, the addition of several strategically placed lamps has chased away some of the shadows. Even the furniture has been rearranged in a way that better suits the room.

"Can I get you some coffee?"

I turn to face Franny, lingering near the threshold behind me. "No, thank you."

Her expression softens, takes on a wistful look. "You know, I've been trying not to drink. Been doing my best to stay sober for Greg. He needs me right now." She glances hungrily at a bottle of bourbon visible on the kitchen table. "I wish he'd hurry up and get home. It seems like too much effort to make a pot of coffee for just one person."

A spasm of guilt tightens the muscles in my chest. Franny and I haven't always seen eye to eye, but the woman is trying. I give her a small smile. "On second thought, I'll go ahead and have a cup, if you're still offering."

She nods almost enthusiastically and beckons for me to join her in the kitchen. Nudging a chair away from the table with her foot, she gestures for me to sit. I hesitate. I don't recognize this Franny. It makes me nervous.

"I know I've given you a hard time over the years," she says. "Too much of the drink will do that to a person."

It seems like an apology, but Franny has never struck me as the type to make amends. Then again, she has a point. Alcohol has a way of making people behave in ways they normally wouldn't, every cop knows that. I've seen soccer moms spit and claw like they were on an episode of *Jerry Springer*, frat boys curled up in corners sobbing. I take the offered seat.

Glancing at the bottle of bourbon on the table as she moves behind me to prepare the coffee, I wonder if I should suggest she remove the temptation by pouring it out. Then again, some people feel less desperate just knowing their crutch is there.

I wonder which type she is as cabinets open and close. Ceramics clink. The coffee machine hisses and drips.

"How do you take it?" she asks, her voice startling me from my thoughts.

"Black is fine."

"One of those, huh? I used to be the same. Drank it simply to serve a purpose, not for enjoyment. But now?" She sets a steaming cup in front of me and settles into the chair opposite, her hands curled around her own drink. She takes a sip, swallows, then releases a satisfied sigh.

"How is it?" she asks.

I try it and smile. "Surprisingly good."

"I bought these fancy flavored grounds. A little pricey, but since I'm saving so much money on other... expenses." She shrugs, watching me as I drink another sip. "Why are you really here?" she asks. Her voice is a raspy whisper as she adds, "Please don't tell me my son's done something he shouldn't have."

I feel so tired. Drained. Sometimes it just gets to be too much, always being the bearer of bad news. Maybe I should wait until tomorrow to speak with Greg, bring Kal with me.

When I don't answer, Franny swallows hard, nodding vacantly as she stares into her mug. Judging by the way her hand is shaking, I suspect she already knows why I'm here. But I'm just doing my job. I can't allow myself to feel bad for that, and yet, there's no denying that I do. I can't help it.

After a moment, she pushes her chair back and stands. Grabbing my cup, she walks behind me to pour us some more coffee. I watch her distorted image in the microwave, wondering if she'll lose her newfound sobriety over this—the charges I suspect Greg Warner will be facing.

And will it be my fault?

"You know, I've screwed up a lot over the years," Franny says from over my shoulder. "And poor Greg, well, he's borne the worst of it. I'm hoping that one day, I'll be able to make it up to him."

I track her reflection as she replaces an orange bottle inside a cabinet. It looks like a prescription vial. I wonder what it's for. With as much alcohol as she regularly drank, she probably has a whole slew of medical issues. Then again, maybe not. Healthy people take medications too. Sometimes to help them with anxiety, or sleep, or...

It strikes me like an electric shock. The Ambien that Dr. Ricky found in Jenny Warner's system during her autopsy. I jolt upright, spinning just as a dish towel loops around my neck. I manage to get a hand beneath the fabric before she pulls it tight, my own knuckles digging into my throat, gagging me, making me expel precious air.

"It's not like I meant for any of this to happen," she says from between gritted teeth. "The boy's mother should have been here. I wouldn't be in this mess if it wasn't for her."

I try shoving back from the table, but Franny has me pinned. Doubling over, I pull her partway onto my back, straining to get to my feet with the woman's weight added to my own. I can't do it. The edge of the table rams painfully into my ribs as I collapse against it.

Franny grunts. Her elbow digs into my spine, tightening the ligature. "What was I supposed to do? The kid woke me up. I was trying to help. I only shut my eyes for a minute. How was I supposed to know he'd drown?"

I force my eyes open wider, but it doesn't help, my vision is still fuzzy. I need air, fast. My free hand struggles to reach my gun, but it's pinned tight to my hip by Franny's thigh.

"I knew no one would understand. So I dried him off, put him in his pajamas. Tucked him in bed, knowing Jenny would check on him when she came home. But when she didn't notice he wasn't breathing, I realized I was being given a second chance."

I flail desperately for anything to use as a weapon as my surroundings fade into narrowing tunnels.

"I had no idea he'd be found so soon. Or at all. Bad luck, that. Still, things would have been fine if Jenny would have just moved on and let it drop. But I saw the way she looked at me. I knew what she suspected. She left me no choice."

My palm finally hits against something hard. I grab the bottle of bourbon by the neck and slam it with everything I have over my shoulder, against the side of Franny's skull.

The woman slides off my back. I drop to the floor, landing in a heap by my fallen chair, gasping. As the haze swaddling my head starts to clear, I see Greg Warner standing in the doorway, gaping at the scene before him.

"What the—?"

"Sit down," I croak. Pulling my firearm from its holster, I use it to gesture toward the chair his mother so recently vacated. "Interlace your fingers and put your hands on your head."

I wait for him to comply, then I flop Franny over onto her stomach with a grunt and cuff her.

"What happened here?" Greg's voice sounds almost as froggy as my own, his eyes wide and flashing, trying to make sense of what he's seeing.

"You and Jenny used PJ to help you move drugs," I say, a statement, not a question.

For a moment he looks like he's going to protest, but then his body sags and he nods guiltily.

"But you didn't kill them."

"No."

"Your mother did."

Greg closes his eyes and draws a shaky breath. His arms tighten against his head as he nods. "I didn't know at first. I didn't even suspect, not until you returned the pajamas that PJ was wearing when he was found."

"Which wasn't what you put him to bed wearing."

"And he wouldn't have worn them even if I tried. He was creeped out by the cartoon eyes on those dogs. Had an absolute meltdown when Jenny gave them to him for his birthday. Everyone was there, everyone knew except..."

"Your mother?"

He nods again. "She passed out long before we got around to opening presents. Even his screaming and crying didn't wake her up. But I don't think—" He hiccups and stares at her as she groans from the floor beside me. "I don't think she hurt PJ on purpose."

By Franny's account, she hadn't. It's quite possible that PJ's death really had been an accident. But what she'd done to Jenny —and tried to do to me—was absolutely intentional.

My chest tightens as the businesses clustered together at the center of Coyote Cove thin. In my rearview, the police department fades until it disappears from view. I grip the steering wheel with sweaty palms as we leave the town behind, nothing but miles of empty road before us.

"Where—?"

"Just drive."

The silence is overwhelming. I glance at Wesley, sitting in the passenger seat beside me. At the gun, no longer in his pocket, put perched on his lap, aimed in my direction. With his other hand, he rifles through my wallet.

"Your middle name's Percy?" he snorts, reading my driver's license.

"It's my mom's maiden name."

"Huh. Good to know."

It feels like he's taken a spoon and scooped a chunk out of me as he tucks the ID into his own billfold.

"Credit or debit?" he asks, holding up a plastic card.

"Debit."

"What's the daily limit?"

"I'm not sure. Three hundred, I think."

He grunts. I watch helplessly as another piece of me disappears into his possession.

"Take this turn coming up on the right," he says.

"What?" A jolt of panic electrocutes my body. I feel myself twitching with the shock.

"Here."

This can't be happening. I hit my signal, staring desperately at the entrance to the logging road ahead. A fresh layer of sweat rises to the surface of my skin as I realize this is it. The end. I thought I'd have longer. I thought he'd at least wait until we reached the next town. My heart spasms. I can barely breathe.

I glance around, desperately seeking rescue. There's a car behind me in the distance, but it's too far away to signal for help. I drop my speed, dreading the fate that awaits me around the bend.

"Your passport up to date?"

"No." I feel the heat of his gaze as he stares at me, trying to determine if I'm lying. I am, but I can't risk him going back to my house to search for it. "I haven't left the country since the last time we went to Canada together in college."

He makes a noise of disbelief. I slow to a crawl as he continues ransacking my belongings. I use his distraction to my advantage, finally coming to a stop in the road.

It's not the ending I had imagined for myself. Not the gentle fading away in the comfort of bed in my old age, leaving a long and fulfilled life behind me, that I had hoped for.

I wonder where in this rural wilderness he's going to leave my body. How long it will take for someone to find it. What will be left by the time they do. If they do.

I remind myself that Wesley's doing this because he wants my identity. Which means it's in his best interest to make sure I disappear forever.

Is Maggie going to think that I left her? Abandoned her like everyone else she's ever loved? Will she try to track me down?

Wesley shoots me a dirty look, gesturing with the gun for me to make the turn. I debate disobeying. Maybe this is where I should make my final stand. Why make things any easier on him?

I flinch as he racks the gun, sending a round into the chamber. Curl my fingers tight around the steering wheel and squeeze my eyes shut. Yet, somehow, I still see the bright white flash.

69

MAGGIE

Five years ago

Maggie stares at the cardboard boxes around her. It seems strange that her former life, which had once felt so full, can fit into only a dozen containers. Then again, she's leaving plenty of baggage behind...

Her parents, who still haven't responded to any of her attempts at contact. She wonders what they thought every time they saw her name pop up on their caller ID. When the letters she wrote arrived in the mail. When they stared at her through the peephole in their door, refusing to answer.

She doesn't understand this sudden break between them. She knows she should have found a way to bring her brother home, but she'd had a late start. If only they had contacted her immediately, maybe she would have gotten to Will Todd before... She sighs, turning her back on the boxes.

Like her parents, no one will listen to her about Todd. Her former colleagues at the sheriff's department think she planted her brother's shirt there in a desperate attempt to cast suspicion on someone other than her parents. They know she was in his house. Suspect that she was the one who beat him, though they were unable to prove it, thanks to Linda. The lamp that may have held her fingerprints is at the bottom of a river across the state, deposited during Linda's reluctant return home.

Regardless, she was released from the force permanently. Not that she cared. She was too busy trying to track Todd's past movements in order to find where he'd left her brother's remains. Had landed herself into even further trouble getting too rough with some of his associates, though she'd never said she was a cop then, had just worn her sheriff's department ball cap, so they'd been unable to make the charges stick.

Even so, news about her "break" traveled through the forensic community like wildfire. The once rising star had crashed and burned. Some said it was inevitable. Others that it was a tragedy. Yet supporters and detractors alike all stood by from a distance and watched with fascination as she continued to self-destruct.

Because she couldn't give it up. Todd is a murderer. And if only someone would listen, she could get them the proof they need.

While Maggie was searching his house, Linda was exploring his property. That's why she hadn't noticed that Todd had returned home until it was too late. She'd been too excited by her discovery, half a dozen rectangular patches of plant growth. Species that tended to grow over where decomposing organic matter was buried. In other words, she'd found graves.

Whether animal or human, she couldn't say without excavating them, but the burials weren't fresh. They weren't Maggie's brother. There had been no recent signs of soil disturbance.

Still, it could be exactly what Maggie needed to get people to listen to her. But when she'd tried to go back and dig up the proof herself, she couldn't. Todd had secured his house. Fenced his yard. Got a couple of savage-looking dogs that he kept hungry.

Then Todd had turned the tables. Had started watching her.

Showing up wherever she went. At the grocery store. In parking lots. Sitting in his car across the street from her house at night.

And he'd become the one with the law on his side.

In the end, she was forced to concede. The game had gotten too dangerous.

So Maggie's come up with a new plan. She'll be waiting for him when he least expects it. One day, her time will come.

70
STEVE

I'm seasick. Bile rises in my throat and my head throbs with each violent rise and fall of the ocean. I've never liked boats. Always hated open water. Especially when it's storming. It's too choppy to be out. Doesn't feel safe.

The vessel bucks with a particularly large swell. My neck snaps and my teeth gnash together. We're listing to the side now. Are we sinking?

Then, miraculously, the storm calms and the motion stops. I try to use the opportunity to fall back asleep, but someone turns on the lights. I flinch against the brightness, pain stabbing through my skull as rough hands seize me under the armpits, fingers digging painfully deep as I'm pulled from my bed and flung through the air.

Landing, the surface beneath me hard and unforgiving, I groan, breath hitching in my chest, shocked back into consciousness. Rocks dig into my bruised spine, feel like they're embedded into the back of my raw scalp.

As I stare up at the skeletal branches dangling overhead like bony hands, it all comes back in a rush—Wesley, the gun, the tire iron he beat me with before throwing me into the trunk of my own car, my imminent death. Before I can get my bearings on where I am now, fingers claw through my hair, nails scraping against my scalp as they tighten into a fist, using the grip to drag me down the road.

I'm not ready to die.

"Wesley," I choke out. I flail my limbs, doing my best to roll onto my side, to curl into a ball, to do anything to make whatever he has in mind more difficult. It must work, because he releases me, my head dropping painfully, stars bursting behind my eyelids as my skull strikes the ground. A second later, a boot lands a solid kick into my stomach. My insides turn liquid, molding around his shoe like Jell-O.

"You don't have to do this," I groan.

"Probably not." He sounds so casual, so flippant.

"Then why?"

"Because we were both there that night." He drives his point home with another kick. And another as he says, "Because you deserve it."

Coughing, I spit out a mix of blood and bile. He pins my cheek under the heavy steel toe of his boot, grinding my flesh into the stony ground, holding me still as he stares down at me.

"And if none of those answers are good enough for you, because I want to. I spent fifteen years penned inside a ten-by-ten cell like some kind of animal while you were free to come and go and do whatever you wanted with your life, and when I got out, I found that what you chose was to hide up here in the middle of nowhere. You could have done anything. We could have done anything together."

For a brief moment, Wesley's expression almost looks sad. Then it morphs back into a mask of rage. "You were my best friend, and you turned your back on me."

"I'm sorry."

"But you're not." He shoves my head with his foot in disgust and withdraws the gun from his jacket pocket. Squatting beside me, he says, "Poor little Wesley Banks was never good enough for Steve Winters. Admit it."

"That's not true."

"Please. I saw you pulling away. I knew that I had to think of something to bind us together, to keep us from going our separate ways after college."

Something colder than the air surrounding us runs through me. He killed that girl on purpose. He did it because of me. This is all because of me.

"I panicked," I explain, trying to appeal to him. "The way I reacted, that was about me, not you."

Wesley shrugs, using the gun to accentuate his point. "Regardless, the outcome was the same."

"But it's not too late." I'm desperate, grasping at straws as I say, "We could be friends again."

"Nah, it's a little too late for that, Steve-o. But, hey, I'll tell you what. I'll do you a solid and keep your bed warm for you after your girl finds out you left her."

The thought makes me sick. I squeeze my eyes shut, blocking out the sight of his evil grin, wondering if Maggie will recognize this man for what he is. Almost hoping that she doesn't. She might be safer that way.

My thoughts quicken, becoming frantic. I can't leave Maggie alone, not with this monster, or any of the others she faces. There has to be a way out of this. But as I feel the barrel of the gun dig into the soft spot under my chin, I fear it's too late. And as the crack of the shot thunders, I know it is.

71
MAGGIE

I can't remember the last time I've felt so exhausted. Every part of me aches, every movement feels like I'm fighting against quicksand. But it's more than just a physical weariness. I feel fragile. Emotional. The kind of raw where a commercial might make me cry.

No matter how much I've tried to deny it, this case has affected me more than I'm willing to admit. All the headway I thought I had made with my grief was merely an illusion. The truth is that there's still a huge gaping hole in my heart. The place that my baby brother and parents once filled. I thought I had regained some of the strength that had been stolen from me with my brother, but now I wonder if that's really true.

Because I live in constant fear of failing again. Of losing what little I have left. That's why I've turned such a blind eye to what's been going on with Steve. I'm not sure I have the courage to face another loss. But what if I don't have a choice?

None of us can control the future. I can't even control the dark thoughts that come to me at night when I should be sleeping. The ones that make me wonder if I can trust Steve. The ones that make me question whether I can even trust myself.

This case has brought everything I've been trying so hard to bury to the surface. Secrets I've been keeping that I can no longer deny if I want to move forward. The question is, which way do I plan to proceed?

Because there's a reason why I'm here, in Coyote Cove. One that I've been struggling with.

The truth is, I didn't apply for the police chief position because of my limited options, although it's true that there wasn't much else available to me. But I had already given up by then. Reviving my career in any form wasn't high on my list of priorities, or even on the list at all.

Because after I'd lost everything, when I hit against that rock at the bottom of my fall, I wasn't interested in trying to climb my way back up to the top. It didn't even feel like an option. No, all I was interested in was exacting my revenge.

So when I learned that Will Todd, the man who'd gotten away with stealing my brother, had family in northern Maine, that's where I went. And I've been lying in wait ever since, a spider spinning her web.

And though I thought my relationship with Steve had helped me move past that, the need for vengeance is back now, just as strong as I've ever felt it before. There was a time when I'd used it to survive, to fuel each breath I no longer had the desire to take. To keep me upright, putting one foot in front of the other.

But now that it's no longer necessary, it's become something worse. It's become more than an idea I use to keep me going. It's become a possibility.

I watch as Kal drives off with the two remaining adult Warners handcuffed in his back seat, on their way to the county jail, relieved to finally find myself alone. Though I'd pretended not to notice Kal's reaction when he'd seen the bruises circling my neck, it had been clear—he felt as guilty as if he had put them there himself. But he shouldn't.

He had offered to come with me. The decision to go alone had been mine. And on some level, I knew what I was going into. It's not the first time I've run headlong down a path that could lead to self-destruction, and I suspect that it won't be the last.

Flipping down my sun visor mirror, I gently touch the red, broken, cloth-burned skin across my throat. I don't know how I'm going to explain this. It's bad enough when it's just Steve looking at me like he's wondering how close I came to not making it home this time, but what's his family going to think?

I don't think I can face them right now.

Steve's family is just so... good. So normal. And me? I knew I was damaged. I just hadn't realized until now that I was beyond repair. What would they think if they knew the real me?

I need to speak with someone who does. Patting down my pockets, I find my phone, the screen cracked from my struggle with Franny. Sometime during the fight, Linda had left a voice-mail. I want nothing more than to speak with her right now. I press dial, crossing my fingers and my toes that this will be the call where we finally connect.

Tears fill my eyes as, a moment later, her prerecorded voice answers. Swallowing a sob, I clear my throat and whisper, "Tag. You're it."

Fisting my eyes dry, I start the engine and put my Jeep in gear, even though I have no idea where I'm driving to. I can't go home. I consider calling Kal, having him turn around and let me make the forty-five-minute drive to the jail, but that doesn't seem fair. I could stop by Margot's, but Steve's grandfather might be there. Looking into his kind eyes, so similar to those of the man I love, might make me crumble.

No, I need to bolster my courage first. Even if it's temporary and fake.

I pull into the lot just as CeCe is locking up. Anxiety knots inside my chest as I worry that she'll turn me away. Guilt sours my spit, because I know I should leave on my own, go home, and face my fears.

CeCe gives me a friendly wave, then ducks down to look at me, shading her eyes with a hand. Gestures for me to roll down my window.

"You look like you're ready for that drink."

I find myself nodding, almost against my will.

"Well, come on, then."

My lower lip quivers as I walk inside. I bite the inside of my cheek to quell it. But if I thought I'd pull anything over on CeCe, I was mistaken.

"Oh, honey." Her face crumples as she spots the injury around my neck. She passes me a full shot glass and squeezes my shoulder so softly, it's as if she knows I might shatter. "You look like you've had a heck of a day. I won't even try and talk you into letting me cut your hair."

"No, do it."

"You don't mean that. It's never a good idea to make a decision about your hair when you're feeling emotional. How about I just help you cover those bruises, instead?"

"It's now," I say, lifting my chin with the challenge. "Or never."

"That's a dangerous game you're playing, girl. You know how desperate I've been to get you in my chair."

I sit in the nearest pink vinyl seat, tug out my ponytail, and hold up my now empty glass for a refill. "Free rein. Whatever you want to do."

Her eyes light up, the sparkle growing as she passes me the bottle to serve myself in order to free up both of her hands, running them through my hair. "If you're sure?"

I'm not sure about anything anymore. About whether I'm the good guy or the bad or something in between. All I know is that I feel the overwhelming urge to escape—to be someone else and to live their life, if only for a while. I just want a break from being me.

So I toss back another shot, even though I'm the only officer in the Cove at the moment. I give CeCe a smile that feels like a lie, and conjuring confidence I don't possess, I say, "I'm sure."

But how could I possibly be confident in any of my decisions? If there was at least one thing that I could have faith in and hold on to... Just last week, I thought that could be my future with Steve. Now I can't swallow my misgivings. Instead, I gulp another shot of whiskey. And chase it with regret.

72

STEVE

I can't breathe. I'm trying, really I am, but my lungs refuse to inflate. My vision is hazy, gray splotches popping like dirty bubbles. I can't feel my hands. Or my arms or my legs or any of the rest of me, for that matter. I try to rise but fall instead.

There's blood on the ground, so fresh that the puddle's still growing. I kick my feet, trying to move myself backward, out of its path.

I scrape my palms against the gravel in my desperation, and my focus shifts. I stare at the raw patches, at the flecks of rock and dirt embedded in my wounds. At the specks of red staining my sleeves. Notice that the pool of blood has almost reached me again, grind more debris into my torn flesh as I push myself farther away.

The tortured cry of a fox sounds nearby, an eerie howl of despair that makes my flesh prickle. Only, it's not a fox. It's not an animal at all.

"Izzy."

There's a buzzing in my ears. The rush of my pulse, the echo of the gunshot.

"Izzy."

I force myself to look at the body on the road. But it's not my body.

It should have been. Those bits of skull and brain and blood should have been mine. They almost were. But instead—

"Izzy!"

I groan, struggling onto my hands and knees. Crawl forward, until I'm beside the corpse. Feel a flood of regret as I stare at the slack mouth, the open yet unseeing eyes, the waxy skin. A lifetime of memories bombards me, threatening to crush me under their weight.

This is all my fault.

"Izzy, breathe," I beg.

A ragged gasp sounds. Tearing my eyes from Wesley's body, I continue crawling until I've reached my sister's side.

Izzy's back is pressed against a tree, her knees curled tight to her chest, arms wrapped around them. The gun dangles limply from the forefinger of her right hand. My gun. The one that I'd left under the driver's seat of my car. But how?

Gently, I take the weapon from her and lay it on the ground by her feet. Scoot forward until I've reached her side. Putting an arm around her shoulders, I draw her to me and hold her tightly, hoping to quell her violent trembling.

"Are you okay?"

She turns to stare at me, and I can see that she isn't. She might never be again.

"How?" I ask.

She looks away, returning her gaze to Wesley. She whispers, "I've known him my entire life. As long as I've known you. My own brother."

I nod, knowing it's true. Wesley had always been a part of our lives. My first memories include him.

"I was on my way back to your place after dropping Grandpa off at Margot's." I have to strain to hear her, to understand the words through the thick emotion clinging to them. "I saw your car. I knew I shouldn't follow you. But I couldn't help it. You've been acting so odd, and I— What have I done?"

The car I had seen in the distance—it had been Izzy. My baby sister had trailed us here. Had followed us down the pitted dirt road we're on now.

She must have discovered my car, abandoned. Must have found the gun I'd kept under my driver's seat since the day of my first meeting with Wesley.

Her teeth are chattering. I think she's in shock. She shouldn't be here, shouldn't have been put in this position, yet if she hadn't...

"Where's your phone?" I turn her gently so her face is close to mine. "I need to call Maggie."

And suddenly, whatever spell she's under is broken.

"No." She says it firm, her eyes flashing.

"We need help."

"No!" This time it's a scream. She grabs my hands, twisting them in her own. "You can't tell, you can never tell, not anyone. Promise me, Steve."

"Izzy, you saved me. It was self-defense."

"Promise!" Her shriek is loud enough to rival any noise. The breaking of glass. The crunching metal of a car crash. The crack of a gunshot.

"Iz, calm down. It's okay. You won't get into any trouble, I promise."

She shakes her head from side to side, tears running in trails down her skin. "You don't understand. I've been struggling for so long. In life, my career... And things have just finally gotten good. I love my job. I *really* love it. And the kids, they need me. And I need them."

"Izzy—"

"Steve! Don't you get it? I killed a man."

"But—"

"No. It doesn't matter how or why. I. Killed. A. Man. I took a life. Do you really think they let people who do that work with children? Especially troubled ones?"

I don't answer.

"You have to promise me that you'll never tell."

"I can't keep this from Maggie."

"You have to."

"I can say that I did it. I shot him," I offer. "We can pretend that you were never here. It's my gun."

She doesn't even consider it for a second. "They'll know."

I glance around desperately, as if the solution is written somewhere in the dirt and the blood and the woods around us. "We can't keep this a secret."

"We can. Look at how steep this embankment is. We'll roll him down the ravine. No one will find him there. If we're lucky, the animals will take care of him."

Now I'm the one shaking their head. She grabs me roughly by the arm. I wince, suspecting that the bone beneath is broken.

"We went hiking. You fell. Far. Your injuries are from an accident. We were never here. We never saw Wesley. Promise me." She holds my gaze. "I'm your sister. Do you really think that if Maggie had the chance to help her brother, that she wouldn't do anything for him, even if it meant lying to you?"

My mouth opens, but no sound comes out. I can't lie. But I can't tell the truth, either.

"Promise me," she whispers, the whites of her eyes flashing. "You'll never tell anyone what I've done."

I'm not sure if my sister has ever seen me cry before. I've always done my best to be strong for her, to be her hero. But the tables have turned. I don't try hiding the tears that etch trails of defeat across my face as I nod.

Izzy squeezes my hand gently as she whispers, "Thank you."

I can't bring myself to look at her, to acknowledge her gratitude, because it never should have come to this. She shouldn't be here, shouldn't have pulled the trigger, shouldn't have to live with the memory of what took place. I failed my sister. Don't I owe her whatever she asks in return?

"Wait here for just a moment," she says. "This shouldn't take me long."

"No, I... I'll help."

We work together soundlessly, the two of us unwilling or simply unable to break the silence between our grunts of exertion as we roll Wesley's corpse to the edge of the ravine. No doubt, this is the same fate that he had intended for me, but being the survivor doesn't feel like a victory. It feels like something else, poisonous and sickly, a cancer lodging itself deep inside me.

I pull the body along the crest until its path is clear, positioning it between the rocks and trees. Then, with a final shove, it's out of my hands. We watch as my former best friend rolls down, down, down until he disappears from view, hopefully to never be seen again.

I kick gravel and dirt over the blood on the road, then cover it with a layer of pine needles. Way out here, in the middle of nowhere, there shouldn't be much traffic. There's no reason for someone to exit their vehicle. With an ounce of luck, if someone does notice the blood, they'll think it's from an animal that got hit.

Taking a final look around, I make sure that we aren't leaving anything behind. It's done. And looking at the devastated expression on my sister's face, I worry that so are we.

73

MAGGIE

As I watched Steve's family gather their luggage two days after arresting the Warners, I wasn't sure whether to feel relieved or panicked. On the one hand, we'd be getting our privacy back. On the other, that meant that we'd be alone. I didn't know if either of us was ready for that.

We've been dancing around each other, sidestepping the elephant that's been in the room since he got injured. I'd known that he was hiding something from me. We'd both been playing that game. But until he came home battered and broken, I hadn't known how close I really was to losing him.

I didn't for one second buy the story he told about falling while he and Izzy were hiking. I've been on the receiving end of enough brutality to know human-inflicted wounds when I see them. Someone had given him a beating, and a serious one at that. One that he might not have been intended to survive. It kills me that he lied about it, that he doesn't trust me enough to tell me who.

Not that I need him to. It hasn't escaped my attention that his "best man" has mysteriously faded from the picture. I just wish he could be honest with me about why.

It's not a way to start a marriage, at least one that I'm interested in entering. And yet, at the same time, when I think of my future, I can't help but imagine Steve in it. Steve, and Grandpa Joe, who gave me a tight hug as he told me to keep his boy out of trouble. Izzy, who trembled and clutched at me so desperately that I was hesitant to let her leave.

Even Diane, who waited until the other two were in the car before giving me that steely look of hers and telling me, "There's a present for you, dear. In the room I was staying in."

I was afraid to ask. I was almost afraid to follow as she took me by the hand and led me down the hall. Her lips twitched at the corners as she opened the door wide and gestured for me to go inside. It took more nerve than I'd like to admit for me to step up to that threshold and take a look. When I did, what I saw took my breath away.

I turned to her with awe, feeling the stone inside me that keeps me upright starting to crumble. "Oh, Diane. I can't accept this."

"You can and you shall, my dear. I can't wait to see you in it."

And when she wrapped her arms around me, I felt myself melt a little. Because it wasn't just a hug she gave me. It was a mother's embrace.

Now, sitting here on the edge of the bed, staring at the wedding dress hanging from the closet door, I find that I miss them already. The house feels too quiet and empty. Without the distractions, I can't help imagining what it would feel like to put on the gown before me, the same one I'd seen on the screen of Diane's iPad and instantly fallen in love with. But I can't let myself think about that. Because what if I never get the chance?

My phone rings, disturbing my pity party. I pat my pocket, withdraw it, and answer it absently, my eyes still on the dress. Relief wells inside me as Linda's voice fills my ear. My vision blurs, the gown growing fuzzy. After countless rounds, our game of phone tag is finally over. I've needed to talk to her so badly. But now that it's happening, I'm not sure what to say.

We make small talk, and though my voice sounds level and calm, all the things I've longed to tell her are building up inside me, threatening to erupt. And yet, I realize that if I tell her my concerns about Steve, I can never go back. Once they're out there, I can no longer claim ignorance. I'll have to make a choice. I'll have to either move forward or put an end to things.

"The wedding's getting closer. You must be getting so excited."

I open my mouth to respond, but no sound comes out. Linda is my closest friend. I know I need to confide in her, have her tell me all the things I keep telling myself, the things I don't want to acknowledge or hear. Because I love Steve. I want to be his wife. Or is it just that I don't want to be alone? How can you know for sure?

Linda takes my silence as agreement. "Have you found a dress yet?"

I stare at the gown. Linda's been married before. She's been divorced. What would she tell me if I told her I was having second thoughts. That it's just cold feet?

"Yes," I answer.

Or that I should listen to my gut? But what is it, exactly, that my gut is telling me? I've always been able to trust it before, but now it's like we're speaking different languages.

"Linda." I have a long history of pushing people away. Is that what I'm doing? Making a mountain out of a mole hill so I have an excuse to run? Am I really that afraid of being vulnerable? I suspect that I already know the truth.

"I—"

I glance up as Steve appears in the doorway.

"I have to go. I'll call you back later."

I don't wait for an answer before ending the call.

My fiancé enters the room silently, head hanging. "You

didn't have to do that," he mumbles, barely louder than a whisper. "I know you've been trying to get in touch with Linda for a while now."

My voice shakes as I say, "Something tells me we need to talk more."

Steve nods and takes a seat gingerly on the bed beside me. I can't help noticing how much space is between us. Then again, haven't I been feeling that space figuratively for a while now?

"I have to tell you something," he says. "But I'm not sure how."

This is it. The moment I've been waiting for. And dreading.

Steve clears his throat, tracing the pattern of the quilt beneath us with a finger. "That guy who came to the house? Wesley?"

"Yes?"

"He really was my best friend. Once. The entire time we were growing up. All through college. Until one night."

He stops fussing with the blanket and lays his hand flat next to mine. I watch as his little finger inches closer. I don't move to meet it, but I don't pull away, either.

"We hit a girl with my car. Wesley was driving. I was sleeping in back, but... but I was there. I agreed not to call the police. I helped him cover it up and bury her under a tree not far from the road."

I suck in a sharp breath, trying not to judge. He was young. It was his car. He was scared. It's understandable. But is it unforgiveable?

"I knew it was wrong, but at the time, I didn't realize..."

He falls silent.

"What?" I ask, more sharply than I intended. You didn't realize what?"

"That it might not have been an accident," he admits.

"What do you mean?" My skin goes cold, my toes suddenly freezing in my shoes.

"Later, after I sobered up—I think he drugged me—I realized that I'd seen him talking to the same girl at a party earlier that night. And there was no way she just happened to be walking alone in the middle of nowhere without a car. And..."

"And what?"

"And there was another girl. Later. He spent fifteen years in prison for manslaughter."

"Why are you telling me this now?"

"Because." Steve licks his lips nervously. Raises his eyes to mine, then immediately shifts them away. "When he got out, he decided to blackmail me."

"That's why he showed up here?"

Steve nods. "As a threat."

"Why didn't you tell me?"

"I wanted to. But I was scared. At first, I thought that I could handle it myself, but then, when I realized I couldn't, it was too late. Wesley headed me off and stopped me."

"Your fall?" I fail to keep the sarcasm out of my tone as I eye his bruises, even more tender looking today than when I first saw them.

"Yes."

"How long has this been going on, Steve?"

"Four, maybe five months."

"Five months! We have to stop this..."

"It's taken care of. Wesley won't be a problem anymore. I promise you."

My chest tightens. I don't want to know, but I have to ask. "What do you mean?"

"I know it's ridiculous to ask you to trust me right now, but I need you to. It's over."

"How can you know that?"

"Because Wesley won't be bothering anyone ever again."

My pulse throbs hard against my bruised throat. I pull my hand away from his, rub my palms on my thighs to dry them.

"Did you?"

"Please don't ask me that. I can't tell you any of the details. Just know that he was threatening you and my family. And when the time came, there was no choice."

I believe him. But that doesn't change the fact that my future husband helped cover up one murder... and may have committed another. Yet, who am I to judge? Because if there's one thing that I've learned about myself this last week, it's that I still haven't moved on from my brother's death. If I found myself alone with his killer, I might do more than simply contemplate homicide.

That makes me worse, doesn't it? Steve might have killed to protect his loved ones. But I would kill to avenge mine. Maybe we belong together after all.

"I know that I'm not the man you thought I was," he continues. "But I'm going to start being that guy. I'm going to turn myself in, bring that girl's family some peace. And maybe one day, you'll be able to forgive me."

"Wait. What?"

Steve swallows hard. "They've waited long enough for answers, and I'm the only one who can give them, now."

His little finger brushes against mine as he stands. I stare at my pinky, feeling the ghost of his touch. My mouth forms the word, though no sound comes out. "No."

I look up, panic surging through me as Steve walks toward the door, shoulders high and rounded beneath his ears. "No," I whisper. He pauses, and I say it again, louder.

He turns toward me with a tormented look. "I have to do this. You're a cop, Maggie. I can't let you risk your career. I can't ask you to keep this secret for me."

"I moved here to murder my brother's killer."

Steve's mouth drops open. I can't believe I said it, but now that I have, I can't take it back. Though I want to look away, I force myself to maintain eye contact as his search mine, finding the truth. My heart pounds so hard it threatens to break through the walls of my chest as I wait for him to react with disgust.

"Oh, Maggie." His tone holds none of the revulsion I expected. None of the pity. He closes the distance between us and sinks to his knees before me, taking my hands in his. "Trust me when I say that no matter how much you might want to do that, you never actually would."

"And neither would you." I wasn't sure until right this second, but now I'm positive. "You didn't kill that girl. You didn't pull the trigger in that carjacking. And..." I draw a deep breath, keeping my gaze locked on his. Because somehow, I know. "You didn't kill Wesley."

His reaction confirms what I already believed in the one part of me I'm terrified to trust—my heart. But I know this man in front of me is good. That he'll always believe the best about me, even when I believe the worst. I can't lose that.

"Stay. Stay and marry me."

Steve's face lights up with hope, then dims.

"But what about her family?"

"We'll find a way to bring her home to them. One that doesn't involve you going to prison."

"But—"

"Shhh."

I cup his face in my hands and press my lips to his. Love is messy and irrational and scares me more than just about anything else in this world. But once you find it, you'd be foolish to throw it away. What Steve and I have? It's worth fighting for. And that's exactly what I'm going to do, no matter what it might cost me.

A LETTER FROM SHANNON

Dear reader,

First, a very big and most sincere thank you for choosing to read *One Little Sigh*, the fourth installment in the Chief Maggie Riley series. If you'd like to keep up to date with my latest releases, you can sign up at the following link. Your email address will never be shared, and you can unsubscribe at any time.

www.bookouture.com/shannon-hollinger

I always have a great time when I find myself in Coyote Cove. I hope you enjoyed your stay there just as much, and I can't wait for you to discover what I have in store for Maggie and the rest of the gang. If you enjoyed the story, I would be so very grateful if you'd leave a review and recommend the book to your fellow readers. Please know that your review makes a huge impact! On future books, future plots, future character development... I love reading what you think. Your review is also incredibly important in helping other readers find my books for the first time, which is an amazing gift to give an author.

Writing can be a very lonely endeavor, so please feel free to get in touch and keep me company. You can find me on social media or my website.

Thank you so much for your support—it really is hugely appreciated!

Until next time,

Shannon Hollinger

facebook.com/thiswritersays

x.com/thiswritersays

instagram.com/thiswritersays

goodreads.com/shannonhollinger

ACKNOWLEDGMENTS

Writing a series can be a daunting task because you don't want to let your readers—or the characters—down. And as your fictional world grows and you get to know your characters better, somewhere along the way, it becomes like torturing your family. Some days it's fun, but others you feel kind of bad about it... Luckily, characters can't pay it back!

I am so grateful to all the readers who have reached out and emailed, messaged, and tagged me in posts sharing their love for the Chief Maggie Riley books! Your support means the world to me, and I really can't thank you enough!

For everyone who has left a review, I am so very, incredibly grateful! Even just a few words can have a huge impact on a book's success, and you have no idea how much I appreciate you taking the time to let others know when you think one of mine is worth reading!

Endless thanks to all the readers, reviewers, BookTokers, Bookstagrammers, book tweeters, bloggers, book clubs, and librarians out there who spend so much of their valuable time sharing book love and reviews!

Please don't underestimate how important you are! Knowing that there are people who enjoyed reading the book you've spent so much time, sweat, isolation, and occasionally tears on is a tremendous feeling, and your kind words get me through the days when I want to pull my hair out while obsessing over a plot twist, character arc, or sometimes even just a single sentence or word.

The best part of this journey has been "meeting" all of you. I love reading all of your posts and am astounded by how gorgeous your bookish pictures are—I need lessons!

A special thank you to Angela Goyette Frank, founder of the Big Comfy Couch Book Club, for hosting me not once, not twice, but three amazing times! She's amassed such a wonderful group of readers, and chatting with her club is always a pleasure!

To my mom, Stacy, who instilled in me my love of both reading and writing, thank you for all your encouragement, for always being there for me, and for our lunches, where I arrive clinging to the peaks of Stress Mountain and leave with a full belly and a happy heart.

Thank you to my dad, Bob, who never got to see me live my dream but had faith that I'd one day make it happen.

Thank you to my grandmother, Marvis, for introducing me to the work of so many great authors over the years who have influenced my own writing, and for always feeding my book addiction!

Thank you to my husband, Ben, for pep talks and days of fun, for hiking, camping, and adventuring, and for being my partner in crime (while at the same time doing your best to keep me out of trouble).

Thank you to my constant companion, Sully, for making every day brighter and every night more interesting while we prowl around and "night wolf" at 3 a.m.

Special thanks to my editor, Susannah Hamilton, for her excellent guidance, keen insight, and indispensable input! She always knows what's needed to make my books better and stronger!

Many sincere thank-yous to the publishing team at Bookouture, especially those whose hands, talent, and skill have touched this book and helped make it into what it is today! Thank you to the amazing publicity and social media team who work tirelessly to get our books out there, and to my fellow Bookouture authors, who are unbelievably friendly and supportive across both genres and oceans. I'm so very grateful to have found such an amazing tribe, one that feels more like a family than a publishing company. You guys rock!

PUBLISHING TEAM

Turning a manuscript into a book requires the efforts of many people. The publishing team at Bookouture would like to acknowledge everyone who contributed to this publication.

Audio
Alba Proko
Sinead O'Connor
Melissa Tran

Commercial
Lauren Morrissette
Hannah Richmond
Imogen Allport

Data and analysis
Mark Alder
Mohamed Bussuri

Cover design
The Brewster Project

Editorial
Susannah Hamilton
Nadia Michael

Made in United States
Orlando, FL
25 June 2024

48282966R00203